Death at the Old Asylum

Adrian Magson has written eighteen crime and spy thriller series built around Harry Tate, ex-soldier and MI5 office, and Gavin & Palmer (investigative reporter Riley Gavin & ex- Military Policeman Frank Palmer). He also has countless short stories and articles in national and international magazines to his name plus a non-fiction work: *Write On! – the Writer's Help Book*. Adrian lives in the Forest of Dean, and rumours that he is building a nuclear bunker are unfounded. It is in fact, a bird table.

D1638277

Also by Adrian Magson

Smart Moves

Inspector Lucas Rocco

Death on the Marais
Death on the Rive Nord
Death on the Pont Noir
Death at the Clos du Lac
Rocco and the Nightingale
Rocco and the Price of Lies
Death at the Old Asylum

The Gonzales & Vaslik Investigations

The Locker
The Drone

ADRIAN MAGSON

DEATH AT THE OLD ASYLUM

CANELO

First published in the United Kingdom in 2021 by Canelo

This edition published in the United Kingdom in 2022 by

Canelo
Unit 9, 5th Floor
Cargo Works, 1–2 Hatfields
London, SE1 9PG
United Kingdom

A CIP catalogue record for this book is available from the British Library.

Print ISBN 978 1 80032 718 4
Ebook ISBN 978 1 80032 685 9

Look for more great books at www.canelo.co

Printed and bound in Great Britain by Clays Ltd, Elcograf S.p.A.

1

Ann, without whom this simply would not happen.

Chapter One

Late summer 1964 – Picardie, France

Fouad Hamal eased the Mercedes-Benz 220S to a stop at the top of a gentle rise and turned off the engine. It had been giving off a harsh, metallic *click-clack* ever since leaving Marseille. The sound was at one with its silver-grey coachwork, now much faded and bruised by time and wear, and the stained and battered hand-written TAXI sign in the front window. As a taxi driver himself, Hamal knew cars, and there were signs that this one had been given a cheap rebuild after being written off in an accident. The doors didn't close properly, the chassis creaked incessantly and only the quality of German engineering beneath the bonnet had kept it going this far.

In any case, there was nothing he could do about it; it wasn't his car and the sooner he could get shot of it along with the three passengers sleeping in the back, the better.

He eyed the soft, rolling landscape of Picardie, northern France, with a growing sense of unease. Unlike the streets of his home in Marseille, the near-featureless fields and slopes here, revealed in the growing light of early dawn, were unwelcoming and scarily open.

The air was chilly to his sun-baked skin, and he wanted nothing more than to be back to the warm and familiar and his wife, Simone. He'd even begun to fantasise about the pleasures of a pleasant breakfast for two; maybe fried eggs, yoghurt and *rghaif* pancakes, all washed down with mint tea... although right now a large black coffee, strong enough to float a dead dog and with a side order of a *jambon beurre* would do fine.

Dealing with the promised hell and eternal damnation could come later.

'What is it? Why have you stopped?' The old man, seated centre back between his two sons, was awake again. When not asleep he'd grumbled incessantly for most of the long overnight drive, about the suspension, the roads, the discomfort and everything else that seemed to displease him. Clearly sleep had done nothing to sweeten his sour disposition.

Hamal seriously wanted to tell him to shut the hell up, but he'd seen the weapons carried by the two younger men. All three were, like himself, Moroccan, and newcomers to France. They were unshaven and wore crumpled suits and shirts showing signs of the long, cramped journey. Worse, the two younger men were either cops or military, he wasn't sure which.

Two sides of the same dangerous coin.

'Answer me, damn it!' The old man again, voice gravelled by fatigue and more than a hint of spite.

'Just checking the map, sir,' Hamal replied softly, eyes flicking from the road in front to the rear-view mirror. He was exhausted after the long drive, with only one decent halt at a truck stop, where he'd been able to make a brief telephone call, and two comfort breaks on quiet stretches of road to interrupt the monotony. Not that there had been rest or comfort; even when the two younger men were out of the car, the air had been punctuated by hissing arguments between them about the need for progress, while the old man, when awake, had been staring at him throughout the journey as if trying to bore a hole in the back of his head.

And therein lay a disturbing element for Hamal: he'd recognised the old man the moment he'd seen him, bringing back memories of Morocco before he'd fled to France. He'd tried to brush them off but the thoughts were too embedded to dispel easily.

Perhaps the old man remembered him, too. If so, it made matters worse. It was like travelling with a scorpion in his back pocket.

Hamal started the engine and made moves as if to drive on, shifting in his seat and adjusting the mirror. He was playing for time, his mouth dry and sour. Surely the men in the back must be able to hear the pounding of his heart and the blood racing through his veins? He had no idea what was about to happen but he hoped it would bring a sense of relief and allow him to go home. Whatever their reason for travelling in this furtive and joyless manner, he had a growing feeling of dread hovering around him like a storm cloud.

'Let us go on, then!' The old man sank back with a sigh and rubbed his lined face with a sound like sandpaper on wood.

The younger man on the old man's left back-handed Hamal hard on the shoulder. 'You heard him, imbecile. What are you waiting for?'

Hamal didn't respond. His eyes were on a vehicle coming up behind them. It had appeared out of a side road a few kilometres back. A brief flash of its headlights was the signal he'd been told to look out for during his call at the truck stop, and it had followed him at a distance. Now it was approaching at speed, kicking up a dust swirl in its wake and pulling up behind.

Chapter Two

It had begun with a call three days ago on the apartment block's shared telephone. An urgent airport trip, the caller had said, naming a pick-up point outside the Musée des Beaux-Arts. Hamal didn't mind; it was easy money and airport passengers usually tipped well. He was surprised that a stranger had got hold of the number, since he relied entirely on street pick-ups. But money was money so he'd set off for the rendezvous point.

The reality had turned out to be entirely unexpected. Lasting less than three minutes in total and not moving away from the kerb, he'd been given orders to collect a car and three passengers from a garage in the south of the city and take them to Picardie.

Hamal had never been that far north and sensed that something was not right about the job. A quick glance in the mirror had revealed a face in shadow. In a former life in the streets of Casablanca, before escaping to France, he'd witnessed too often the forced conscription of individuals by political and criminal organisations to undertake tasks that had often carried little chance of survival for the unfortunate person selected.

'It's a long way. It will be expensive,' he said, hoping the customer would change his mind. The sunny day, with the Boulevard Longchamp busy with smiling tourists and promise in the air, had turned suddenly sombre and cold.

The man had ignored him. 'Time your arrival in the region for the early morning, then stop at a point of your choosing and call a number for further instructions.' He was given a telephone number to write down, followed by the address of the garage where the car and passengers would be waiting. He'd never heard of the establishment and began to suggest he could use his own vehicle, but to no avail. The silence alone made him realise that his move to France for a better life had not distanced him from the snake-like tendrils of religious and extremist forces in his home country.

For just a few fleeting moments he'd considered pleading incapacity before realising that nothing short of genuine hospitalisation would be enough. The future was set.

And now he was here.

'We have been followed.' He'd first mentioned the possibility earlier after leaving the truck stop as a way to allow him to cut off the main routes and use back roads instead, avoiding any large urban areas. It would also bring him closer, he'd been told, to the location for the handover and preferably nowhere near any houses.

'A handover?' he'd queried. The voice had replied that it was the point where his task was done and he could return home. Someone else would take over from there.

The two younger men had argued against the deviation, citing the need for speed over caution and insisting that he was imagining things; that nobody could possibly know they were here in France, let alone in which direction they were moving.

The comment had done nothing to dispel his concerns, but it was too late now to back out. Better to complete the job, collect his money and move on.

Fortunately, the old man had agreed with him, stilling his sons' voices with a sharp command. Caution had kept them alive thus far, he'd reminded them, and he wasn't about to relax until they arrived at their destination. Back roads it was from this point on.

Hamal didn't wish harm on anybody, but for the two younger men, so openly contemptuous of him ever since he'd picked them up, he was prepared to make an exception. It was an attitude he'd come across before, common in someone from the old country when confronted by one of the many who had left Morocco years before in search of a better life. They didn't use the word 'traitor', but the contempt in their eyes was enough.

He took a deep breath and tried not to think about what might be lying in wait for them at the end of their journey. Instinct told him it would not be pleasant.

The approaching car had stopped a short distance behind them. Was this the handover or simply a Samaritan stopping to offer help? It was a maroon Renault, dusty and nondescript, and looked like a hundred other cars on the road, albeit not this one in particular, which was more of a forgotten route to nowhere. He hadn't seen another vehicle for over an hour. The Renault driver's door swung open and a man stepped out. He was tall and thin, one hand in his pocket like a man out for a casual stroll.

'What's happening?' the old man demanded. 'Why aren't we moving?'

The two sons craned round to look out the rear window, confused by their father's sudden agitation, picking up on his air of alarm.

'Why aren't we moving?' he repeated.

'Because,' said Hamal, turning off the engine again, 'there is no point.' He opened the ill-fitting door and got

7

out, then walked back along the side of the road, passing the newcomer on the way. The man didn't even look at him, eyes focused on the Mercedes.

'*Hey!*' one of the sons cried, eyes growing wide. He wound down his window and called out, 'Where are you going? Get back here now!'

Hamal ignored him. The Renault looked like a shit car pulled from a wrecker's yard but he could hear the engine ticking over sweetly enough. Just as long as it got him home safely, that's all he asked.

–

In the other car, the older son had realised what was unfolding. He scrambled to throw open the door, telling the old man to keep his head down. As he jumped out, he reached inside his suit jacket and took out a semi-automatic pistol, swinging to face the oncoming threat.

Far too late. A single shot took him in the head, spinning him around. The sound of the report was flat and snappy, flicking away across the open fields. A nearby family of crows, the only witnesses, scattered in noisy panic at the rude disruption to their morning.

The other young man pushed his father down and leaned over to cover him. But by then the gunman was moving swiftly up on his side of the Mercedes and levelling his weapon. He fired twice through the open window, killing both men instantly.

Fouad was about to climb behind the wheel of the Renault, his mind already picturing the long road south to Marseille, when he heard the first shot. He spun round and saw the older son lying dead in the road. The newcomer was walking across the rear of the car then down the side, a gun levelled at the windows. Two more shots followed, then silence.

He was momentarily rooted to the spot in horror. Then he realised there would be no going back to his wife in Marseille; no early morning breakfasts; nothing more of the new life he had made here.

Instinct took over and he began running, the taste of bile rising in his throat, eyes fixed on the long, empty stretch of tarmac in front of him.

Chapter Three

By the time Inspector Lucas Rocco arrived, the scene looked very different. Several police vehicles and uniformed officers were present along with a heavy tow truck, awaiting instructions.

Violent death wasn't unknown in this rural area – at least, not so much in peacetime. Place any number of excitable and alcohol-fuelled hunters in proximity on the annual wildlife slaughter and sooner or later one of them would fall victim to a careless blast of buckshot. But a triple killing of this nature was a different story altogether.

Rocco saw the familiar pale figure of Doctor Rizzotti, the local stand-in forensic pathologist at the commissariat in Amiens, kneeling at the side of a grey Mercedes, his wispy hair blowing in the gentle breeze off the surrounding fields.

'Nasty business,' Rizzotti murmured, looking up, and gestured at the three bodies, one on the ground, the other two inside the car. He stood up with a groan of tortured knees and shook hands with Rocco, blinking behind his wire spectacles and brushing a fly away from one cheek. 'A gang execution, do you think?' He knew Rocco had extensive experience in gangland violence from his time in Paris before being posted to the Amiens commissariat, and would probably have a suggestion. 'Three in one, though – that's intense.'

'Just a bit,' Rocco agreed. He gathered up the hems of his long coat and bent to study the man lying on the road outside the car. He looked to be in his late thirties, dark-skinned and well-dressed, if a little rumpled. He'd been shot once in the forehead. Just edging out from beneath his jacket was a dark leather strap. Rocco eased the fabric to one side to reveal a leather shoulder holster, shiny with use. The holster was empty. He turned his attention to the pistol on the ground, which he guessed would fit snugly into the leather. It was a MAC 50 9mm and looked in excellent condition, clean and free of scratches. That in itself was telling: most gangland members were accustomed to treating their weapons with casual indifference as if such care showed a form of weakness.

He bent and sniffed at the barrel without touching it. No signs of being fired recently but Rizzotti would confirm that later. If it was the case, the man had been taken by surprise before he could defend himself.

Rocco stood up, brushing dust from his coat. The beginnings of a scenario were building in his mind, and he turned to check out the other two bodies in the rear of the Mercedes. One old, the other young. Like the man outside, they looked of North African heritage, and he thought he saw a certain resemblance in their jawlines. Family members, then. Another MAC lay on the floor of the car by the younger of the two men. Also clean and shiny. He reached in and eased the man's jacket aside. Another shoulder holster.

The evidence was unsettling. In common use by the French police and army, the MAC had spread out over the years to other countries such as those along the North African coast, including Morocco, Algeria, Tunisia, where France had interests. But most had been acquired for police or military use. Looking at the two younger men and the state of the weapons suggested the guns were service issue, which made these two cops... or body-guards. Gang crime was problematic enough, but the possibility of outside government forces being victims on French territory was something that would have the Interior Ministry in turmoil.

Still, he preferred to reserve judgement. He'd seen other killings like this, albeit not this neat. They were usually the result of gangland disputes that had been building for years and had finally erupted like an over-heated boiler when tensions and rivalries had become too much to contain. And gang membership sometimes included former military personnel who had respect for their weapons if little else in life.

The usual format for a gang killing would be for a targeted vehicle to be stopped by some innocuous incident such as an apparent motorcycle accident or a broken-down tractor in the middle of nowhere. The attackers would be lying in wait for their moment, and as soon as the target vehicle came to a stop the gunman or gunmen would emerge from hiding and strike.

Depending on the gangs involved there was often more than one killer, usually as a display of overwhelming force to discourage any thoughts of payback. In the aftermath of such a killing, the norm was that those who understood all too well what had taken place would retreat silently to wait for the inevitable violent repercussions to follow while the innocent – and the police – were left to pick up the pieces.

'No sign of a driver?' Rocco asked.

'Not so far.'

Rocco stared out across the landscape into the sun, which was growing hotter by the minute. They were at the tail end of summer and the fields were little more than brown stubble where the harvest had been completed. A nice day all in all; too nice for this kind of horror to be visited on it. But why here? If there was some kind of tie-in with the area, he was damned if he could see it yet. Sure, there was a criminal element in this part of France, like everywhere else, and his own experiences here had included visits by gang members intent on revenge or escape or even extending their criminal influence.

If this was an arranged killing, this site was a classic. On a quiet road and away from witnesses, it offered a perfect escape route either way once the job was done.

He could just make out the outline of the cathedral in Amiens many miles away through the heat haze. Elsewhere the swath of fields showed that whatever had happened here over the years up to and including this brutal act, the farmers would continue regardless to produce their crops. Clumps of trees were dotted here and there, along with a line of telegraph poles and a solid, unromantic shape of a water tower on the horizon. The roof of an ancient barn was just visible in the distance, its structure showing light through the sagging walls and framework. But no houses. Any that were there would be too far away to provide reliable witnesses to what had occurred.

'Do we know who called it in?' The radio message on his way to the office had mentioned a killing and the location but no other details. It was probably kept deliberately brief to avoid media interest and to allow Rizzotti and the team to get the investigation under way in relative peace. Give it a couple more hours and the press pack from Paris and further afield, alerted to a new sensation, would be crowding the scene and creating its own brand of mayhem.

Rizzotti said, 'A farmer on his way to market in Amiens. He found this lot just before seven. The officer on the front desk knows him well. Says he's a religious man and wouldn't know how to use a gun if his life depended on it, much less kill three men.'

'If only,' murmured Rocco dryly. He'd known several very ordinary people use weapons for the first time in their lives when desperation had called, and it was amazing how quickly they had managed to find their way round an unknown piece of deadly engineering when the occasion demanded. But he knew what the officer had meant; some people would not pick up a gun under any circumstances.

He made a circuit of the Mercedes, leaving Rizzotti to do his work. Although originally a doctor, Rizzotti had been co-opted to his role when no available expert could be found to match the local budget, and the position was now more or less his by default. He'd proven himself skilled at reading crime scenes and understanding what detectives like Rocco needed to know to help in their investigations; he needed no hand-holding.

Rocco tasked two uniforms to check the fields on each side for tell-tale tracks away from the road. The driver might have made a run for it, but it seemed unlikely; the stubble was short enough to reveal bare earth in every direction and the undulations in the terrain here were barely visible. He looked down at the road surface behind the rear wheels, then did the same at the front. No skid marks to indicate the driver had slammed on his brakes or been forced to stop by another car cutting in on him.

Odd.

Chapter Four

Rocco walked along the road away from the rear of the Mercedes, trying to read the scene for himself. It was mostly guesswork at this stage because only the assailant knew for sure what had happened here. But he was already certain that a key person – the driver – was missing. The dead man lying in the road had clearly exited from the rear of the vehicle, and in any case was too tall to have needed the booster cushion in the driver's seat.

He heard a shout and turned. The uniforms had completed their search through the short stubble, signalling no tracks in the soil and no further bodies. He waved them back in.

Had the driver committed the shooting? If so, where the hell was he?

Rocco chewed his lip in puzzlement. He was about to turn back to the car when he spotted a gleam of reflected light on the surface of the tarmac a few metres away. It came from a small puddle of oil at the side of the road. He bent and dipped his finger in it and studied the result. There was the beginning of a skin forming but it was relatively free of dirt. If it had been lying here overnight it would have become covered in a wind-blown layer of dust and begun to dry. But that hadn't happened.

'Found anything?' It was Detective René Desmoulins, Rocco's younger colleague. He was keen and reliable, which was more than could be said of his thin moustache. He was fingering it now as usual, as if tugging the embryonic hairs could encourage them into a respectable burst of growth.

'Not sure yet,' said Rocco. He held up the oily finger. Desmoulins had been a mechanic before joining the police. 'You're the expert. What do you think?'

Desmoulins looked at it, then bent and examined the patch. 'Pretty recent, I'd say. An older car, too, to have left that much behind. If the oil was hot it would have flowed quite easily.' He looked along the road surface in both directions. 'If it was a serious leak there would be other splashes but I can't see any. I'll check the Merc to see if it's losing any. You think this was connected?'

'Possibly. My gut says probably. But we'll see.'

'Judging by some old paperwork I found in the glove box,' Desmoulins added, 'the Merc comes from Marseille. But it doesn't list the owner's name. I'll give the local police a call and see what they come up with.'

Desmoulins walked back to the Mercedes and knelt to study the ground beneath the engine. He stood up and shook his head in Rocco's direction, holding up his thumb and forefinger with barely a gap between them. Nothing serious and nothing like the patch Rocco had found.

Rocco hummed. It was pure speculation but it looked as if the Merc had stopped and the other car had pulled up a short distance behind it. Maybe the second car had flashed it to a stop or, if the driver was a key component, it had been his choice. Which spoke volumes.

He took another careful look around at the immediate area. There was nothing here to provide cover for anyone lying in wait, which ruled out the idea of a pre-arranged ambush. Yet the location made it ideal for an attack. Even if there was anyone within earshot, gunfire in the area would be dismissed as an early hunting party or bird-scarers. People around here tended to mind their own business unless trouble rumbled up to their doorsteps.

Walking back to join Rizzotti, he asked him to take a look at the oil patch to confirm his thoughts. Another view was always useful. He considered the bodies again. Three men, North African or Middle Eastern in appearance: two in their thirties, armed and fit-looking, and an older man somewhere in his sixties, seated in the protective centre of the vehicle. Sadly, it hadn't done him much good.

'Any signs of a robbery?' A brown envelope was now pinned to the jacket on each body, and Rocco recognised Rizzotti's attention to organisation and detail.

'No,' Rizzotti replied. 'Desmoulins checked. Wallets, ID cards and money are all intact.'

Rocco opened the envelope on the older man and took out an identity card, a passport and a wallet. The latter held some folded Moroccan dirhams and French francs and three family-style photographs of innocent-looking faces smiling goofily at the camera, all light years away from this sad ending. A business card bore a telephone number and a name: Hafid Benhamid. A folded, dual-language entry permit to government buildings showed his age to be sixty-eight years, and gave an address in Rabat.

The face in the photograph was a slightly younger version of the dead man, unsmiling and stiffly formal in a dark suit, high white collar and a tightly knotted tie. Clearly a studio shot against a bland background, it told him nothing useful about what this man was or had been, save for the fact that he'd been a government employee of some kind with the clothes then and now indicating a certain level of money or class above the norm.

The other two men carried similar documentation but less in the way of personal effects. Saad Benhamid, the man who had exited the car, carried a service card bearing a red-and-gold government crest and listing him as a captain in the Royal Moroccan Police. Mohamed Benhamid was a lieutenant in the same organisation. Their faces matched two in the photographs from the old man's wallet.

So, sons and bodyguards, Rocco concluded. Or maybe nephews. Clearly the three Moroccans had been travelling north and dressed for trouble they had not seen coming in time to save themselves.

Two faded service invoices lay on the front passenger seat. Both were dated from three years ago. The garage was named Autos Samat and located in Rue Samatan, which, if he remembered correctly, was a mere spit from the Old Port of Marseille. It was a predominantly residential district with a few shops and small businesses housed in narrow streets, all overhung, as he recalled, with the smell of industry, oil and the many boats using the busy southern harbour.

Having spent more than a few days and nights down there in abandoned buildings on surveillance for gangs smuggling drugs and other contraband coming in from across the Med, Rocco knew it as a place where criminal organisations of every hue had ruled their patches with violence and fear.

Had they now exported that violence here?

Chapter Five

Rocco left his colleagues and Rizzotti to their work and made his way back to the office. He had enough inform-ation for now to begin the hunt for some background details on the three dead men, as well as the last recorded origins of the Mercedes, which might lead him to the driver. Follow the trail, he had learned very early on in his career, and you would usually get at least some of the answers you were looking for. If you were lucky, more than a few.

As he entered the outskirts of the town, he saw flashing blue lights ahead and a cluster of vehicles at a junction in the road. He was about to take a turning off to skirt the problem when he noticed a police car had become wrapped around a lamp post and a small Renault was buried nose deep in the front of a flower shop, the driver, an elderly man, waving his arms in the air. Both were surrounded by a carpet of colourful blooms and shards of glass glittering in the sun. A third vehicle, a white Citroën DS, wallowed inelegantly thirty metres further on outside a pavement café. The car had badly crumpled side panels and a buckled front wheel.

The avenue here was particularly wide, unlike in the centre of town, but even so traffic was building up and he could see why. He climbed out of his car to a caco-phony of noise from impatient motorists and onlookers and walked across the junction to where a cop in uniform was slumped unconscious against an electric junction box. He was surrounded by the broken remains of a wooden chair, with another cop tending to him. Nearby, a man in everyday shirt and trousers lay on the ground with his hands cuffed behind his back. He was struggling to get free and cursing at the cops, but unless he was related to Houdini he wasn't going to get very far.

Rocco ignored him and focused on the injured officer. He didn't try reading this particular scene; road traffic incidents involving multiple cars were often too complex to understand at first sight. Unfolding out of nothing in a matter of seconds, they were often beyond any rational explanation save that someone had made a mistake and someone else had paid the price. The question of who did what would come later.

The officer tending his colleague saw him coming and stood up. Rocco thought he recognised the man from somewhere but couldn't place him. In his late twenties, he looked fit and capable. He was slightly out of breath and his tie was askew.

'Morning, Inspector. Officer Mathieu Pouillot.' The man nodded briskly, adjusting his tie. 'Sorry – we had a bit of a tussle here.' He nodded towards the man in handcuffs.

'I can see that. At least it looks like you won. Do I know you?'

'Yes, sir. We met a while back after a bank robbery in Lille. I transferred in a couple of weeks ago.'

Then Rocco had it. 'I remember. You and a colleague cornered two armed men near an abandoned café.' The scene came flooding back. Another Mercedes that time, he remembered, a new model, unlike the one he'd just seen. It had been stolen by a devotedly under-accomplished Parisian street criminal named 'Bam-Bam' Fontenal for a raid on the Crédit Agricole in Lille. They'd ended up trying to hide from the police in a building standing on what had been discovered to be an enormous ammunition dump. It had seemed rather typical of Fontenal to have tempted fate in such a dramatic fashion.

Rocco bent and checked the wounded officer, who was breathing steadily but with one leg bent at a critical angle. 'What happened here?'

'We were on routine patrol outside town when we were overtaken by the DS being driven erratically. I signalled him to stop, but he refused. He tried to side-swipe us, then hit us hard just up the street. I'm afraid I lost the wheel and hit the lamp post. He tried to get away but when he got to the junction he broadsided the Renault and drove it across the pavement before losing control himself. The old guy cussing up a storm is the driver.'

'What about your colleague?'

'Officer Cabaud. He was first out of the car and tried to arrest the driver, but the man went berserk. I thought I could smell alcohol on him but he was rolling around so much I couldn't be certain. If he's not drunk, he's on something stronger.'

'And the chair?'

'He picked it up from the café near where he crashed and attacked Cabaud. By the time I got to him he'd laid Cabaud out and given him a broken leg and some busted fingers. There's an ambulance on the way now.' To confirm it, the tinny sound of an emergency vehicle could be heard over the rooftops. Seconds later it appeared at the top of the street, closely followed by two police cars, which disgorged several officers who set about clearing away sightseers and moving the backlog of cars while the medics attended to the injured officer.

Rocco was impressed by Pouillot's calm explanation. 'What did you do? I don't see any obvious bullet holes.'

Pouillot nodded at the people watching the events on both sides of the street. 'I can't say I wasn't tempted, but there were too many pedestrians about so I decked him and put the cuffs on.' He shrugged. 'I was lucky; it was only when I checked him out that I found this.' He held up a paper bag and showed Rocco. Inside was a revolver. 'Lucky he didn't get it out. We'd have been in real trouble.'

'A Browning,' said Rocco. 'And yes, you were lucky – you'd likely be dead if he'd used it. Still, good work. You know what to do: all the usual details and names of any eyewitnesses. And get your prisoner to a nice cell where he can't hurt anyone else.'

'Will do.' Pouillot grinned. 'They said in Lille that this area was more exciting.'

'Be careful what you wish for,' Rocco advised him, reminded of what he'd seen earlier. 'And remember the paperwork.'

'Will do.' He nodded towards Rocco's car, a Peugeot 403. 'Weren't you driving a black Traction Avant when we last met?'

'I was. It got bent.' He walked over to the car and found a radio message summoning him to a meeting at the station in one hour. The topic was a review meeting about the three deaths, confirmation that the identities and nationality of the three dead men had already filtered through the chain of command and was causing a flurry of anxiety at senior levels. That meant news would have got to the Interior Ministry, which in itself would be a cause for concern for everyone lower down the chain. The suits in the Ministry didn't like anything that might threaten their calm existence, and foreign nationals killed on French soil was a problem they wanted to avoid at all costs, as it usually brought questions, protests and demands for action against those suspected of the killings.

It took him five minutes to reach the Café Schubert, just round the corner from the station. A few uniforms on shift-change were sinking early drinks or late breakfasts, surrounded by a veil of cigarette smoke hanging overhead. It was clear from their expressions that they were discussing the latest event here in town and the shooting further out, but none of them made a move to ask any questions, merely nodding in greeting. He waved back, grateful for the break. Maybe they'd heard about the meeting and knew he was on the clock.

Rocco ordered a large black coffee and took it to a corner table where he stirred in several sugar lumps and sank a mouthful. It was bitter and gritty, and he quickly felt the shock of it hitting his system. He'd had a series of late nights and early mornings and the effects were beginning to catch up on him. Not that he could expect a let-up any time soon; being called into the meeting would make certain of that. But for now he was out of the way.

He drank his coffee while marshalling his thoughts on the few facts available. He had a feeling it was going to be laborious and involve a lot of telephone work with other regions and *départements*, some of which would be slow in returning anything useful. Typical police work, in other words.

Coffee done, and ready for the fray, he thanked Schubert and headed to the station, where a buzz of conversation in the ground-floor office proved that a multiple 'slaughter' was the main topic in town, along with the case of a lunatic driver who'd put one of their colleagues in hospital with life-threatening injuries and caused untold damage to several cars and buildings in the very centre of town.

He didn't waste time correcting the more outlandish speculations or suggesting that they should get out more; the actual details would emerge soon enough and until then, the rumour-mongers would enjoy the drama spicing up their day.

Chapter Six

Rocco was surprised to find Commissaire François Massin chairing the early review meeting, already seated at the head of the table in his office with two buff folders in front of him. He preferred to leave the day-to-day investigations to his subordinates, focusing instead on running the ship of local law-enforcement while preferring to be briefed in summary fashion later. In addition, Mme Ignace, his secretary, a mild-mannered and reserved lady in her late fifties, was seated just behind him and to one side with a notepad at the ready. She smiled nervously at everyone as if the nature of this meeting had suddenly dawned on her – that it was likely to discuss violent death and bloodshed.

Rocco saw what was at play: Massin, once totally in thrall to every demand of the Interior Ministry in Paris, had recently become more adept at keeping official fingers from probing too deeply into the way things were done here. His team's success rate at solving crimes had helped but it wasn't always enough, and Rocco was willing to bet this was one of those occasions. He could understand why; throw in foreign nationals being shot to death on his patch and Massin had little choice but to ensure everything was recorded carefully for his superiors to pore over endlessly before releasing anything relevant to the media.

Alongside Massin was his deputy, Commissaire Perronnet, tall and slim with a reputation for doing things by the book and who invariably backed Massin in all things. Captain Eric Canet, genial and nodding a welcome, represented the uniformed branch, along with the imposing figure of Deputy-Sergeant Godard of the Gendarmerie Mobile. Last was Dr Rizzotti, grinning at Rocco in his amiable manner.

'This business of the three men murdered in our area has already caused considerable ripples,' Massin began after the customary greetings. He opened one of the folders. 'The identity of the older man appears to have been sufficient to have raised eyebrows in certain quarters, so before the questions start flying in I'd like a review of where we are so far, to show we're on top of it.' He tapped the second folder and looked at Rocco. 'I also have details here of the brutal attack on two of our officers here in town. I'll discuss this with you later as there is an issue we need to be aware of.' Before Rocco could query what he meant, he gestured to his secretary. 'Mme Ignace will take notes for my report on the killings. I realise Dr Rizzotti has to complete a more detailed examination of the bodies and there is much we do not know, but, Inspector Rocco, let us start with your summary of what we have so far from the scene.'

Rocco nodded. Keeping it brief wasn't going to be a problem, but he could see where Massin was coming from. 'It's not much, I'm afraid. The three victims, all male, were carrying Moroccan papers. One held what appeared to be a government pass and two carried Moroccan police IDs. They were travelling north in a taxi, although there was no indication of where they were going or why.'

'I think the Ministry might have a view on that,' said Massin. 'But we'll see. Please continue.'

Rocco nodded. The Ministry would undoubtedly have a lot to say, which was their gut reaction to anything out of the ordinary. In fact, he'd be surprised if there wasn't already a flurry of activity heading their way to make sure no blame was attached to Paris for the deaths of the Moroccan nationals on French soil.

'All three were shot dead by an unknown assailant on the old Caix road, with what might have been the cooperation of the driver, who is missing. The vehicle, a Mercedes, is from the Marseille area but that's being checked out right now by Detective Desmoulins. From what we understand it stopped at the side of the road and another vehicle pulled up a short way behind. It's only guesswork at the moment but this second car might have belonged to the assassin. It's a quiet country road with no obvious witnesses as yet, and might have been chosen for that reason.'

'Chosen how?' This from Perronnet. 'If they were all strangers to the area, as it seems, they wouldn't have known what location was convenient or not.'

'That's a fair point,' Rocco agreed. Perronnet tended towards an air of aloofness that kept him apart from most people, but had recently adopted a tendency to marshal the facts and avoid indulging in politics, preferring to raise genuine queries. 'If the driver was involved, he would have likely been responsible for selecting a quiet location to stop. All the following driver had to do was wait for that to happen and move in.'

'And there are likely to be no witnesses?' Massin interjected.

'Not there, no. It's not used much and it's possible whoever planned this chose the route deliberately.'

'So somebody local might have been involved,' Captain Canet suggested.

It was another point to consider and Rocco knew he was going to have his work cut out; the Ministry might jump to the same conclusion and expect results quickly, as always.

'That's something we have to determine. If the actual location for the killing was down to the driver, then yes, he would have used his initiative to choose the best opportunity for the hit.'

'It makes you wonder if the passengers were aware of being followed,' said Godard. 'They seemed to be travelling in expectation of trouble, being armed.'

Rocco agreed. 'It's possible. We'll know more about that when we have confirmation of their identities and why they were here.'

Massin pulled a sour face. 'I'd be interested in knowing whether they had permission to be carrying weapons over here – and their point of entry.' He looked to Rizzotti. 'Anything to add so far about the killings?'

Rizzotti nodded. 'As Rocco has mentioned, the victims are three males, two in their thirties and one aged sixty-eight. All looked in good physical shape, were well-nourished and well-dressed. From their documentation, they shared the same family name. Each victim was shot once in the head. I don't have the facilities here to open them up and find the bullets but I know a surgeon here in Amiens who can perform the autopsies for me under controlled conditions so it doesn't spoil any chain of evidence. It will be quicker than sending the bodies to Paris, if you agree to that?' He looked at Massin for permission.

'Excellent,' Massin agreed. 'Do what you need to and I'll sign if off. What else?'

'From the wounds, my initial view is that the weapon used was a small calibre, but I need to check the bullets to be certain of the size.' He blinked. 'I must say, one shot each, that's remarkable – especially considering two of them seemed to be at least prepared for some form of retaliation.'

'Sounds like the work of a professional to me,' Godard murmured. 'That kind of shooting takes skill, not luck.'

'I would think so,' Rizzotti agreed. 'As Rocco will probably confirm, it doesn't have the look of a gang killing, which would have been much more messy and dramatic. Unfortunately we have no links to the weapon used because there were no shell casings left at the scene. Either the killer used a revolver or he used an automatic and picked up the ejected shells before leaving.'

'Would he bother doing that?' Massin queried. 'They could have fallen anywhere and I'd have thought he wouldn't want to waste time getting away.'

'If he was very careful,' Rocco said, 'and to a professional it would be second nature. Besides, the area around the car was fairly clear. He'd have seen where the ejected shells fell.'

Nobody spoke for a few seconds, absorbing this latest information and knowing that while every detail of this matter pointed to a professional hit, what they didn't know was why.

'It would help,' Perronnet said, glancing at Massin, 'if the Ministry could provide us with what they know of these three men. Coming from Morocco, it suggests that's where this business began.'

'I agree,' said Massin. 'It seems there's a lot more for us to do.'

'What about the thug in the cell?' Captain Canet queried. 'Koutcheff.' He was holding up a black-and-white photo of the man arrested at the scene of the crash. He sounded angry, as if he'd been waiting for his chance to speak about it. 'He put one of our men in hospital with broken bones but he's refusing to talk to anyone. And he was carrying a weapon. All he has said is that his employer is a very important person and we will have to let him go.'

Massin looked at Rizzotti. 'Have you examined him?'

'I took a quick look to make sure he was not incapacitated in any way. There were definite signs of alcohol on him but the effects were fading, I think. Some people process it faster than others. But that doesn't rule out the use of another intoxicant. They can produce a range of effects from stupefaction through to extreme excitability, which this case might well be. But whatever emotional state he displayed earlier seems to have abated.'

'Can you run a test for drugs?'

'Not reliably. I don't have the equipment and would have to rely on sending a sample to a laboratory in Paris. It might show a presence, but I gather from current studies that there is insufficient reliability because the presence of a narcotic wears off after a while.'

'So what do you suggest?'

'Charge him with assault on an officer,' Sergeant Godard rumbled pragmatically. 'Throw in criminal damage of property, resisting arrest and carrying a deadly weapon – a nine millimetre no less, which is a serious gun – and drop the key down the nearest drain. It might keep him off our streets for a while.' He looked at Massin, who seemed about to interrupt, and added, 'Officer Cabaud is currently assigned to my unit but on temporary duties with the traffic unit while recovering from a training

30

injury. It's typical of him to step up first and I hope the man who did this is going to be punished.'

'And,' suggested Perronnet, 'we should try to find out if he has some kind of mental deficiency. I gather the officer who detained him said he appeared out of control… like a berserker.'

Massin gave a hint of a smile. 'God help us. Vikings in northern France? I'm inclined to agree with Godard, personally. But maybe we need to see if there's more of a problem here.' He looked at Rocco. 'I know you have this triple killing to deal with but I'd like you to do an initial interview with this man to see what you can turn up. I'm damned if I'm going to have a gunman smashing up cars and assaulting officers in our streets, no matter who his employer might be.'

'About that,' Rocco reminded him. 'You said there was an issue we should be aware of. Is it the employer?'

'Indeed. From the papers he was carrying, Koutcheff appears to be in the employ of a man named Guy De Lancourt, an attorney with offices in Paris and an address not far from here. He does a lot of work for various government offices and has a habit of using his contacts with them if he feels like it, which is why we need to tread with care.' He tapped the folder in front of him. 'I don't care who his friends in Paris might be but let us make sure we have ample evidence to proceed before we go tripping over ourselves.'

'I'll bear it in mind,' said Rocco. It was all he needed right now: a high-priced city attorney with top-level contacts, who wasn't shy of using them. He'd come across people like this before and it was akin to swimming in shark-infested waters.

Massin gathered his papers and stood up. 'In the meantime, let's get this shooting investigated and I'll deal with the Ministry to see what they're willing to share with us.'

Chapter Seven

Rocco made his way down to the cells where Georges Koutcheff was being held. Given the choice he'd rather have been looking into the triple shooting of the Moroccans than the brutal rampage of an enraged motorist, but orders were orders.

He opened a folder carrying the man's personal effects and scanned the contents. Apart from some coins and car keys, it held a faded green ID card and a wallet, which told him that Koutcheff was employed as a secretary with a home address in Amiens. A confirmation of employment letter dated a year ago detailed the address of G. De Lancourt as near the village of Petit Montgallet, some dozen kilometres away.

'Times are changing,' said Perronnet dryly, looming up behind Rocco and peering at the contents of the wallet. 'My wife's a secretary and she can't even step on a spider in case it has a soul, much less beat someone up in a mad rage.' He gave a smile. 'I suppose I should be grateful.' He walked on, leaving Rocco wondering if the normally stuffed-shirt officer was beginning to unbend a little like his superior.

At Rocco's signal, the custody officer unlocked the cell and ushered the prisoner into an interview room with a table and two chairs, then remained in the room as a witness. Koutcheff looked unconcerned by the procedure or the cold grey walls and chipped paintwork, and sat on the chair with his hands on his thighs, staring straight ahead.

Rocco recognised the stance; he'd seen it in many men in military circles, waiting in the presence of a senior officer to be judged, punished or praised, conditioned by their training to remain at attention even while seated. It had served many as a safeguard against nerves and for keeping up a staunch show of bravado in the face of whatever bad was about to come their way.

He took the other chair and said, 'I'm Inspector Rocco. Can you confirm your name, please?'

'You've got my stuff. Why do you need to ask?' The prisoner looked at him with a steady, challenging gaze. He had cool blue eyes, short-cropped hair and the sturdy build of a man who kept himself in good physical shape. He was also displaying a level of defiance that was somehow different to some of the most hardened criminals Rocco had confronted. They were mostly in angry denial, resentful and brash, while playing a role that they imagined was somehow expected of them, part tough guy, part bluster. Koutcheff, however, possessed something else, as if he were above anything Rocco or the system could throw at him, too distant even to be frightened about what lay ahead.

'Ex-military?'

'It shows, does it?' His lips moved in what might have been a smile. 'How about you? An office boy, I bet; never been near a front line in your life. Never had it tough, either, like most cops.'

Rocco ignored the taunt. He'd heard far worse before now and allowing it to affect him would merely put him on the back foot. He wondered whether Koutcheff, like himself, had seen service in Indochina. It would be something to look into. 'What was your regiment?'

'That doesn't concern you – it's in the past. You wouldn't understand, anyway.'

Rocco allowed a few seconds to tick by. It was an odd thing for the man to say, and he wondered what lay in his background. He resolved to find out. 'When did you leave the military?'

A shrug. 'A year ago. What does it matter? Can I go now?' He got to his feet and the custody officer was instantly ready to step in. Rocco signalled for the officer to stay where he was, but stayed seated himself, hands at rest on the table.

'Sit down, soldier,' he said easily. 'You'll leave this room when I'm ready.'

Five seconds went by, the tension in the room accentuated by the sounds of breathing. Koutcheff calmly took in Rocco's position and the guard's, as if assessing the situation, then shrugged and resumed his seat. 'You'd like that, wouldn't you,' he murmured, eyeing them both. 'A chance to bounce me around the room a few times to soften me up? I wouldn't try it.'

'Why didn't you stop when indicated by the patrol car?'

'I didn't feel like it. Next question.'

'You committed a serious assault on a police officer trying to execute his duty. Do you deny that?'

'No comment.'

'You were found to be carrying a revolver. Do you have a current permit for it?'

'No comment.'

Rocco held up the man's wallet. Apart from the ID card, the employment letter, a faded photo of three soldiers in full battle gear and some paper money, it held nothing of any use. 'You don't have much of anything, do you?'

'I prefer to travel light.' Koutcheff yawned and added, 'Do I get something to eat and drink here? I'm starving. Why don't you toddle off and get me something, there's a good boy.'

'Of course. We have a contract with a local Michelin-style restaurant. Answer my questions and I'll see what I can arrange. Would you like the menu of the day?'

Koutcheff's mouth moved into a sneer at the sarcasm and he said, 'I won't be here long enough for that, so why don't you let me go now and save us all some time?'

'Koutcheff – that sounds Russian. Is that where you're from?' Get a resentful and angry prisoner talking about something close to them and not on the subject in hand, he usually found, and it began the task of unlocking their unwillingness to talk.

But Koutcheff wasn't like most prisoners; bigging himself up in the face of adversity was clearly not part of his character. 'I've no idea. I never asked.'

'I see you're employed as a secretary for a Mr...' He made a show of scanning the letter although he knew the contents perfectly well. '...Mr Guy De Lancourt. What kind of business is Mr De Lancourt engaged in?'

'That's not relevant. Next question.'

'In a way you're correct: it's not really relevant to the charges you're going to be facing. But I'm wondering who employs a gun-carrying ex-military man as a secretary. The gun might pass muster in Paris where there are all sorts of reasons for someone to employ a professional bodyguard, but out here in the sticks?' He shrugged. 'Not so much. Maybe a typewriter really is more your style.'

There was a flash of something deep in Koutcheff's blue eyes that might have been anger, impatience or resentment. For a split second the man looked as if he might leap up and go on the attack. But the light faded as quickly as it had come and he blinked and looked away. It was another surprise; he clearly possessed, when it suited him, some powers of self-control. Did that mean the opposite was also true – that he could turn on the aggression when needed and become a completely different animal?

'You do know there are serious consequences for assaulting a police officer?'

No reaction.

'It's even worse for putting that officer in hospital. And that's without adding the possession of the gun, the considerable damage to property and failing to stop for a police officer when indicated. Unless you can explain why you did it, they won't just throw the book at you, they'll bury you underneath a pile of paper so deep you won't see daylight for a long, long time.'

'Like I said, Rocco, I won't be in here long, so drop the threats. You're wasting your time.'

'Fair enough.' Rocco stood up. 'You will be charged with the various offences in the next few hours and held until your case comes up before the court. Whenever that may be. I should warn you there's a bit of a backlog. The rest is up to you.'

The custody officer opened the door and ushered Koutcheff out of the room and back to his cell, with Rocco following close behind. As the cell door closed, Rocco felt Koutcheff's eyes on him as if he were memorising every detail of his face.

As he turned to leave, he saw Perronnet hovering at the end of the corridor.

'Any response?' the deputy commissaire asked.

'No,' said Rocco. 'I don't think he's going to crack easily.'

'Seriously? I thought you'd have him eating out of your hand.' He gave a hint of a wry smile.

'Quite the opposite. He seems to think he'll be out soon.'

Perronnet pursed his lips. 'Yes. Massin is concerned about that.'

'This De Lancourt,' Rocco asked. 'Do you know him?'

'I do, although not well. I take it you haven't had the pleasure?'

'Not yet. The only place I mix with lawyers is in court.'

'Lucky you. Well, there is a bit of a problem.' He gestured for Rocco to follow him into the interview room and explained, 'Outwardly – at least around here – De Lancourt is one of the region's more artistic residents. As well as being a lawyer he has a certain reputation among some as a writer and historian, among other things. I've known of him vaguely for several years, although we don't move in the same august circles.' His face clouded momentarily in what might have been disapproval, although since that was one of his more common expressions it was hard to tell.

'So where does the trouble come in?'

'That's his other side – and why Massin wanted you to get involved. He's an active lawyer with chambers in Paris, which places him close to the seat of power and influence. He knows all the right people, if you understand my meaning, and tends to fight dirty in court by summoning expert witnesses of high calibre and position. God knows how he does it but he seems to be able to exert some pull in certain quarters. I know that has never deterred you before and nor should it, but it's something you should bear in mind should you ever come into contact with him. He doesn't fight without having all the advantages and weighing up the opposition carefully.'

'Am I likely to come into contact with him?'

'Absolutely. If he values this man Koutcheff, he'll likely want him out on the street rather than in a cell. De Lancourt does not like publicity unless it helps him, especially right now. It might put a little crimp into his reputation if he were found to have employed an armed thug who beats up policemen in public. He'll fight it because it's what he does.'

'You said "right now". What does that mean?'

'Simple. De Lancourt aspires to membership of the Académie Française, a position that's been denied him for some time.' He sniffed. 'Along with his friends in high places he has attracted enemies, too, over the years. But times and attitudes have changed and he now seems to be in the running for a seat, which will give him even greater influence. I take it you have heard of the academy, at least?' His look suggested there might be some doubt.

'Yes. A bunch of poets and writers.'

Perronnet almost shuddered at the words. 'Good God, Rocco, if they heard you dismiss them so casually they'd demand your head on a spike – and they'd probably get it served up on a silk cushion.' He took a small notepad out of his jacket pocket and scribbled a name on it. 'Gérard Jeunet is a former academy member who lives locally. He resigned due to ill health a couple of years ago and now prefers to live a quiet life free of pressure and competition. He's an art historian by profession but now stays out of the limelight. Every Wednesday morning at eleven he visits the cheese market here in town followed by taking coffee and cognac at one of the local cafés. Look out for the tallest man in the place and it'll be Jeunet. He'll give you a few pointers about the academy and its members… most importantly, if he's in the right mood, about De Lancourt. Jeunet voted against his membership at least twice in the past.'

'You've primed him?'

'I gave him a subtle pointer, yes. You might find a chat with him useful before you think of going anywhere near De Lancourt.'

'You said Jeunet is a former member. Don't they serve for life?'

Perronnet's eyebrows lifted in surprise. 'That's correct, they do. Some may lose their seat due to misconduct or unseemly behaviour, but that's rare. Others, like Jeunet, resign due to ill health or old age, or they drop gracefully off the perch when their time is up. There are far more who fall into the two latter categories, of course. Time and tide and so forth.'

'But is Jeunet likely to tell me anything useful that will help keep Koutcheff locked up?'

'That I can't guarantee. But he's bored and a little ill-tempered about the state of his health, and feels the academy moved with uncommon speed to fill his seat. I get the feeling he'll be happy to get some of that off his chest. Good luck.'

With that, Perronnet breezed out of the room as if he'd never been there.

Chapter Eight

The afternoon whirled away with surprising speed, with Rocco and his colleagues busy working the telephones in search of answers to the origins of the three dead Moroccan nationals. The Mercedes had been through a number of hands before being reported as stolen several days ago from a used-car garage in Nice. Calls to the police there had provided no solid leads and little enthusiasm to help. It was an old car and they had more pressing crimes to deal with.

Predictably, calls to the Moroccan consulate and the Royal Moroccan Police headquarters in Rabat asking about the Benhamids were met with long delays or the dialling tone, and eventually an official comment that any questions about Moroccan nationals should be addressed by the French Foreign Ministry to their embassy in Paris.

In the end, Rocco had recognised that they were getting nowhere and suggested that everyone call it a day and resume investigations in the morning. He drove home with a feeling of frustration familiar to all police officers in the course of their enquiries when getting stuck in mud seems a pleasant alternative way of passing the day, and the reminder that nothing ever came easily, even at an official level. Like surveillance work, waiting was part of the job.

As Rocco pulled into his driveway in Poissons-les-Marais and switched off the engine, he saw Mme Denis, his elderly but sprightly neighbour bustling towards his gate bearing a small basket. He was prepared to bet it carried vegetables, eggs or, he would not be surprised to find one day, a dead rabbit. She had taken it upon herself to look after him from the time he'd arrived in the small village just over a year ago, and delighted in plying him regularly with whatever produce she thought was necessary to keep his body and soul together. She'd also helped him fit into the community when few others had shown anything but suspicion about the arrival of a police detective in their midst. At least he now had a passing familiarity with some of the more prominent residents, such as Georges Maillard, the café owner, Claude Lamotte, the local *garde champêtre* or rural policeman and a regular colleague, and M. Thierry, an odd-job man who also looked after the churchyard. Thus far, Rocco's standing with the village priest, whose name he still didn't know, had remained on the cool side as he never attended Mass and had shown no interest in doing so. His feelings for the church in any guise were less than friendly and he didn't want to encourage any false hope.

'Here,' she greeted him, as he climbed from the car. 'A few things to be going on with.'

Rocco smiled and thanked her for the basket but she showed no sign of moving away. She had obviously heard something on the village grapevine and wanted to pick his brain for scraps that would enhance her position as a source of privileged information courtesy of the cop next door. It was a game she'd played before and he usually dropped a few hints her way without breaking any rules of confidentiality.

'Come on,' he said finally, and walked to the house, unlocking the door. 'You get the drinks and I'll bring you up to date.'

'Really? About what?' Her innocence was as transparent as mud but she lost no time in finding two wine glasses and taking a bottle of Muscadet from a picnic cooler in the corner.

'You start first,' he responded, 'and I'll tell you if what you've heard is rubbish.' He checked the basket and saw a selection of apples, potatoes and eggs, all from her garden. He thanked her and watched as she poured two half glasses and pushed one across the table towards him before sitting down. He knew from previous occasions that Mme Denis would only sip hers while she listened to what he had to say, just to be sociable.

The old lady tasted her wine and said, 'Three dead, I hear, shot along the old Caix road. Is that right? What is this world coming to?'

Rocco marvelled as always at the expertise of the local bush telegraph. How they transmitted information from village to village was a mystery, as telephones were few and far between. But it was never long in moving around and usually uncannily accurate apart from a few outrageous embellishments to spice things up. It had occurred to him before that if the police could transmit bulletins with such efficiency and speed, they'd solve a lot more crimes.

'Who gave you the nod this time?' he asked. 'Mme Duverre? Or Sylvia?' They were two of the local links that he knew of, but there were others he'd never met strung out across the surrounding villages, all eager to be in on the latest gossip.

'Neither, actually. But I expect they'll both know by now... although of course they won't have any first-hand details, will they?' Her eyes twinkled teasingly, waiting for him to give up what he knew.

'Sorry to disappoint you,' he said. 'There were three men killed but I can't give you the details. Three unknown men in a car, that's all we've got. It's a mystery.'

Mme Denis looked momentarily nonplussed, then shrugged. 'Ah, well, what you don't know you can't tell, I suppose.' She peered at him over the rim of her glass as if trying to tell if he was lying. 'I hear they were from the south… like, across the Mediterranean. Just nod if I'm right, there's a dear.'

'No comment,' he said with a firm smile. 'And stop asking. You're going to get me shot one of these days. But' – he held up a hand to forestall her next question – 'I will have more information tomorrow.' He did a sign of the cross. 'Hot off the press, I promise.'

She grinned and stood up, her wine barely touched. 'That's good enough. As long as I get it before anyone else. Have you seen your young lady recently, by the way?'

'Which young lady is that?' He knew who she meant but liked to play hard to get. If he gave even a hint that there was any kind of change to his status, she wouldn't stop asking questions until he folded like a rickety old fence in a high wind.

'The artist's daughter from the old chateau near Passepont. She seems a nice girl… from what I've heard, anyway.'

'Her name is Eliane,' he told her, 'and she's not my young lady. She doesn't count as even a friend. Her father helped us with our investigations, that's all.'

'Ah, yes.' She narrowed her eyes. 'The art fraud thing. I remember. And of course you must have found it *so* tiresome having to go back there to see him more than once. You poor boy!' She laughed at the expression on his face and walked to the door. For good measure, she made a noise of disbelief. '*Pffit*. Not a friend… pull the other one, Inspector. Don't worry – I'll see myself out.'

Chapter Nine

Next morning, before leaving for Amiens and his meeting with the former academy member, Rocco drove to Claude Lamotte's house at the other end of the village. As the local *garde champêtre* or rural policeman, Claude had proved himself invaluable in dealing with the local area and sharing his knowledge of the population and its quirks. He lived alone, although he had two daughters, one of them a police officer in Amiens.

'I was hoping you'd come by,' said Claude, opening the door with an expectant grin. He was dressed in a dark green shirt and brown corduroys, his usual working attire, and his stocky build made him look impregnable and anchored to the ground. 'A triple shooting, I hear. It never rains, eh? D'you want coffee?'

'No thanks. We're pressed for time before the Ministry gets involved.'

Claude grinned, aware of the uneasy relationship Rocco had with the suits in Paris. 'Good luck with that, then. What can I do to help?' He knew Rocco wouldn't have come here unless he could add something to the investigation. Strictly speaking it wasn't part of his job but he was glad to throw his cap into the ring because Rocco, unlike some other officers, didn't treat him like a simple country cop but a valued member of the force.

Rocco described the scene and the location of the shooting and summarised what little they knew so far. 'The investigation team and Rizzotti covered the immediate area but I need a fresh pair of eyes to go along the route both ways, and check the area for signs of disturbance.'

'Sure. Anything specific?'

'If the driver wasn't involved in the shooting, he might have legged it along the road before heading off across the fields. But I need to be sure we haven't missed anything. You know that area better than I do so perhaps you could take a look.'

Claude nodded and pursed his lips. 'That road doesn't get a lot of use so a body could lie out in the fields for a while before anyone noticed. It looks flat but there's quite a bit of dead ground all over there with old shell holes and the remains of trenches that never got filled in properly or have sunk over time. Easy to miss something if you don't know it.'

'Good point. I'm not saying the uniforms didn't do a proper job, but another pair of eyes is always helpful.'

Claude nodded. 'Other than the driver is there anything you're looking for in particular?'

'Nothing I can put my finger on. The victims' car stopped there for some reason, and I've a feeling the killer was in another vehicle that followed behind or intercepted them. You'll see the signs on the road. See if you can spot anything that stands out.'

'Will do. I hear there was a bust-up in town yesterday, with an officer put in hospital.'

Rocco gave him the basic details. At mention of Koutcheff's employer, he raised his eyebrows. 'De Lancourt? Now there's an odd fish. He's a big cheese

47

lawyer in Paris and lives in a former mental asylum out near Petit Montgallet. It's little more than a hamlet and I don't have cause to get out that way much. The locals say he employs some pretty rough types as gardeners and general workers.'

'Rough in what way?' If they were anything like Koutcheff, it made Rocco wonder if there wasn't a pattern here.

'There's been the occasional bust-up in the local café and one or two further afield. In fact, they've been banned from a few from what I hear. I'm only going on local chit-chat, but you know how the people around here talk. Rumour is he likes to do good works on the side and gives work to former military men having a hard time, although that's not so good for the locals.'

'Is he ex-military?'

'No idea. He's a lawyer, so I doubt it.'

'Is he at home much?'

'He spends a lot of time in Paris, but he has weekend gatherings on a regular basis with a few of the high and the mighty coming down for cocktails or whatever it is they drink. He's quite the social animal among his own kind.' Claude's voice left little doubt about his feelings; he liked lawyers about as much as Rocco did. He gave Rocco a knowing look. 'Are you thinking of paying him a visit?'

'Maybe. Why?'

'Just asking. You know I'm here if you need me. And I wouldn't mind a closer look at the place. I hear he's made quite a transformation.'

Rocco smiled. 'I'll bear it in mind.'

Rocco bade him goodbye and made his way to the office, where he checked on the prisoner, Koutcheff. There had been no response to further questioning other

48

than demands that he be released without further delay. Rocco couldn't decide whether the man was in denial or simply insane, and left him to stew. As he walked back to his desk to organise a list of calls to be made and check on progress so far, he saw two men in suits enter the building and make their way upstairs. One was tall, lean and moving fast; the other was built like a truck and struggling to keep up, his face red with effort.

'This doesn't look good,' said Detective Desmoulins, watching them go. 'Do I smell the Ministry?'

'More like Laurel and Hardy come to entertain us,' muttered another officer nearby, causing a ripple of laughter.

By ten o'clock, Rocco decided to get along to the cheese market for his meeting with Gérard Jeunet. He wasn't sure just how much use it would be but at this stage he wasn't about to turn down any background information he could get, especially if it helped him stay out of trouble with friends of friends in high places. And if Perronnet thought there could be a problem, it was worth taking heed.

As he walked towards the door, Dr Rizzotti intercepted him. 'I hear we've just received representations for the prisoner's release.' He nodded towards the ceiling. 'A couple of lawyers came by earlier, one of them from Paris. They're waving lots of official-looking paper around. I hope you've got your long underwear on.'

Rocco was surprised. 'I wondered who they were. Release on what grounds?'

'Unfair arrest, assault and claims Koutcheff didn't realise it was a police car but was in fear of his life due to battle trauma.' He gave a sour smile. 'Amazing to think that a car with a blue light, badge and siren might belong to anyone else.'

'And?'

Rizzotti laughed. 'Not a chance... for now, anyway. Massin's holding the line.'

'Long may it last.' He had a thought and pulled Rizzotti to one side. 'I'll be going to see De Lancourt later for some background information. What's your opinion on Koutcheff's state of mind?'

'That's a broad question. Going on what we know, he evidently exhibited extremes of unexplained behaviour leading to serious assault, then shifted to a state of calm once he was in the cell. It's not exactly normal but I've heard of it before, although usually involving intoxicants. If it was I can't tell which one, but there's clearly something amiss. That's something his lawyer might claim as a defence, but we'll have to see.'

Chapter Ten

Claude Lamotte drove across country towards Beaufort until he reached the old road running from the village north towards Caix, the next commune. He turned and headed that way and soon came across the site of the shooting outlined by police markers. The suspension on his grey 2CV squeaked in mild protest as he bumped up onto the grass verge out of the way and switched off the engine. There were few cars to trade the space with out here, but he didn't want to risk his car being sideswiped by a tractor and trailer driven by a careless local with his brain in neutral.

Claude eased his frame out of the old canvas seat, which had long ago given up any idea of tension, and stared around at the scene. There was little sign of the actual shooting described by Rocco save for a patch of dried blood on the road where one man had fallen and a few chalk marks left by the investigation team. The Mercedes had gone, taken away for further examination in Amiens.

The fields on either side were covered in a short, beige stubble running into the distance like the bristles on an upturned curry comb. Claude tried putting himself in the mind of a man in fear for his life after witnessing a gunman shoot three men dead in the back of his car, and wondering what that man might do. Run, certainly; instinct alone would make him do that – that's if he didn't freeze with shock on seeing such horror. As to which way, there was a wide swath of countryside to choose from. But where? Which direction offered the best hope of survival?

Avoiding a bullet in the back by hiding in cover would be impossible – there was none immediately to hand. And from what Rocco had said, the gunman had demonstrated considerable skill by despatching three men with three bullets. Another one to add to the score would have been an easy task.

There was also the basic question of outrunning a bullet. Nobody could – and taxi drivers were not generally known for their athleticism, due to sitting behind a wheel for hours each day and snatching meals whenever they could. Claude himself had once been a taxi driver in Paris and knew the downsides of the calling first-hand.

Still, maybe sheer blind terror had turned this one into a gazelle, and he'd hoofed it over the horizon before the gunman could stop him. Unlikely but worth considering.

Claude walked a good three hundred metres along one side of the road before branching off into the field, looking for signs of a man on the run. The ground underneath was soft enough to show the boot-prints left by one of the uniformed cops Rocco had sent out here, the imprints of his gait shallow and even. The tracks of a man running for his life would have been much deeper, desperately uneven and unlikely to have been in a straight line, but more of a mad, lurching dash to avoid the red-hot burn of a bullet.

The stubble rasped against his gaiters, the sound setting up a flurry of small ground birds followed by a hare bouncing away into the distance. Claude swore mildly at the last one, a lost opportunity; one shot and he'd have had dinner taken care of.

In the end he turned back, finding no dead ground here save for one sunken shell-hole barely big enough to hide a small dog. Crossing the road, he repeated the exercise on the other side.

There was a little more dead ground here, with the snake-like signs of an old World War One trench system in the earth, the in-fill soil marked by the tell-tale scar of chalk. As always at times and places like this, he found himself wondering about the men on both sides who had fought, survived or died here, each one leaving their mark on the ground for generations to come.

But there was no sign of disturbance anywhere save for the footprints left by the cops. He performed a zig-zag pattern over the whole area until he was certain he'd covered every possible angle. If the driver had come out this way, he must have grown wings – or run along the road. And that would have made him even easier for the killer to catch.

Claude returned to his car and stood for a few moments, trying to visualise the unseeable. Skylarks high above provided their unique background music along with the buzz of a tractor far in the distance, and a few small birds whirled and jumped close to the ground, snatching up grains from the completed harvest. Apart from that, nothing to get excited about. If the driver wasn't out there, where was he? There was no way any gunman would have allowed a witness to escape; it simply didn't happen. Witnesses to a killing were to be despatched, not allowed to run free and spread their tales.

Climbing back in the car, he opened up the soft roof, flooding the inside with light. He drifted slowly along the road, one eye on the mirror and stopping occasionally to climb on his seat and peer around him like a tank commander surveying the battlefield. But nothing showed up in the fields.

Then he spotted the dark shapes of crows, wheeling and circling in the sky over what looked like a statue of the Virgin at a small crossroads. He pulled up near the statue, its metal surface weathered by time but carrying a small clutch of dead flowers nestled into a crevice by the Virgin's foot, a sign that someone locally still valued its presence and potential support. The birds' collected cries of disgust echoed around him before they gave up and moved away towards the horizon, leaving behind a heavy silence save for the sound of the breeze hissing over the landscape.

Claude climbed out and looked around. There were no hedges here, simply small grass-covered berms running along the side of the road with a shallow ditch on the far side and a similar arrangement delineating one field from another. Why pay for the cost of a wire fence when a ditch performed the same service?

He looked down at the road surface, which showed a streak of black rubber. Further over, where the verge began, was a long rip in the grass. He bent and flicked the grass to one side for a better view, revealing a shallow gouge in the soil beneath.

A vehicle had braked fiercely here, leaving its marks.

Claude looked up. The crows had gone but this was where they had been focusing their attention. But on what? Crows were driven by an insatiable curiosity and an investigative nature allied to their ongoing hunt for food. Yet there was no sign of roadkill here, and they had neither the time nor energy to waste on empty stretches of tarmac with no pickings.

Stepping past the statue and up onto the berm behind it to get a better view, Claude looked down into the ditch behind, expecting to see little save for a shallow dip in the earth filled with grass and weeds.

He felt his gut go cold.

It was the body of a man. He was lying on his back, his limbs thrown out in an untidy star shape. The face was ravaged by deep tears and scratches in the skin made by the crows' beaks, and one eye was gone, leaving a mess of gore deep in the socket. The remaining eye was staring up at the sky with a look of shock.

Chapter Eleven

Rocco entered the cheese hall just before eleven and began a circuit of the stalls. The various aromas from the products on display enveloped him immediately in their embrace, hanging in the air like intertwined layers of curtain material, each one waiting for appreciative customers to push their way through and savour their peculiarities like the fine wines they so often accompanied. His nose wrinkled. He enjoyed the many cheeses France had to offer as much as the next man, but not when they ganged up on him.

Perronnet must have been enjoying the slight air of mystery in arranging this meeting, rather like a spy movie but without the need to sport a red buttonhole or a carry a copy of *Figaro*. Rocco hoped it was going to lead to something useful.

The customers were mostly women with shopping bags and a handful of older men with a vague air of having come in here by mistake and yet to find the exit. Then he spotted the only person who could be Jeunet, hunched over one of the displays. As Perronnet had described, he was exceptionally tall. He looked frail, a tweed jacket hanging loosely from his shoulders, and wore a plaid peaked cap pulled low over his forehead. His feet were encased in brown brogue shoes, which Rocco recognised as English; he had a similar pair in black.

Jeunet was prodding a small round of creamy Boursault from the Loire Valley, under the watchful eye of the stall owner, and looking as if the cheese might leap up and bite him.

'You must be Rocco,' the man said without looking round. 'I was told you had a certain presence. I swear I felt a shudder of apprehension run through the place the second you walked in.' He glanced up and smiled, his deep eyes rheumy but bright with a twinkle of humour. 'Coffee, I think. Then we can talk?'

Rocco nodded towards the cheeses on display. 'Are you sure I'm not interrupting something?'

'Not at all, dear boy. Don't worry, they know who I am; I come in every now and then just to put the frighteners on them. He'll have an excellent selection set aside for me later; my weekly treat. My doctor tells me I should stop eating so much of the damned stuff, but that's like denying a man a glass of wine. Or cognac. Don't you agree?'

Jeunet turned away without waiting for a reply and led the way out of the market at a brisker pace than Rocco had expected to a café in a quiet side street away from the crowds, where they found a corner table. The café owner came out from behind his counter like a sprinter on a starter's gun the moment he spotted Jeunet and fussed over him, serving black coffee in sturdy cups alongside small balloon glasses of golden cognac. When Jeunet waved him away with a casual hand, he almost bowed on the retreat and disappeared through a plastic curtain into the back of the café like a genie.

'He's an old fraud.' Jeunet watched as the man picked up a telephone and started dialling. 'And he knows it. He's currently ringing his competitors in the neighbourhood, telling them he's just served me and wishing them a thoroughly depressing day. Give it ten minutes and they'll all be round here peering through the window and pretending not to. It's a game they enjoy.' He winked at Rocco and added, 'So do I, if I'm honest. It helps pass the time.'

Rocco held up the short-stemmed glass and wondered if he should give it a miss. A clear mind was a necessity for police work and he had a feeling this current task was going to be a blinder.

'Don't worry,' said Jeunet with a mild chuckle, 'I won't tell on you to your superiors. Anyway, one glass is a powerful aid to digestion and concentration at any time of day, so they should be grateful for your devotion to duty.' With that he drank half his cognac and poured the rest into his coffee. 'Now, Eugène said you needed some information about the Académie Française, correct?'

For a split second Rocco had no idea who Eugène might be, before realising he was talking about Perronnet. He'd never heard the officer's given name before. 'That's right. Thank you for agreeing to meet me.'

'Why would I not? It sounds intriguing. Now, how can I help and which one of us old fossils are you going to arrest?' He grinned and signalled to the café owner for a refill of his cognac. Rocco declined with a quick wave of his hand. Another one of these so early in the day and he'd likely end up in the adjacent cell to Koutcheff. For all his faint display of humour yesterday, Perronnet did not approve of police officers rolling around the station under the influence of alcohol.

'Not you, I can assure you,' Rocco said.

'That's a shame. I could do with some excitement and the tinge of disapproval from some of my over-elevated colleagues. Still, maybe another day.'

Rocco smiled. He found he rather liked this man, who had none of the pretensions he'd been expecting of a member of the august body he represented. Perronnet had said nothing about him but Rocco got the sense that they had known each other for many years.

Sipping at his cognac, he felt the soft burn of the alcohol in his throat. He followed it with some coffee and reflected that there were far worse ways of starting a discussion.

'I'm working on a case that involves a person connected to a potential applicant to the academy,' he said carefully. 'The case doesn't involve the applicant himself, but I wanted to find out more about the academy as background to avoid tripping over any potential problems.'

'I see. Very wise of you. We can be a vicious load of old bastards when the moon is full. Is it a serious crime?'

'Serious enough. Assault on a police officer, property damage and possession of a gun.'

'Right.' Jeunet gave a faint smile. 'Well, that lets me off the hook. I've often thought of assaulting someone but never have. Not yet, anyway.' He toyed with his glass. 'How much do you know about the academy, Inspector?'

'Lucas, please. Let's pretend I know nothing.'

'Thank you. I'm Gérard. In that case I won't bore you with a lengthy history lesson as it would serve no purpose. In brief, the council was set up by Cardinal Richelieu in 1635, and known informally as *les immortels* – the immortals.' He wagged his head. 'Sadly it doesn't mean that we gain everlasting life – although many would prefer that it did – merely because that term is on the charter seal granted by Richelieu. Quaint, don't you think?'

'What's the specific purpose of the academy?'

'Simply? To protect the French language, grammar and literature from, among others, the invasion of modern idioms such as Americanisms and the ghastly predations by the modern youth's lack of respect for our language.' He grinned. 'Not my words – I'm paraphrasing a member of many years ago. It's a losing battle in many respects, but we have a duty to perform and we all take it seriously. Or took it, I should say.'

'You no longer do?'

Jeunet winced in a mild show of embarrassment. 'Let us say, not so much. I absconded. I no longer have the passion or the energy, if I'm honest. It's like facing a tide that threatens to overwhelm us... although that shouldn't stop us trying. I'm sure you feel the same way about policing.'

Rocco didn't comment. He understood the man's feelings but didn't know him well enough to say anything that might come back to bite him later. 'How long do you serve?'

'For life... unless serious illness or something else gets in the way.'

'Something like... bad behaviour?'

Jeunet laughed. 'That's a quaint way of saying it. But yes, like that. There have been one or two members in the past who have been unseated for such things. But most of us die in service, like carthorses, past their best but occasionally useful. We number forty in all, and your mention of an applicant reminds me that there are currently two vacancies up for grabs.' He looked Rocco in the eye. 'I suppose you can't drop a hint as to who this applicant might be, can you?'

'I'm afraid that would be unethical.'

'Damn. An honourable cop. Just my luck.' He stuck a finger in his cognac and licked the tip with appreciation.

'How powerful are the members?'

'By themselves, not at all... although some have powerful friends, which I suppose amounts to the same thing.' He pursed his lips. 'You're no doubt concerned by the possibility that this unnamed person could seek the protection of the unnamed applicant to dodge an investigation.'

'Yes.'

'It's a possibility, but in my experience, members of the academy have far more to lose by standing up for a dubious friend than stepping back and keeping their counsel. It's not that they – we – are moral cowards, far from it. But our responsibilities are to the state. Our acquaintances come second to that.' He peered at Rocco from beneath his brows, and suddenly his face changed as if a radical thought had come to mind.

'Did I say something?' Rocco asked.

'You did indeed. Damn. I think I know to whom you're referring. It's De Lancourt, isn't it? Guy bloody rotten De Lancourt.' The words were uttered with a degree of venom. 'Go on – admit it. He's been trying to get a seat in the academy for years and no bugger has allowed it – me included.' He chuckled to himself with a delighted expression. 'I knew this chat would make my day, and it has!'

'It sounds as if you don't like him much.'

'Not at all, as it happens. He's not exactly one to bring credit to the academy in my view, although don't quote me on that. He's deeply litigious and fights his corner like an angry polecat. He pretends to do good works but

61

frankly, I'm not sure how wide that goes. And he changed his name, the sure mark of a scoundrel in my view.'

'Is that relevant?'

'Probably not, but it's an indication of vanity, don't you think?'

'It depends. Was there a family problem in the past?'

'Hah!' Jeunet gave a bark of sour humour. 'As far as I know all the problem lies with De Lancourt himself… or should I say Delancourt, its original spelling. Not many people know it but he changed it some years ago.' He shook his head. 'So arrogant he even capitalised the De to give it more gravitas.' He made a rude noise with his lips.

Rocco said nothing. Jeunet really didn't like the lawyer, which was interesting. He wondered how much Perronnet had let slip while priming this man to talk to him. On the other hand, how many potential or hopeful members of the academy could there be living in this part of the country? Whatever his state of health, Jeunet was no idiot.

After a period of silence, he prompted him. 'You say he does good works?'

'Yes. He "employs" – and I use the word loosely – former military men who have fallen on hard times. I'm not sure why but word is he takes them in, gives them employment for a while, then sends them on their way to who knows where. He calls it rehabilitation but I've never seen what happens to the men who move on. All I know is, they don't seem to stick around very long, but he seems to think he's doing a decent job.' He shrugged. 'Maybe he is, I don't know. I'm probably being a bitter old fool.'

'Why don't you like him?'

'Search me, Inspector. It's probably bad chemistry or something like that. I've rubbed up against him a couple of times when he was after my support for election. To be blunt I didn't like his approach, which was impolite, and refused. He got, shall we say, a little spiteful, which I believe shows the inner spirit of the man. There was nothing I could put my finger on, but I was being dogged by a series of incidents at the time from some local street criminals who were never apprehended, and my change in health made me decide to vacate my seat. That made me instantly less than useful and he stopped badgering me. I haven't spoken to him since, thank heavens.'

'What professions are represented by the members?' Rocco asked, hoping to put the subject on a different course.

'Mostly the arts and letters, as one would expect, but there are those with other backgrounds. Like philosophy and history.' His eyes glittered wickedly. 'Some serious, some less so.'

'Politicians?'

'Those too, along with priests, former military persons and, I suspect, the odd farmer here and there.' Another laugh, which led to a short coughing fit. 'My apologies, Lucas,' he muttered finally, slapping his chest. 'The sudden excitement is too much for me. I'm a terrible gossip.'

'Farmers?'

Jeunet nodded. 'There will be another one soon, if he gets his way: De Lancourt's family were in farming for over a century, if you can believe it. Not that I have anything against farmers, you understand. My grandfather was one, too, God rest his soul.'

'I'm going to have to meet this De Lancourt. Is there anything I should know?'

'Just remember he has his eyes on a seat in the academy, which will give him a great deal of social satisfaction and an entrée to various government circles that may have been denied him so far. First and foremost, however, he's a working lawyer with many contacts he's not afraid to use, so he's not a man to cross without being very sure of your ground.'

Rocco finished his cognac and chased it down with the last of his coffee. He handed Jeunet his card. 'I'll make sure to remember that. If you think of anything else, please feel free to call me. For now, thank you for your time.'

Jeunet chuckled. 'My pleasure, Lucas. Any time you need cheese or a chat, I'm usually around somewhere.'

–

Rocco walked back to the office deep in thought. As interesting as Gérard Jeunet's gossip about academy members had been, it had been of little immediate help save for the obvious grit that existed between the two men. But he knew that wasn't unusual; take any group of elderly men and women and there were bound to be a mix of friends, conspirators and competitors, each with their own loyalties and perspectives. If there was going to be trouble from this man De Lancourt over the arrest of his so-called secretary, the fact that he was a high-level lawyer in Paris was likely to be the biggest threat. Rocco had long experience of their kind, and although they weren't all painted with the same dark brush and did not all harbour suspicion or antipathy towards the police, he knew their instinctive position was combative. And combat invariably got in the way of progress.

As he walked up the steps to the building's entrance he was stopped by Desmoulins, who was on his way out.

'Officer Lamotte called in from Caix,' Desmoulins told him. 'He found a body in a ditch not far from where the triple shooting occurred. It could be the missing driver.'

Rocco nodded. 'I'll follow you over there. Have you told Rizzotti?'

'Yes. He's getting his stuff together.' He gestured at the office behind him. 'You might not want to go in there. The two men who came in earlier are demanding Koutcheff be released but Massin and Perronnet are putting up a united front pending your investigations.'

'Mine?'

Desmoulins grinned. 'I think they're using you because you've already spoken to the prisoner and you're out of the way. They'll probably want you to stay like that.'

Rocco changed direction and made for his car. The first thing he did was to turn off his radio. Desmoulins was right; he didn't want to get stuck in the office dealing with a violent thug or playing hide-and-seek with unfriendly lawyers and Ministry officials. Massin and his deputy should be more than capable of dragging their feet, and in the meantime he could get on with the investigation.

Chapter Twelve

Rocco spotted Claude Lamotte sitting by a forlorn-looking statue near a crossroads when he and Desmoulins pulled up nearby. Claude stood up and pointed to an area behind the statue and said, 'He's down in the ditch. I'd bet my ears he's an immigrant... possibly from Algeria or along that coast somewhere. I haven't touched anything.'

'Well done,' Rocco said, and walked up the berm and looked down at the body. Claude's judgement was correct; the man looked North African. The clothes looked workaday, available anywhere.

'That's nasty,' muttered Desmoulins at the damage to the face. 'What the hell did that to him?'

'Crows,' Claude informed him with a tone of relish, and pointed a thumb at the now empty sky. 'I saw them circling overhead and came for a closer look. It was easy pickings for them. Lazy bastards don't like working if they don't have to. Eyeballs are a special delicacy; they like to suck out the juices.' He grinned at the expression on the younger detective's face.

'Have you seen anyone else in the area?' Rocco queried. It wasn't unknown for killers to revisit the scene although he was pretty sure that would not happen here. A small hole in the side of the man's head was testament to that, and the connection with the three deaths back along this same road was obvious.

'Not while I've been here. It's not used much except by farmers getting to their fields, and the harvest is all done for now.'

Moments later a small van driven by Dr Rizzotti pulled up across the road. He got out and joined them on the edge of the mound, carrying a large black box.

'So, is this your missing link?' Rizzotti asked, eyeing the body. 'He's very efficient, I'll give him that.' He was referring to the killer.

Rocco nodded. 'We don't know yet. Maybe you can tell us. If he is the driver and left the scene of the shooting with the killer, why did he end up here with a bullet in his head?'

Rizzotti pulled a face. 'Thieves falling out?'

'Could be.'

While Rizzotti got down to work examining the body, Rocco turned away and ran through the possibilities that had brought a working driver, possibly from Marseille if the papers in the car were any guide, to this undignified and brutal end in a ditch in northern France. The choices were limited: he'd either served his purpose, bringing the three men here to be killed, or he was innocent of complicity and had actually made a decent attempt at getting away until being tracked down and disposed of; a witness the killer did not need.

But why had any of them been along this deserted back road that was hardly ever used? Was the taxi heading for Amiens or one of the many villages in the area – or even further north to the channel ports? If the latter, it was doubtful they'd get across to England using their Moroccan ID cards unless they had secured some kind of safe passage with official help. But that didn't gel; if the French government was involved, they'd have made sure the three men got through France and away, even if only to pass the problem, if there was one, on to someone else. As far as he knew the British had few specific connections with anyone in Morocco.

Claude read his expression and said, 'This road is the middle of nowhere for any of these people. But at least we know from the position of the Mercedes that they were heading north.'

'And being chased,' said Rocco. 'What we don't know is by who.' And that, he figured might only become clear if the Interior Ministry shared what they knew about any of the three passengers, especially the old man. Furthermore, if they had been killed by a professional, that person had either followed them all the way from Marseille or had been recruited from Paris, perhaps, to intercept them. The capital certainly held a concentration of men willing and capable of doing that kind of work, and they usually plied their trade where there was both money and regular demand, unlike in this part of the country.

Rizzotti turned and looked up at them, shaking his head. 'The body's clean. The pockets are empty and the clothes have no readable labels. There's nothing to indicate who he was. Sorry.' He looked disappointed, keen as always on using his skills to present good news, not bad.

Claude pursed his lips and called down, 'Hey, Doc, check his socks.'

Rizzotti looked puzzled, then shrugged and did as Claude suggested, peeling back the dead man's trouser hems and removing his shoes. Seconds later he gave a grunt of astonishment, and held out some items for Rocco to take.

A piece of card and some folded low-denomination bank notes.

'How the hell did you know to look there?' Rocco asked.

Rizzotti clambered up to join them. 'I'd like to know the answer to that, too. Is it science or some kind of rural hocus-pocus I could tap into?'

Claude grinned. 'Not that. It's an old habit among some drivers working late shifts in case they get robbed by drunks or opportunists. The money's for getting home if the car gets stolen or damaged, and acquiring a new ID card is a bureaucratic nightmare, especially for immigrants, so they hold on tight to it.' He looked at Rocco. 'Drivers carry all sorts of crap on them, like squirrels storing nuts. If his pockets were empty it's because they were stripped.'

Rocco knew what he was driving at. People carried stuff around with them that was no longer useful out of sheer habit, forgetfulness and even out of a sense of comfort, as familiar reminders of good times.

The scene looked pretty self-explanatory and Rizzotti's examination would centre more on the body than the surrounding area. He looked at the card. It was grubby and stained and the spidery handwriting overlaid with official stamps informed him that the bearer was Fouad Hamal, born in 1928 in Casablanca, Morocco, now with an address in Marseille.

No doubt whoever had dumped the body here was trying to delay identification. Leaving the other three bodies with full ID on them, however, might have been a clear signal to anyone allied to them: this is what happens to anyone we don't like.

At least the driver's address, if this was he, would tell the police where this business had begun and lead to a possible chain of evidence. Trying to delay that even for a few days by emptying his pockets, as the killer had done, was meant to inhibit the investigation and allow time for the guilty party to fade into the background.

'I think you're right.' He handed the card to Desmoulins. 'Some phone work for you, I'm afraid, René. See what you can find out about Hamal from the local cops.'

Desmoulins nodded and headed to his car.

Rizzotti joined Rocco, wiping his hands on a small towel. 'I know you're going to ask, so here's what I know so far: your man was shot at close quarters going by the burn marks around the wound. Whether in a car or outside, I can't tell. There's no dirt on his shoes so I'm guessing he didn't come across the fields, but by road. The shoes are badly scuffed and his trousers are torn at the knee. My guess at this stage is that he might have tripped at some point.' He jerked a thumb behind him. 'It's a fair distance from the other location but if he was chased by car he'd have been caught much sooner and further back.'

'So he was brought this far,' Rocco said, 'before being disposed of.'

Rizzotti smiled. 'That's your conundrum to deal with. I'll know more about the scuff marks when I get a closer look back at the station. Can I get him moved? It's getting warmer and the body's already becoming a bit public.' As if to confirm it, he looked up to where a dozen or so crows had settled on a phone wire a hundred metres away and were now watching the scene with interest.

'Do it,' Rocco confirmed. 'No shell casing?'

A shake of the head. 'Sorry. Same as before. Whoever did this was very careful on that score. Careful and efficient.'

Rocco turned towards his own car. He had some questions on an entirely different matter to ask, and the quicker he got them dealt with the sooner he could get on with investigating this particular conundrum, to use Rizzotti's word. He used his radio to issue instructions to the despatcher in Amiens, and set off for Petit Montgallet.

Chapter Thirteen

Les Cyprès, according to Claude Lamotte, where Guy De Lancourt lived, had been built in the 1890s as a mental institute before being abandoned ten years ago in favour of smaller, more modern units in the region. De Lancourt had bought the old building and made extensive renovations, transforming what had been a typically utilitarian style of the times into a private residence with elegant shutters and windows, a cream render and a Mediterranean-style tiled roof. He had also added the cypress trees along the drive, no doubt as a nod to the building's original name, which he had kept.

The man hadn't done a bad job, Rocco thought, pulling up at the front gate and staring down the tree-lined gravel drive towards the house. He'd seen state institutions like this before and whatever the original lines lacked in style or appeal, the changes made to this particular one had served to soften the overall brutalist effect. The grounds were laid to flower borders and stretches of neatly cut grass, the latter showing signs of serious browning under the summer sun. The building was elegantly set against a backdrop of mostly dark conifers running into the distance, their spiky tops moving under a faint breeze, and he could just make out the corner of a secondary building at the rear.

Rocco followed the drive, the tyres crunching pleasantly and the cypress trees causing a fluttering of light as he passed. As he pulled to a stop by the front steps and cut the engine, a dark Simca Aronde saloon drove out from behind the house, kicking up gravel. He noted three men inside but they didn't look his way, and the car disappeared out of the gate in a cloud of dust.

When he turned towards the front door he saw it was already open, with a man standing in shadow just inside, his features indistinct. De Lancourt, he hoped. He'd radioed the despatcher after leaving Rizzotti and Claude, and got him to check if the lawyer was in and, if so, to inform him that a police inspector was on his way. No ifs and buts. The despatcher had come back with an affirmative on both counts.

As he climbed the steps, the figure inside moved forward with an outstretched hand.

'Rocco? De Lancourt. I was advised you were coming. Please come in.' The tone of voice was polite, but lacked warmth, and the outstretched hand was there for the briefest instant, cool and perfunctory, before being quickly withdrawn. Most people being visited by the police expressed surprise, even innocence, real or feigned. This man was annoyed and doing nothing to hide it.

Rocco stepped inside. Close to, De Lancourt was tall and slim, with pale skin and fine features, his high forehead capped by long, grey hair swept to one side. Facially he had the melancholy look of an old teenager but with the air of one stuck in the Left Bank era of an older Paris, when a deliberately casual manner was an affectation worn like a second skin. He was elegantly dressed in a sports jacket and white shirt with a high collar and wore impressively sharp slacks ending in casual leather loafers.

'Mmm... not quite what I was expecting,' the man said, studying Rocco with a faint look of surprise. 'In my experience most of the police around here have yet to shake the farmyard mud off their boots.'

It was an odd jibe, coming from a farming family man, if Jeunet's information was correct. It was meant to elicit a reaction, he was sure, but he ignored it and handed over his card bearing his name, rank and telephone number. There was a procedure to follow here and he wasn't about to be put off; anything an aggressive lawyer could use would be remembered and come up later, and he wasn't going to leave this man such an opening.

De Lancourt didn't bother checking the details but tucked the card in his jacket pocket. 'I trust you have some news for me about my employee, Captain?'

'Inspector,' Rocco corrected him. 'Not so much news, more a request for some background information.'

'Really? You would have done better to have brought him with you.' De Lancourt turned and gestured for Rocco to follow, leading the way across a long, tiled hallway running the entire front length of the building. It was lined with chairs, wooden chests and a large grandfather clock, all highly polished but carrying the air of having been left there casually many years ago and quietly forgotten, save for a regular clean. A selection of paintings also adorned the walls, mostly scenic in nature, interspersed with an occasional portrait of a figure in eighteenth- or nineteenth-century dress set against a pastoral landscape. Rocco had been in grand houses like it, usually on the heels of a robbery or worse. The style of the furnishings spoke of money, status and lineage, all extensive and solid, lacking any degree of true comfort but there to fill a space and impress observers.

Rocco suppressed a shiver, which he at first put down to having just come in from the sunshine. On reflection, though, there was a definite coolness in the air that had nothing to do with temperature, rather the impression of atmosphere caused by the nature of the building. Whatever he'd seen from the exterior was somehow muted compared with the feeling in here, of walls so thick they allowed nothing inside, the interior holding still some remnants of the original nature and purpose of the place.

One of the paintings stood on the floor covered by a large cloth. He lifted a corner of the fabric to one side and saw a small brass plate at the base of the heavy ornate frame. It carried a name in barely legible script, as if it had been scraped away: Pascal Delancourt. The date was 1824. The one above it on the wall was similarly titled, but with a newer, shinier name plate. Daniel De Lancourt – 1880.

Interesting. Jeunet had been right: there had been a name change. He wondered what had brought that about.

'Inspector?' De Lancourt returned to see where he was.

Rocco followed him into a room furnished with comfortable armchairs, two settees piled with scatter cushions, and a long coffee table with an inset glass top. More paintings here, too, bigger, grander and all with gold frames, each lit by wall-lights to show off their subjects. Each one was dark, impressive and collectively they dominated the room.

'Nice,' Rocco said. 'All family members?'

De Lancourt nodded and looked pleased that Rocco had noticed. 'Indeed they are. I like to think they match the setting. It's taken a lot of work – still does, in fact.' He hesitated, then said, 'Let me show you around.' He led the way to the back of the room and through a door into another long hallway, which looked out onto the rear grounds, talking all the way. He was evidently proud of what he had done to the place. He pointed to the building Rocco had glimpsed from the front. 'That is the staff quarters where the men who stay here are housed. I like to give them a sense of space while being in the company of others. Beyond that is a large, wooded area, which provides tranquillity for all of us. I like to wander there myself. Beyond the trees are some fields where we grow vegetables to sustain the household.' He led Rocco out through a glass door and took him on a tour, expanding on his aims for the men in his temporary employ.

Rocco was only half listening, wondering if this grand tour was an attempt to derail his questions about Koutcheff or whether De Lancourt simply wanted to show off, the rich man in his gilded palace anxious to be held in awe. There was certainly an unmistakable tone of pride in his voice, but the words were spoiled by an odd delivery, more the style of the curator of an ancient setting rather than an owner, as if he wasn't quite sure of his feet.

At the end of the hallway, he noticed two doors. One had a frosted glass panel in the centre, like in a restaurant, and Rocco heard the sounds of machinery and of pans clattering. The other door was fitted flush into the wall and looked to be made of steel.

De Lancourt noticed his interest. 'I decided to keep the original kitchen,' he said, 'brought up to date, of course. I employ a chef who comes in to prepare meals for the men every day and to produce refreshments for a number of small functions I like to host.' He waved a casual hand and turned away, saying, 'Just because I live in the country doesn't mean I have to be a hermit.'

'What's the other door?' Rocco asked.

De Lancourt hesitated, then said, 'It's an underground space. Not so much a cellar but it was used as a place of restraint by the people who originally ran this place as an asylum. Their methods were not exactly admirable, but they were of the time. I understand particularly violent patients were kept down there to cool off.' He gave a brief smile. 'I now use it as my wine cellar. I like to keep the temperature consistent, so you'll have to excuse me not taking you down there. I have a champagne function in a few days and don't want to disturb the atmosphere.'

With that, De Lancourt turned and led the way back to the room where they had started out.

'So what's the problem, Inspector?' De Lancourt waved him to one of the settees and took the one opposite, sitting neatly and staring at Rocco with the blank eye of one who did not expect the meeting to last long. Gone was the sense of pride, replaced by something else, as if he had thrown a mental switch. 'If one of my boys has been misbehaving, I'm happy to offer my apologies.'

Rocco felt instantly on the alert at the change in atmosphere; there was now a frisson of hostility in the air, like electricity held in check. It was sufficient to make the apology false and forced. He wasn't sure if it arose out of an inner arrogance, the characteristic of someone who was above any kind of reproach, or if De Lancourt simply didn't like policemen. He'd met more than a few men like him, in the military and more recently in various courtrooms. Invariably high-born or excellent actors, they carried an air of absolute and unassailable confidence in their position.

He was glad Perronnet had advised him to seek Jeunet's counsel before coming here; he had a feeling he might need it.

'Boys?'

De Lancourt gave a thin smile. 'I employ several men here, former military individuals who have served their country with fortitude and courage. I call them boys because I'm old enough to be able to grant them that distinction.'

'I see. Can I ask what sort of jobs they do?'

'Certainly. They work in the house and on the grounds around here: gardening, landscaping, painting, decorating – anything that needs doing.' He gestured towards the window. 'As you've seen, it's a large building and needs regular upkeep. You might even have spotted some of the men out there. They work for me but in all other respects they're free to come and go as they wish. Most choose to stay here for a while until they're ready to move on. It's safe.'

'Safe from what?'

A shrug. 'From ghosts… from the images that follow all men who have seen war. Men possibly like yourself, I would hazard a guess.' He waited for a reply but when Rocco said nothing he added, 'Or perhaps you were one of the lucky ones who saw no conflict?'

Another dig, Rocco thought, aimed to get under his skin and deflect the conversation from wherever De Lancourt thought it might be going.

'I served in Indochina. Georges Koutcheff, he's your secretary?'

A space of a couple of seconds went by before De Lancourt answered. 'He is. Why is that relevant?'

'Because he is a person of interest, as I've just indicated. He put an officer in hospital and caused serious damage to property in Amiens. He was also found to be carrying a firearm. It's hardly normal behaviour. He says he was in the military until about a year ago, is that correct?'

'It is. I only bring in men who have served. I want to help them, you see. Others can… well, they can seek help elsewhere.'

'Do you know where Koutcheff saw service?'

'You haven't asked him?' A brief pause. 'Then it's not my place to tell. Why are you really here, Inspector?'

'To find the truth. I asked him, but he was evasive so I'm asking you. It's a simple question of detail, that's all. I can look up the military records, but you can save me the time.'

De Lancourt considered it and said, 'Well, that's what you will have to do, isn't it? I don't ask many questions from the boys who work here; there is little need and I don't wish to remind them of the harmful period to their service. All I can tell you is that they come from various regiments and theatres of conflict.'

Rocco resisted the temptation to call the man a liar. It might have been mildly satisfying on a basic level but ultimately pointless. And he had ample instincts already about the line the man would take if he gave him the opportunity. Instead he asked, 'Why do you help them?'

'Because it seems a worthwhile venture. While they work for me they can revitalise their old selves, banish some of the horrors they have witnessed and regain some kind of normality in their daily lives. After a while they're free to go elsewhere if they wish.'

'That's very decent of you. And do they – leave, I mean?'

'Most, yes – to one degree or another. Some find it more difficult to adjust so take a little longer. As I'm sure you know some refer to it as shell shock or battle fatigue, although there are fancier names.'

'Do you ever have any trouble from them?'

De Lancourt puffed his lips as if it were no great matter. 'Some, occasionally, but nothing serious. They are young men and tend to go off-course from time to time. Alcohol is banned here although they can easily acquire it outside, which they do. As long as they don't bring it back there's little I can do. One thing I can assure you of, Inspector, is that I take a very robust – some would even call it a very *military* – stance with anyone who steps out of line. But there's been nothing serious that would warrant the police being involved.'

'Until now.'

'You mean Koutcheff.'

'Correct.'

'Frankly, I can't see why you're bothering. The boy saw admirable service for France and carries the scars of that period with him. Why is he being hounded?'

'We're not hounding him. To paraphrase your word, we tend to take a very *police* stance with anyone who fails to stop after committing a motoring offence, who puts an officer in hospital with broken bones and who is found to be armed with a deadly weapon for which he readily admits he has no permit. You're a member of the legal profession, so what else would you suggest we do?'

There was a fractional tightening of De Lancourt's lips. 'Treat the boy for what he is, of course, which is a hero of France who has suffered for his country. It shouldn't be too difficult.'

'I'm a policeman, M. De Lancourt, not a psychologist. Koutcheff's military service might explain his actions but doesn't excuse them. I'm merely carrying out my duty, which is to investigate crime and protect the public.'

'So do your duty; there was an armed robbery in Compiegne last week – was anyone arrested for that?'

'I have no idea. *This* is my case, not the one in Compiegne.'

De Lancourt pursed his lips briefly, then said, 'For now, maybe. But not for much longer. I would hate for you to be under any misapprehension about your powers, Inspector.'

Rocco felt a chill around his neck, the tone having taken a much darker turn, the throwing of another switch. He'd come across it before, usually with men who exercised a much more open threat to those opposing them and showed no reluctance to displaying it even to a police officer. It wasn't something he ignored.

'Meaning what?'

'Meaning this is victimisation and I will be moving heaven and earth to make sure Koutcheff is released without charge so that he can get on with his life, such as it is.'

'You sound as if you're saying he has suffered more than most – is that correct?'

'It's a defence that any right-thinking society should be prepared to take into account, and that is the direction his legal team will take.'

'You won't be representing him, then?'

For a brief second there was a flicker deep in the lawyer's eyes, as if of uncertainty. Rocco wondered if the man had considered defending him but couldn't. Or was there some other reason, such as not wishing to get too close to what might turn out to be a flame, perhaps?

'What I intend to do or not is none of your concern, Inspector. Or are you willing to risk a confrontation with your superiors at the Interior Ministry simply to prove a point? If so, I should warn you it will not end well.' He stood up smoothly and made a gesture towards the door. 'I think we are done.'

Rocco stayed where he was for a few heartbeats, leaving De Lancourt on his feet and waiting, suddenly off-balance. He couldn't quite fathom whether the man was blindly arrogant or whether he had so little regard for the police that he was willing to trample over anyone he saw as an obstacle. Either way it was clear he wasn't getting very far in this conversation.

'Thank you for your time,' he said. He stood up and headed for the door, ignoring the usual etiquette of a handshake. He caught a glimpse of a clock on the way out and was surprised to find he'd been there nearly thirty minutes.

As Rocco drove back down the drive, he passed two men standing on the verge. They watched him go, their stances reminding him of sentries on guard duty. The only things missing were their uniforms and rifles. Neither man looked friendly.

Chapter Fourteen

Before reaching the outskirts of Amiens, Rocco pulled into the side of the road and cut the engine. He climbed out of the car and walked over to a gateway of a newly ploughed field, where a flock of gulls was wheeling over the fresh earth, protesting loudly at each other.

Rocco knew how they felt. Police work involved going back over much ground previously covered without turning up anything useful. Most investigations took time and hard work and this one was promising to go the same way. A hard-nosed prisoner on one side was echoed by an unhelpful employer on the other, and neither seemed the kind of man to give way easily. Adding to his problems were the killings of the Benhamids and now, it seemed, the taxi driver.

Running over the conversation with De Lancourt in his mind and trying to tease out any inconsistencies, he heard a squawk from his car radio. He walked back to the vehicle and picked up the handset.

'Rocco.'

'Inspector?' It was the despatcher at the station, and he sounded anything but his usual calm self. 'I've got some bad news for you, sir.'

The line went quiet and Rocco said, 'You'd better tell me what it is, then.'

'Sorry – of course. I've been asked to advise you that the prisoner, Koutcheff, has escaped custody.'

'Jesus, how?' Rocco demanded, then added, 'Don't answer that – put me through to Captain Canet.'

'He's busy organising the search. Can I put you through to anyone else?'

'Commissaire Perronnet or Massin.'

A few clicks and Massin came on. He sounded tight-lipped as if holding in a great deal of anger. 'I'm sorry, Inspector. The prisoner was taken to hospital suffering what appeared to be a serious breathing problem. Once he was inside and away from his escort he managed to slip out. We've got all hands out now looking for him.'

'He didn't have any breathing problems when I spoke to him,' Rocco muttered. 'He's played us. Who authorised his release to hospital?'

'Maybe so. But it was on the orders of the Interior Ministry and arranged via a local lawyer and De Lancourt's legal representative from Paris. Koutcheff was found choking in his cell less than an hour ago. We had no choice but to comply with the order. He was accompanied by two uniforms but they were obstructed from going in with him because of multiple casualties from a factory fire arriving at the same time. In the confusion Koutcheff absconded through a side door.'

Rocco swore silently. It sounded too contrived. Funny how the legal rep and a lawyer happened to be on hand so conveniently, and all while he was engaged talking to Koutcheff's boss.

'Are you still with De Lancourt?'

'I was but it wasn't helpful. I'm on my way in.' Rocco disconnected and drove back to the station, wondering if he was letting his imagination run away with him as far as De Lancourt was concerned. Not everything that happened carried traces of a conspiracy or the involvement of the Interior Ministry, and the fact that he had experienced problems with lawyers and the Ministry before did not damn them both entirely. Yet De Lancourt's manner had been at times bellicose and defensive, treating his employee's behaviour as little more than a misdemeanour. And now that same employee was out of custody and on the run, assisted in some way by the intervention of a legal rep and the Ministry itself.

The station was eerily quiet when he entered, the usual desks deserted. He made for the stairs and Massin's office and found the commissaire and Dr Rizzotti in conversation.

'Come in, Inspector,' Massin said, and looked at Rizzotti. 'Tell him.'

'I wasn't long at the scene out near Caix,' Rizzotti said. 'When I got back here I found the custody officer attending to the prisoner. Koutcheff was coughing and appeared to be unable to breathe properly.'

'Seriously?'

'He seemed in a genuinely bad way: face deep red, eyes bulging and clearly distressed. I tried to calm him down to slow his breathing rate and check his airways, but then he began vomiting.'

'Was anyone else with him before you got there?'

'Apart from the custody officer, just the lawyer. Koutcheff's legal representative arrived within minutes. They had a signed order for Koutcheff to be given a medical check-up in case of matters arising.'

'What does that mean?' Rocco asked.

Rizzotti shrugged. 'Literally anything, but it's usually reserved for prisoners with known medical histories like asthma or other ongoing illnesses producing breathing difficulties and so on. Claustrophobia is one fairly common cause.'

'I can't imagine that. He seemed pretty calm when I spoke to him, considering he was in a cell. Can it come on spontaneously?'

'I'm not sure. Perhaps in extreme circumstances but it's not a condition with which I'm very familiar. In any case the lawyer had already deposited the order so we had to comply. I called for an ambulance and he was taken away accompanied by two escorts.'

Rocco felt instinctively sceptical. 'Is there any chance he was acting it out?'

'To be fair, it looked and sounded genuine. I thought he was going to explode, the coughing was so violent. You can ask the custody officer – he was scared stiff the prisoner was going to suffocate and I must say I couldn't disagree. However' – he picked up a folded envelope from the desk in front of him and said – 'after they left I happened to spot this under the bunk-bench where he'd been sitting.' He opened the envelope and showed Rocco the contents, which consisted of a yellowish-brown powder.

Rocco peered at it. 'Is that heroin?' He knew the drug to be mostly white when it hit the streets, but it depended on what other substances it was cut with by subsequent dealers to make it stretch further.

'It's snuff.'

'You're joking.'

'I think he ingested it deliberately to produce the coughing fit.' Rizzotti shrugged. 'It certainly fooled me.'

Rocco looked at Massin. 'Where could he have got it?'

86

'A good question.' Massin looked uncomfortable at the admission. 'It wasn't on him when he came in – he was searched very carefully. It must have been brought in from outside. The only people who had direct contact with the prisoner as far as we know were the custody officer, the lawyer and a legal representative.'

'So one of them, then.'

'Perhaps. Unfortunately there's nothing to stop anyone else from up here going down to the cells without being seen, so we have no way of knowing who else could have got to him. It's not exactly a maximum-security unit, although I will be reviewing our procedures in future. The custody officer didn't see anyone who shouldn't have been there but we'll be speaking with him at length on that.'

'Do we trust him?' Rocco asked. He had no reason to think ill of the man, but Massin would have a better feel for his integrity.

'I trust all my officers equally,' Massin replied levelly. 'But the officer on duty this morning was new to the job. He didn't think to question the presence of the two visitors so he might not have done so for anyone else. We will investigate his background, of course.'

'And the two legal people?'

'The legal representative is named Louis Khoury. He's from a chamber I've heard of in Paris. They have a very good reputation. As far as we know the chambers were retained by Koutcheff's employer, De Lancourt, to avoid a question of bias, as is proper. Khoury was despatched to deal with the matter. We have no reason for thinking there's any link between them, but we will check.'

'And the lawyer?'

'Mmm… that's less clear. His name is Freddy Toussaint and he was retained by De Lancourt earlier today. He arrived recently in the area and opened an office here in town, so other than a few petty offences we haven't seen much of him. Lawyers have to start somewhere, so he may have seen this region as a good place to set himself up in business.'

Rocco stood up. 'Fine. I'll start with him.'

Massin's eyebrows shot up. 'To do what?'

'I'll have a word, just to go over what he can tell me about the incident.' He smiled and said, 'He'll be expecting a visit, I'm sure. Don't worry – I'll be civilised.'

Massin seemed to hold his breath for a moment, then nodded. 'Very well. But remember his profession: we don't want any legal blood on the streets or word getting back to the Ministry.'

'One thing,' Rocco said. 'Could you put someone onto the military records office and find out where Koutcheff served and in what capacity?'

Massin lifted an eyebrow. 'I take it you asked De Lancourt?'

'He didn't know. Apparently he doesn't ask such searching questions in case it upsets the men who work for him.'

Rizzotti scooped the snuff from the desktop back into the envelope, then handed it to Rocco. 'Here, you'd better take this with you. See if he reacts.'

Rocco took the envelope. 'Good thinking. If he sneezes, can I bring him back in the boot of my car?'

He walked out, leaving Rizzotti chuckling uncertainly and Massin shaking his head in doubt.

Chapter Fifteen

It was a short distance to Toussaint's office, but traffic seemed unusually slow. Rocco put it down to the search teams stopping cars throughout the town and causing a ripple effect on movements everywhere else. On the way he listened to radio reports between officers manning the search for Koutcheff and the station, where Captain Canet was fielding calls and directing the teams.

The lawyer's office turned out to be in a quiet street close to the cathedral. He found a parking space right outside, a reminder that the day had flowed by faster than he'd realised and office and shop workers were already beginning to leave.

Rocco entered the building, which was an old town-house converted into a grandly named Centre d'Affaires with a smart plastic name plate on the outside wall.

The interior was tight on space, smelled of new paint and wood dust and echoed with slamming doors, muffled voices and the sound of typewriters and a telex machine chattering in the background. A line of business names on a board fixed to one wall placed Toussaint's office on the fourth floor. *Had to be*, Rocco thought wryly. *And no lift.* He climbed the stairs to a tiny attic landing with an angled roof, which meant he had to duck, and small skylights admitting the barest minimum of daylight. Highest, smallest and probably cheapest, he decided.

The single door bore a nameplate with F. TOUSSAINT – AVOCAT in plain white letters. He knocked and entered.

The room was just about big enough for an untidy desk, two hard-backed chairs, a filing cabinet and a small side table with a kettle and coffee makings. A fat man was squeezed behind the desk with his back turned to the door. He had a telephone clamped to one ear and was shouting at someone to get something done or face the consequences. Dressed in a crumpled white shirt and braces, the thick straps cutting into his beefy shoulders, he had the appearance of being as wide as he was tall. The air in the room smelled of sweat and stale coffee, barely relieved by a tiny open skylight overhead.

The man ended his call without saying goodbye and slammed the receiver down before turning to stare at Rocco with an air of aggression. 'Do you have an appointment?'

'Freddy Toussaint?' said Rocco, ignoring the question. He realised he was looking at one of the men he'd seen entering the station earlier.

'Who else would it be? The name's on the door. Who are you?'

Toussaint had slicked-back dark hair and the biggest glasses Rocco had ever seen. Actually, maybe not; he'd seen pictures of Brigitte Bardot with bigger ones, but she was a film star so could get away with it. Toussaint's seemed to hover in front of his chubby cheeks without quite touching his face, like glass shields against whatever bad weather he might run into.

'Lucas Rocco.' Rocco dropped his card on the man's desk. 'Inspector of police.'

Toussaint sat back, or might have had there been more room, and looked at Rocco with a sour expression.

'Great,' he muttered. 'You must work with the clowns who allowed their prisoner to escape.' He gave what might have been a smile but it worked its way across his face into a smirk. 'That's going to reflect well on all of you, especially… what's his name, Massin? Losing a prisoner is a big no-no in anyone's book.'

'Commissaire Massin, you mean.' Rocco took the spare chair, which was piled with files, and dropped them on the floor alongside an over-filled wastebasket. He sat down without being asked. 'Yes, I work with him and I'm here to investigate the circumstances that allowed a prisoner to get out by feigning a choking fit.'

Toussaint showed his teeth in a snide grin. 'You what? There was no pretence, I can assure you. He was actually choking – I witnessed it. Ask the custody officer.'

'Really? Handy that you happened to be there, wasn't it?'

'I got a call from the custody officer that my client was having difficulties breathing. I live close by the station so I went round there to see for myself.' He leaned forward, his belly straining against his desk. 'Instead of throwing around insinuations, you should be speaking to your custody officer and the idiots escorting Koutcheff to find out what happened and why they weren't paying more attention to their duties. Or is it the case that you people are incapable of admitting that you screwed up?' For emphasis he stabbed the air in front of Rocco's face with a fat finger.

Rocco wondered what the penalty would be for snapping off this idiot's finger and throwing it out the skylight. He sighed and took out the envelope Rizzotti had given him and showed him the contents. 'You think we also provided this for him to choke on?'

He was watching Toussaint carefully and saw a split-second expression of something cross the man's face, before it vanished just as fast.

'How would I know? Are you in the habit of serving pepper to prisoners in custody?'

'Who said it was pepper? I've seen a lot of heroin this colour. It also makes users cough if they snort it in too quickly.' Rocco waited a few heartbeats. The pause seemed to make Toussaint uneasy. He looked as if he were about to say something, then closed his mouth.

'Yes?' Rocco urged him.

'I guessed wrong. So what?' His eyes went runabout as if they had a will of their own. 'I can't help you. Sorry.'

'Who provided the order for Koutcheff to have a health assessment?'

'That came from Paris, via what's his name – Khoury, the legal rep. I've no idea who arranged the order. It must have been put in place earlier in the day.'

If that were the case it meant someone had foreseen a health problem and taken steps to provide help if it arose. That could only have been someone who knew Koutcheff extremely well.

Guy De Lancourt.

'And nobody thought to question it?'

'You'll have to ask the Ministry, won't you? I'm merely acting for the client.'

'I hear you're new to this region, is that right?'

Toussaint's mouth opened as if he was thrown by the question. 'Uh, yes, that's correct. Why do you ask?'

'We'll probably come across each other again. I like to know who I'll be dealing with.'

'Right.' Toussaint nodded vigorously and added, 'I was in Bordeaux for a while but I heard this area was opening up. It seemed a good idea to get in on the ground, so to speak.' He was babbling, and if he was aware of the irony in his statement up in this crow's nest of an office, he didn't show it. 'There's nothing wrong with a man having ambition, Inspector. Do you have any news of the prisoner?'

'Not yet. But he can't have got too far. When he does, we'll soon get him talking.'

'Talking?' Toussaint blinked.

'Sure.' Rocco got to his feet. 'About why he didn't stop when required to do so; why he attacked the officers; why he had a gun in his car. You know how it is with prisoners: if there's a deal on offer in exchange for information, they usually take it with both hands.'

Toussaint said quickly, 'I can account for the gun. I've got a statement from him about that. He said it was something he picked up a few days ago – a collector's piece.' He shrugged. 'He's a former soldier and a gun nut like a few of them, I suppose.'

'A Browning?' Rocco countered. 'It's a service weapon common all over the world, so hardly a collector's piece.'

Toussaint gave a snide smile. 'So maybe he's not the brightest of men. That's not a crime, is it?'

'Why didn't he tell me he collected guns when I asked him about it? It could have explained a lot.'

'It depends how you asked, doesn't it? You don't exactly inspire confidence in a man being held in custody.'

Rocco turned to the door. He was wasting his time. 'I'll see myself out.'

After calling in at a shop just down the street, he returned to the station to find the building still quiet, with all hands out searching for Koutcheff. Perronnet was passing through and stopped by his desk.

'I suggest you go home, Inspector,' he said. 'You're going to need a good night's sleep.'

'That sounds ominous.'

'It is. We have a visitor from the Ministry coming in the morning. Hopefully he'll be able to tell us more about the three men who were shot yesterday.' He tilted his head to one side. 'But I would not bet on it.'

Chapter Sixteen

Rocco was in early the following morning, having slept little, his head rattling with speculation and fragments of evidence popping up about the triple shooting, the escaped prisoner and his talk with Toussaint.

He decided to let the lawyer stew for a while. It might have been coincidental but Toussaint had seemed oddly unnerved after his initial opening. Right now he couldn't decide whether the man was somehow involved in the escape of the prisoner or merely an obnoxious human being who thought being aggressive was a badge of office. He would get back to him later; the pressure of not knowing what was to happen next might tip him over the edge.

He entered the station and found a number of uniformed officers clocking off under Captain Canet's instructions, having been working for much of the night with no results and no sightings of the prisoner. If not already done, the next stage would be for a national alert to be broadcast to all forces to be on the lookout for the man, listed as dangerous.

Detective Desmoulins approached and took him to one side.

'It's been a blank so far except for one,' he reported. 'A woman who lives behind the hospital claims she saw a car with three men inside parked along her street about the time he escaped. She thought they were up to no good and went next door to use her neighbour's telephone to call the station. By the time she came back the car was driving down the street in what she described as a hurry.'

'So she didn't see anything useful?'

'Actually, she did. She swears the car now had four men on board.'

'Did she get a number?'

Desmoulins shook his head. 'I'm afraid not. All she could say was it was quite big and dark in colour, and what she called posh with a rounded shape, so not a 2CV or a van. It's all we got.'

Three men in a dark car. Rocco remembered the men in the Simca Aronde he'd seen leaving De Lancourt's house. As cars went it wasn't what he'd call big or posh, but to anyone who didn't have one it might appear to be both.

'You might like to drive out to De Lancourt's place near Petit Montgallet and ask if he's turned up there? Just a routine visit… nice and polite. Ask Canet if you can take a couple of uniforms with you.' He knew it wouldn't achieve much because it was the last place Koutcheff would go immediately. But a show of strength might put a bit of pressure on De Lancourt, seeing as how he was so concerned about his 'boys'. 'And be careful; he employs ex-military men out there and they might not react too well to the visit.'

Desmoulins smiled. 'Will do. I'll see if Sergeant Godard wants to come with me. He's pretty scary.'

'Do that. Anything useful on the taxi or the driver?'

Desmoulins looked sour. 'I called Marseille as you suggested but got the run-around. I spoke to three officers about Fouad Hamal. One of them said he'd never heard of him, another said he was a jobbing taxi driver but that was all, and a third – a detective – told me not to waste their time because they had grown-up crimes to solve, unlike us sugar-beet pickers in the north looking for a petty criminal immigrant.'

'He said that?' For an officer to refer to a petty criminal and immigrant in one sentence might be a simple matter of discrimination, but it also indicated that the officer was familiar with Hamal's background. If so, why not share the information?

Desmoulins handed over a piece of paper with three names on it. 'These are the only officers I got to speak to.'

Rocco nodded. Regional sharing of resources and information wasn't always what it should be, and he knew some forces felt they were so busy fighting a war it didn't allow for time spent helping others. He took the paper and thanked Desmoulins for his help. He was going to have to think about approaching the Marseille precinct in a different way. Using Massin's seniority wouldn't work, nor would going through the Interior Ministry, which would be like using a tank to knock down a wire fence: cumbersome and unwieldy.

Maybe he'd have to get creative.

One thing was certain: leaving aside the Moroccan end of this affair, Fouad Hamal's involvement meant it had to have started in Marseille. And without any firm leads this far north, starting down there was the best way to proceed.

As Desmoulins walked away, Massin appeared from upstairs. He exchanged a few words with members of the search team, then made a gesture for Rocco to follow him to his office.

Once inside, Rocco saw that the commissaire was not alone. Perronnet was sitting at the conference table and, across from him, a man studying the contents of a plain brown folder. The stranger was sparsely built with shiny, close-cut hair and wearing a dark grey suit, with a gleaming white shirt and a nondescript tie done in a minuscule knot. He looked up as Rocco entered and stood up.

'Inspector Rocco? Jean-Pierre Galland of the Interior Ministry's General Secretariat.' They shook hands and sat down. Galland continued, 'I gather you have an interest in three Moroccan nationals, victims of a shooting near here.'

'That's right. What can you tell us?' He realised that anyone from the general secretariat was unlikely to have specific knowledge of the three dead men, but had probably been sent along to show whatever the Ministry felt was suitable enough to share. As an organisation that did not operate an open agenda, he was certain the information would have been carefully edited before being released here.

Galland opened the folder and showed Rocco a photo. It was the oldest of the three men in the Mercedes, taken possibly five or so years ago.

'Hafid Benhamid,' Galland intoned. 'Aged sixty-eight years, a widower with two sons – Saad, aged forty-two and Mohamed, thirty-eight.' He slid two more photos across the table showing the two younger men. 'Are they the three victims you saw at the shooting?'

'They are,' Rocco confirmed. As usual when seeing photos of murder victims when they had been alive, he felt a sense of waste having seen them at the end of their life. 'Who are they?'

'Benhamid senior was for many years in the Moroccan Ministry of Agriculture; basically a middle-grade civil servant described as efficient but unremarkable. After a few years he transferred into the land and property section where he dealt with land appropriation investigations following the end of the French protectorate situation. That's all we have.'

'Did he have any political sympathies that might have become a threat?'

'I doubt it. As far as we know he leaned towards the nationalist side – a basic requirement of the job over there these days, I should think.' He sniffed as if the notion of anyone outside of the French Republic being a nationalist was somehow unthinkable.

'What about criminal connections?'

'As far as we know, none.' Galland blinked. 'Why would you think such a thing?'

'Because it's my job. What you've just told me doesn't give me much to go on.'

Galland glanced towards Massin. 'I'm sorry. I don't see how you can say that.'

'Well, if there's a country that knows more about Morocco than any other, it's France. Our government and civil service have connections there going back decades. Are you honestly saying we don't know any more about this man than that – or that we can't persuade the Moroccans to tell us something about his background? Surely they would be glad of the assistance.'

'It's not as simple as that. The situation is complicated.'

'Is that your way of saying I wouldn't understand? I might be only a simple cop, M. Galland, but background is everything in an investigation. Everyone has one, no matter how small or insignificant. A civil servant like Benhamid would have more documented information on his life than most. My main question, which you could pass on to your people in Morocco is, why would an efficient but otherwise unremarkable Moroccan bureaucrat be a target of a gunman here in France?'

'How would I know, Inspector? Casablanca might know. We do not.'

'So,' Massin put in, 'are you saying we're free to ask them?'

'Well, I'm not saying that, no,' Galland murmured quickly, shifting in his chair as if feeling he was being hemmed in. 'In fact, we have been in touch with our representative offices in Casablanca and Rabat about this crime and the response from their government contacts has been... discouraging.'

'Meaning?' This time it was Perronnet joining in.

'Effectively our people were advised that Morocco would prefer to regard this event as an unfortunate death of a civil servant while on holiday abroad. There's nothing more we can do.'

'What are we supposed to do with the bodies – bury them in a charity grave?'

'No. The request was that we allow the body to be repatriated as quickly and quietly as possible. We should respect that.'

'Body? It's not just one, though, is it?' Rocco pointed to the photos of the two younger men. 'His sons died, too. Both serving police officers, if their service documents are correct. One was a captain in the Royal Moroccan Police, the other a lieutenant. That makes this investigation a lot more than simply the unfortunate death of a foreign civil servant on vacation. These men were on their way somewhere up here and it would help if we knew more about them and why they came over here armed and ready.'

Galland was beginning to look like a squirrel caught in a trap. His Adam's apple bounced as he swallowed and looked around at each of the men facing him. He chose to attack the most junior man present.

'What are you suggesting, Rocco?' He took back the photos and dropped them into the folder before closing it with a snap, as if that was the end of the discussion. He began to get to his feet. 'I think you're trying to make more of this than there is.'

Rocco said, 'You think? Well, let me make it plain for you, M. Galland. What I'm suggesting is, when you murder a patriarch and two of his sons in close proximity, as happened here, it's not just an unfortunate death. It's a wipe-out.'

'I have no idea what that even means.' Galland sat back down and turned to Massin for support. 'Commissaire, I came here to offer background information, not to find myself defending a situation not of our making.'

Massin said nothing for a moment or two, chewing his lip in thought. He tapped the table. 'I would remind you that these three murders are not of our making, either, M. Galland. Yet we have a sworn duty to investigate them and will do so. And you should listen to Inspector Rocco before dismissing his words so easily. He has extensive experience of gang-related violence in Paris and further south, and knows that if three members of a family – whether blood-related or criminal – die in a professional shooting, it's usually for a reason.'

'What reason would that be?'

'It's either a warning to others,' Rocco said, 'or to stop someone telling what they know.'

Chapter Seventeen

A disgruntled Galland eventually stomped away downstairs accompanied by a uniformed officer, leaving the three policemen in an uncomfortable silence. Massin was the first to break it when he murmured, 'Well, that's going to come back to bite us. Not from him, though; I think he was a messenger sent to see what we knew. Still, when making omelettes… What do you have for us, Rocco – anything interesting?'

Rocco recounted the lack of cooperation Desmoulins had received from the Marseille police regarding the dead taxi driver, Fouad Hamal, and explained, 'If we can find out who hired him for the trip it might tell us more about this business. Without it we're not going to move forward.'

Massin pursed his lips in thought. 'I would normally suggest going through the Ministry and getting their weight behind us, but' – he gave a nod at the door and Galland's receding footsteps – 'I think we might have just shot that particular horse in the ear. I'll see what I can do through the ranks – unless you have another suggestion?'

'I bet he does,' Perronnet murmured softly with a wry smile. 'You worked that area for a while on the anti-gang unit, didn't you, Rocco?'

'I'm not suggesting I go,' Rocco said carefully. He was half thinking it but he knew it was unlikely to go down well. Still, a tilt at the idea to test the water wasn't a total bust.

Massin immediately dismissed it. 'I'm glad to hear it,' he replied. 'I need you here right now. In any case, you might have blended in down there are one time, but there will be people who remember you. And I'd rather the Ministry didn't hear about this if we can avoid it. Sorry.'

Rocco nodded in agreement. Massin was right; he'd been part of a task force from Paris working undercover at the time, fitter, leaner and probably downright foolhardy at times in his desire to make a difference. The senior officers in the local office had known they were there on the ground and had made it very clear that they didn't like it. Eventually, however, their presence had become known among the lower ranks. It hadn't been long before details leaked out to the criminal community. They had been forced to move their base out of the area to avoid confrontations and their movements being monitored.

As far as Rocco was aware, the leak had not been found but there had been a strong suspicion that it had been a local team member talking out of turn, or worse, subverted by one of the local crime syndicates into giving away their presence. Still, they'd had time to identify and scoop up a number of leading gang members in the process, a coup that had aided the Marseille police, so it hadn't been a complete failure.

'I still think it's an avenue worth exploring.'

Massin frowned. 'Are you suggesting someone on the Marseille force might be involved in the shooting?'

'Not directly. But if they've heard about it they'll be on the lookout for anyone asking questions. That would present a danger for Hamal's family, if he has any. They'll be vulnerable.'

'True enough. What are you suggesting?'

'We could send someone clean. Someone trained and experienced.'

'Desmoulins?' Perronnet lifted an eyebrow.

'No. He's good but he'd be out of his element down there. He's better off here helping run the current cases.' He paused, then said, 'I was thinking of someone trained and experienced but no longer a cop.'

'Your friend... Casparon, is it? I thought he was unwell.'

'He's much better now – and probably desperate to do some work. Don't worry, it will be low level and discreet. He knows the area and the people first-hand and he's been out of it for long enough to not be recognised. He also knows people in the North African crime gangs, so he might be able to put out feelers in that direction and find out more about the Benhamids.'

Massin looked at Perronnet, who shrugged in a 'why not' manner. 'It's all we have at the moment,' the deputy said. 'If Rocco is right, we won't be able to move forward without trying it.'

Massin ruminated on it for a few moments, then said, 'This would not go down well with the Interior Ministry. They already think some of the regional forces have too much autonomy and leave them out of the loop on operations. Can you guarantee to keep it off the record for now – at least until we get some results?'

'I believe so,' Rocco confirmed. 'Caspar has always worked that way so he won't have a problem with that.'

'What about payment? We can't expect him to do this for free.' He was looking at Perronnet.

'There's a special service fund we could use.' Perronnet glanced at Rocco. 'If I remember we've used it for paying Casparon before.'

'That's right.' Rocco didn't know the full details but the special fund was for employing outside contractors for things like special mailings, missing person's posters and hiring unmarked vehicles among other services.

Massin grunted. 'Do it. We will need a written recommendation from you, which we can sign off against this investigation. It's purely for your protection if questions are asked.'

'I'll write it now.'

'Good. And make sure Casparon knows that if he gets into trouble down there, he's on his own. We won't be able to mount a rescue mission involving you, Desmoulins and Sergeant Godard riding into town with all guns blazing.'

–

Rocco walked downstairs, relieved and surprised by Massin and Perronnet's support. Massin in particular had shown a complete change of heart. Anything guaranteed to gain the attention of the Interior Ministry would have once been anathema to him, but that had undergone a subtle change over the past few months. Rocco knew that might revert instantly to what it had been but was happy to go along with it while he could.

He sat down and wrote the recommendation, which he passed to Mme Ignace for typing, then picked up the phone to call Caspar. He was hoping the former undercover cop was ready and willing to step in and take on the job at short notice.

Marc 'Caspar' Casparon had worked with the Sud-Méditerranée Task Force for ten years chasing drug gangs operating from the North African coastline through Marseille and all the way to Paris. He was wiry, with skin the colour of stained oak and a scrub of short, black hair, and could blend in with consummate ease, especially among the various immigrant communities.

Unfortunately, living too close to the shadows for too long had taken its toll and he'd been forced to retire due to stress. Rocco had used him more than once since then, as Caspar had found himself bored with inactivity and a normal day job working for a security company, and had enjoyed low-level assignments requiring an experienced operative who could move around without attracting attention.

Caspar picked up after three rings.

'Lucas,' he said, a grin in his voice when he heard who was calling. 'What can I do for you? A job, I hope?'

'Could be. It depends.'

'On what?'

'It's in Marseille. It means steering clear of anyone you used to know unless you can trust them not to talk. Would that be a problem?'

'I doubt it. As far as the local cops are concerned, it's been a while since I was down there so most of the ones I knew will have moved on by now.'

'What about non-cops?'

'You mean the gangs. Are they involved?'

'They might be, especially on the North African side, Morocco especially.'

'Sure, some of them will still be in play. But I know how to avoid them. And I know a couple of former cops who might be able to give me some pointers.'

'Glad to hear it. How's Lucille? Have you married her yet?' Lucille and Caspar had been engaged for a while but neither of them had been in a hurry to set a date and make vows. Rocco had concerns that Lucille might be against Caspar being dragged back into any kind of danger, but he'd have to leave that to Caspar to decide.

'It's still on the calendar but we're trying to save money for an apartment.'

'I might be able to help towards that if you're willing. Where can we meet for a briefing?'

Caspar named a bar on the outskirts of Senlis, a small commune to the north of Paris in the Oise *département*. Rocco agreed. A face-to-face meeting was better than over the phone, as he wanted to give Caspar photos and details of the four dead men. He suggested a time that allowed enough time for him to drive the ninety-odd kilometres then rang off, before heading for his car.

–

Senlis was a historic town, once home to the early kings of France, with a wealth of monuments and a Gothic cathedral that attracted many tourists. Its location also made it easy for people working in Paris to commute into the city. Caspar had chosen a bar close to the outskirts where he and Rocco could meet in relative privacy and away from the summer crowds.

Caspar was waiting for him in the car park and looked much healthier than the last couple of times Rocco had seen him. He had no doubt that was Lucille's doing, quite apart from being away from the dangers of his previous life in the shadows.

'It's good to see you,' Caspar greeted him with a fierce handshake. 'What's the job?'

'Steady on,' said Rocco, as they settled into a table in one corner of the bar with beers. 'First of all, are you sure this is possible? It could mean a couple of days away and I wouldn't want you to run into any of your old contacts down there. In fact, it's best if you could avoid being seen if possible. This job doesn't have Interior Ministry approval.'

'Like I said, no problem. It's good to feel I can be useful. My job pays all right but you have no idea how boring it is talking about security locks and alarms.' He took a sip of beer and sat back. 'Come on, you mutton-head, get on with the briefing. There's a couple of trains leaving for Marseille later this afternoon and I can make one of them without too much trouble.'

'You could fly.'

'No, thanks. The airport's likely to be full of cops and robbers on the lookout for criminals or marks. There's no way of avoiding them all. I can sneak in much easier by train.'

Rocco smiled and opened the envelope containing the photographs of the four dead men and a summary of what Galland had told them, along with Fouad Hamal's address. He described the crime scene and what he needed Caspar to find out.

'No problem,' Caspar said easily. 'I know a couple of people I can talk to… *and* I've got a contact with the Royal Moroccan Police who might be able to help with that end if he's still around.' He slid the photos back in the envelope and stood up, clearly excited to be on the move. 'Let's meet up when this is done. Lucille would like to see you.'

Rocco shook his hand and held onto it for a few seconds for emphasis. 'That would be good. But listen to me: stay safe, don't take risks. You hear?'

Caspar grinned, his face animated at the idea of an assignment. 'Don't worry. I know the game. Anyway, Lucille is a lot scarier than anyone I can think of down there so I'm not going to push my luck.'

Chapter Eighteen

There was little of the afternoon left by the time Rocco got back to the station. He stayed long enough to check the latest details on the hunt for Koutcheff, which revealed nothing new. There had been a few so-called sightings, mostly from citizens who wished to be helpful but who had no real eye for detail. None of them had led anywhere. He made a brief phone call to Claude Lamotte.

'Can you meet me at Les Cyprès?' he said. 'Bring your shotgun and a torch.'

'Damn,' Claude muttered, 'you say the sexiest things. I'll wait outside the gate.'

Rocco drove fast to Petit Montgallet, hoping against hope that De Lancourt wasn't in. He'd checked Canet's log of the search details and found that two officers had visited De Lancourt's house as a first measure and made a brief check of the place in the hopes that they might stumble over some evidence that the escaped prisoner had gone back there. However, ten minutes into the search they had been prevented from proceeding by a telephone call from De Lancourt himself in his Paris office. Outgunned by threats of legal action, and on the advice of Deputy Commissaire Perronnet, they had made their apologies and withdrawn.

In spite of the evident threat still standing, he decided it was time to rattle De Lancourt's cage a bit more. If he or his men were protecting Koutcheff, putting them under pressure might just force something to give. As he'd discovered through his former experiences with the anti-gang unit in Paris, it came down to finding a weak spot. And every group, no matter who they were, had one.

He saw Claude's 2CV at the side of the road and pulled in alongside it. He got out long enough to tell him what he was looking for, then climbed back in and they both proceeded down the drive and stopped along the side of the main building.

Two men appeared from the building De Lancourt had described as the staff quarters. They were both slim, fit-looking and unfriendly. One of them stepped forward.

'You shouldn't be here without permission.' He sounded assured enough but his eyes betrayed him, especially when he saw Claude's shotgun. The over-and-under was held casually enough beneath his arm, but ready for use.

'What's your name?' Rocco asked.

A slight hesitation, then the man said, 'Debac. Raphael.' The delivery was automatic, an ingrained habit. The second man turned away, clearly less willing to respond. Then another man stepped out behind them. He was short and stocky. He stayed briefly in the background before disappearing back inside. Debac followed.

'We'd better get a move on,' Rocco said. 'I think De Lancourt will be receiving a phone call any minute.'

'Suits me,' said Claude. 'Friendly-looking pair, those two.'

Rocco led the way into the trees, the shadows closing over them. The air here was cool, the atmosphere filled with a constant sigh of a breeze passing through the foliage. The ground underfoot was soft with a carpet of needles and long-ago fallen pine cones gone soft. Overhead the birds seemed unmindful of their presence, fluttering around in the treetops and chattering away non-stop. *And why not*, thought Rocco. Even in warzones, sharing their space with men, equipment and the brutality of battle, the sounds of nature did not cease for long.

He was beginning to regret not bringing more men. If Koutcheff were here it would be a job pinning him down among this lot, and if the man knew his way around he'd be able to stay out of their way with ease. But he hadn't come here in the expectation of being that lucky; what he wanted to do was rattle the bars a bit and see what he could find.

Claude was walking along a few paces away to Rocco's left, eyes on the ground. As an experienced country cop and hunter, he could read signs easily, and see things others – Rocco included – would miss.

Rocco was deliberately staying to one side section of the wood, keeping his eye on the light showing through the trunks where the trees gave way to open fields as a guide. He doubted Koutcheff would dare go out in the open, since that offered little to no cover. But if he and Claude could cover one half of the wood, then cover the other coming back, it would give them a chance of spotting any obvious signs left behind by the fleeing man.

They came across a trench system from the Great War. Snaking away in either direction, it was a giant scar on the landscape camouflaged by the trees surrounding it and the thick undergrowth until you were almost upon it. Almost two metres deep in places and as wide, the slopes were grass-covered with the bottom showing a carpet of pine needles, cones and branches from decades of wind-falls. Curls of rusting barbed wire showed here and there, scorpion tails waiting to trip and sting the unwary, and rotting sheets of corrugated metal as sharp as razor blades emerged from the ground where dugouts had been dotted at strategic points along the trench system. It was a silent and melancholy reminder of what had happened here all those years ago, when the deep furrow would have been busy with men, weapons and pack animals, the sounds of the living and those yet to die.

The two men paused involuntarily, picturing the scene from over forty years ago.

'Can't imagine how they managed to get up the sides and out, can you?' Claude murmured, and made a brief sign of the cross. 'Poor bastards.'

They continued on their way, traversing where it seemed safe, sliding gingerly into the depths of the trench and treading warily on the softer ground underfoot. At one point Claude called out for Rocco to stop, pointing to a criss-cross of branches in his path. 'Not there. There's a hole underneath.'

Rocco nodded and moved a few paces to one side, then crossed further down. 'Does this remind you of anywhere in particular?' he said softly.

'Sure. The wood near Poissons military cemetery,' he replied, his voice a whisper. 'Just as dangerous, too. Cut yourself on any of that old metal or barbed wire and you'll end up in hospital, if you're lucky. And that's without the old ammo that could be lying around waiting to take off a leg.' He gave a visible shiver. It was a place both men had been to, not far from here, and where death had been waiting for anyone foolish enough to tread; a deadly legacy-in-waiting.

They stopped and listened every few metres, straining to pick up any trace of sound that could be alien here, any signs that they might be being watched. Then they continued, all the time keeping a view of daylight to one side and the denser part of the wood to the other. They came across another trench, then another, and what looked like a child's fort sticking up out of the ground where the soil around it had fallen in over time.

'I don't see any signs of footprints,' Rocco commented after a while. 'How about you?'

'A couple,' Claude replied. 'But it could be anyone – and they didn't look that fresh.' He stopped, eyes on the trees ahead. 'I didn't expect to see one of those here.'

He was pointing at a large, squat shape thirty metres away. Covered in green mould and a variety of creepers, and with trees crowding in on all sides, it was difficult to distinguish, with only the occasional glimpse of a straight line indicating that it was a man-made structure. It was a blockhouse or bunker built of reinforced concrete, the sides dented and crumbling and showing strands of rusted metal wire that formed the skeleton holding the walls together. If sunlight had ever penetrated here it would have been a long time ago, leaving the area dark, damp and rotten, an ugly reminder of a time long since past.

'No birdsong here,' Claude murmured softly, looking up into the branches where there was an absence of movement. 'Birds can tell, did you know that? I've seen the same at other battlefield sites: they don't like it.'

Rocco hadn't noticed, but he agreed. It was as if they had stepped across some kind of boundary where the pleasing sounds of birds singing were absent as if by common agreement. He reached into his pocket and drew his gun and Claude readied his shotgun. 'Let's take it easy until we find the entrance.'

They made a wide circle of the site, treading cautiously. As they both knew, apart from the narrow firing slits on all sides, blockhouses usually had an entrance at ground level shielded by a wall or sunk into the earth to provide added protection for those inside to come and go. The doors were usually heavy cast iron set on massive hinges, designed to resist explosions and forced entry. This one was a standard design, crablike and ugly, with what had once been steps leading down to the door, but these had now crumbled into dust covered with grass, foliage and detritus from the overshadowing trees. In addition, as they approached the steps, they could see that the firing slits had been bricked up and the door was now buried under a pile of concrete blocks, brick rubble and rusting metal.

Claude tested some of the rubble, but found it had solidified into a mass of damp soil and weeds. He tossed a rotten half-brick to one side and three rats skittered away into the pile and disappeared down a hole to one side.

'Nice,' Claude muttered, and shivered. 'God, I hate rats.'

They completed their tour of the blockhouse until they were satisfied they had covered every side, with no signs of any other entry points.

As they made their way back through the trees towards the house, someone called out, 'What are you doing here?'

The voice was low and hesitant. A man was standing in the trees, half concealed behind a large trunk. He looked as nervous as he'd sounded. When he stepped into the open, Rocco recognised the figure he'd spotted earlier behind the other two men back at the staff quarters. Up close he was soft-looking, even portly, of medium height with thinning hair and glasses. He didn't have the air of a former soldier, but stood head tilted to one side, avoiding eye contact. A tortoise, inoffensive and low-profile, unlike his colleagues.

Right now he looked ready to turn and run.

'Who are you?' Rocco queried, and held up his card. 'We're police – Lamotte and Rocco.'

The man held up both hands to show they were empty. His eyes flicked from Rocco's handgun to Claude's shotgun. He said, 'I'm Dujols. Bruno Dujols. I work for M. De Lancourt. He knows you're here and has asked that you leave immediately.'

'If he's not around,' Rocco said, 'how does he know we're here?' He knew this man or someone else had to have told their boss but he was interested in knowing who. It would tell him something about the hierarchy here.

'I called him. It's my job to keep him informed.' He seemed to gather a measure of confidence the more he spoke, and added, 'He asked me to advise you that a complaint of unauthorised access has been registered with the commissariat in Amiens and with the Interior Ministry in Paris. Furthermore, he says that if you do not leave immediately he will take legal action against both of you and demand your dismissal for provocation, trespass and…' He hesitated as if searching for a word, then added, 'harassment.'

'What about Georges Koutcheff?' Rocco asked. 'Have you seen him recently?'

'No. Please, I think you should leave.'

'Well, M. Dujols,' Rocco said, putting his gun away. 'You can report that we heard the message and are leaving as requested. As long as none of your friends are waiting for us between here and our cars.'

'Friends?'

'The other men.'

'Oh. They're not my... they're protective of the property, that's all.' With that he turned and disappeared, stumbling over the long grass as if the devil was behind him.

'This De Lancourt likes throwing his weight around, doesn't he?' muttered Claude. 'Is he serious?'

Rocco nodded. 'Very.' And clearly capable of calling up whatever big guns he could get on his side, he thought. Time would tell if the threats he'd uttered via Dujols were genuine or bluff.

Chapter Nineteen

It was late in the evening and Officer Mathieu Pouillot was feeling tired and nervy. He'd worked a double shift and badly wanted to get off his feet and head for his bed. Not that he was complaining; being a cop meant doing what was required, especially now the force was stretched working full-time on the quadruple shooting near Caix as well as the assault on himself and his colleague, Oscar Cabaud, by the man Koutcheff here in town and his subsequent escape. As a new member of the local force, he was low on the list for getting time off, and being a single man didn't cut him any favours either. He also had an ulterior motive for doing this extra work, which was to try to catch Koutcheff and bring him in as a matter of pride.

He steered his patrol car out in the direction of the neighbouring small commune of Pont-de-Metz, thankful for the diminishing glare of yellow street lamps on this edge of town. There was very little traffic around at this hour save for a few late workers changing shift and the usual dribble of late-night drinkers making their way home. He was keeping his fingers crossed that none of them chose to drive into a tree or another car, which would tie him up in paperwork for at least an hour.

As he approached a row of side streets, mostly housing but with a few small businesses, he got ready to check for movement among the shadows. He didn't expect Koutcheff to pop up conveniently right in front of him – that would be too much to hope for. But a man on the run had to find a way of staying out of sight, and an empty property was an ideal place to lie low for a while.

He glanced in the mirror as twin headlights appeared behind him, keeping pace with his speed. Someone else having a late night and probably trying hard not to stand out now they'd spotted his police car. He pulled into the side of the road and allowed the vehicle to pass. Two figures showed up inside, neither of them looking at him, and the car disappeared down the road.

He looked around him at houses on one side and open spaces on the other dotted with a few straggly trees. Nowhere to hide there, he decided, and turned his attention to the houses in the two side streets. The buildings were small and far from new although the area looked tidy enough. Further down were small workshops he'd seen on previous patrols. He'd check these last two turnings, which would put him right on the edge of town and within sight of the few lights in Pont-de-Metz. After this he'd head back to the station to clock off. Maybe the Café Schubert was still open. The owner was a fan of the cops and preferred to keep the doors open for late customers if he could. With an empty rented flat to go back to, it would be an easy choice to make, and maybe he'd get a game of bar billiards or spin the players on the table football before heading home. There was always a cop or two passing through ready to while away the time.

He drifted down the penultimate street, his headlights washing over the windows and brickwork, checking the row of small houses on each side and a couple of workshops, which were in darkness. He turned the corner at the end and moved along to the last street, which brought him back to the main road. Nothing doing there; all quiet. He signalled and turned back towards the centre of town.

As he cleared the corner, he saw a car sitting at the side of the road with a figure slumped on the road by the driver's door. A drunk driver or a heart attack? He'd dealt with both in his time and he couldn't drive on by without checking it out.

He passed the car and pulled into the side of the road just ahead. The street lights here were showing very little light and he couldn't see much more than shadows and the outline of the figure on the road. The person wasn't moving.

Pouillot clipped his flashlight to the front of his uniform jacket, got out and walked back towards the other car, which still had its engine running. He bent to check if the driver, who was lying with his back to him, was still breathing and sniffed the air for signs of alcohol.

As he did so he became aware of movement inside the car. What the—

Before he could react, the man on the ground turned over and lifted one hand. Pouillot felt his gut freeze as his torchlight showed up the gleam of dark metal. The man had a gun and it was pointed right at him. And that face…

He threw himself sideways in desperation, reaching for his own weapon, knowing he wasn't going to make it in time. A blast of hot air and a vivid flash of light exploded right in front of him, and he had enough time to hear the noise of the gunshot.

Then nothing.

Chapter Twenty

When Rocco arrived back in Poissons-les-Marais, the lights were still on in the Co-op in the village square. He could just make out through the cluster of special-price offers and posters on the window the neat figure of Mme Drolet, the owner, along with a customer. It reminded him that he hadn't eaten much today and he decided to get some ham or pâté. Add some bread and eggs and he'd be set for the evening. Simple but sufficient. Then head down for some sleep.

'Ah, here's our lovely local policeman.' Mme Drolet looked up from wrapping something on the counter, her eyes lighting up like fireworks on Bastille Day. It was the reaction he'd encountered each time she saw him. She was an attractive woman and always beautifully coiffed, once described by the wife of a local farmer as akin to a black widow spider on permanent lookout for a mate, preferably with an official position in life and a decent pension to go with it. Like a cop, the woman had added with sly malice. Rocco had ignored her but so far had managed to keep Mme Drolet at arm's length.

'Good evening,' he said politely. 'I hope I'm not too late for a couple of things?'

'Never, Lucas,' Mme Drolet purred. 'Any time, you know that.' It wasn't quite a seductive bedroom drawl but a reasonably close neighbour. If she remembered that she had a customer present, she clearly wasn't about to let it distract her.

Rocco glanced at the customer in question, a young woman with her back to him, checking over some plums in a basket. She was tall and slim with dark hair, and when she turned round he realised that he knew her. Eliane Cezard lived in the village of Passepont, a few kilometres away, with her father, Sébastien Cezard, a local artist of some renown.

'Lucas,' Eliane murmured. 'How lovely to see you. I forgot you lived in the area. How are you?'

'Umm… fine, thank you. Just popping in for some ham… or pâté… whichever is available. And bread. You, too,' he added, eyeing her shopping. It was an innocent observation that, even as he said it, sounded more like an addition to the list.

'Yum. Sounds good.' Eliane's brown eyes twinkled with humour and she was working hard to suppress a grin.

'No, I meant…' He stopped, aware that he was rambling like a teenager. Both women were looking at him now as if they had conspired to turn him into a gibbering fool.

Eliane waved a casual hand. 'I know what you meant. I'm just teasing. I'm on my way home from a job interview in Doullens.'

'Anything interesting?' Mme Drolet put in, leaning over the counter and somehow managing to insert a significant part of her upper body between the two of them. Her eyes were fizzing now and aimed at Eliane, who affected not to notice.

'A teaching job,' Eliane replied. 'I think I'm in with a chance, but we'll see.' She smiled and left with her purchases, while Rocco turned and placed his order with Mme Drolet, who was still leaning across the counter.

'Nice girl,' she said, with what sounded to Rocco like a deliberate emphasis on the second word. She wrapped his purchases and handed them over. 'I hear she's engaged, though.'

Rocco escaped as quickly as he could and went out to his car. He was surprised to find Eliane standing nearby, then noticed her car, a sporty soft-top Renault, parked across the square.

'I was going to offer to send in a rescue party,' she said with a grin. 'I think she has her eyes on you. You should be careful.' She made a *grrrrr* sound and laughed.

Rocco shook his head, unsure of what to say. He finally settled for, 'It won't do her any good. By the way, I hear congratulations are in order – that you're engaged.' He blurted out the comment before he could stop himself, then gestured back at the shop. 'Sorry – she mentioned it.'

Eliane's eyes widened in surprise for a second before the smile returned. 'Really, Lucas… and you a policeman. You shouldn't believe everything you hear. I think she was toying with you.'

'So you're not, then – engaged, I mean?' *God in heaven*, he thought, feeling his face blossoming red, and was glad of the poor light. This was getting worse. 'Sorry – it's none of my business.' He threw himself into a change of topic. 'How's your father?' Sébastien had helped him with a recent case of art fraud, after being held by some as the possible perpetrator. He'd come to like the old man a lot. And his daughter, he thought.

'He's fine, thank you for asking. He's in Brussels for a few days discussing a commission for a series of official portraits. And no, I'm not engaged or anywhere close to it.' She turned to go and added, with a delightful curl to her lips, 'But it doesn't mean I can't entertain a friend once in a while. You should come round and I'll cook you dinner. Say, in a day or two? I'll ring you.'

'Umm… yes. That would be nice.' Rocco watched her walk away with an engaging swing of her hips and took a deep breath. He was pretty sure he'd got away with that little bit of awkwardness. Well, mostly. Damn, he needed to get a bit more with it when talking to her, which sounded as if it might be sooner rather than later. How the hell had he got to this?

Chapter Twenty-One

When he arrived at the station the next morning, Rocco found the yard at the rear full of vehicles and uniforms. He found a space a block away and returned to the building to find it abuzz with news of a shooting. Officer Pouillot, he learned, had been on patrol late last night and had been found on the outskirts of town. He was dead, one shot to the head.

As he was absorbing the shocking details, another officer called his name and pointed at the ceiling. A summons had been sent out. He hurried upstairs and found Massin, Canet and Godard in subdued conversation around a large map of Amiens and the surrounding districts.

'Ah, Rocco, glad to see you,' Massin said, and beckoned him in. The senior officer looked ashen. 'I didn't call you because we've got ample hands on this business already, but you should know what happened in case it's connected with our runaway prisoner.' He nodded at Canet. 'Perhaps you could summarise, Captain. I have to go downstairs.'

Canet puffed his cheeks and flicked a hand at the map. 'From what we know, Pouillot was on patrol late last night out towards Pont-de-Metz and stopped at the side of the road. A local householder named Ledran told us he'd seen a car parked there with its engine running, so maybe it was to do with that. Next thing he heard was the sound of a gunshot. When he looked out he saw a patrol car in the road but the other car had gone. The patrol car was still there a few minutes later so the resident went out to look and found Pouillot lying nearby. He'd been shot in the head but was still breathing at that point.' He hesitated and shook his head at the enormity of the event. 'By the time they got him to the hospital it was all over.'

For someone who'd come here looking for some action, Rocco thought grimly, Pouillot had got more than he'd bargained for. 'No clues to who it might have been?'

'Only one I can think of,' said Godard. His eyes were tight with suppressed anger. 'He'd not been here long enough to get under anyone's skin... except for one person.'

Canet explained the sentiment by saying, 'We think he might have encountered Koutcheff. If it was him, that bloody man is racking up some serious jail time.'

'If he makes it that far,' Godard said heavily, his voice low. 'Pouillot was a popular addition to the force here and the others won't be very forgiving if Koutcheff draws down on any of them.'

Rocco sympathised. Most police officers had the same desire for retribution as any normal citizen, and the means to apply it, especially when the victim was one of their own. But he also knew that the hot anger following the shooting of an officer dissipated quickly enough to make any threats unlikely to be carried out unless their hand was severely forced.

'Koutcheff's lawyer said he's a collector, whatever that means,' he told the two officers. 'He's likely to have access to other weapons.'

'I'll put the word out,' said Godard. 'Thanks for the warning.'

'Did you get out to De Lancourt's place? I suggested to Desmoulins that a visit with some uniforms might be in order to see if Koutcheff turned up there.'

'We did. It was like poking a stick in a rat's nest. Men popped out from all over. Some of them looked like they were braced for a fight. De Lancourt wasn't in but we completed a search of the grounds. There was no sign of Koutcheff, unless he was hiding inside.'

'And they let you do that?'

'In the end. I told them that we had a duty to hunt for a dangerous man to protect the local population and property and they backed off – although I think the four of us evened up the odds a little.'

Rocco smiled. Desmoulins had taken him at his word and gone in mob-handed. A wise move as it turned out. He told them what he and Claude had found in the woods, and the difficulty of tracking a single individual among the dense trees and undergrowth.

Massin returned and announced that he'd given the order for all available officers who were not on sick leave or otherwise incapacitated to be called to duty in the search for Pouillot's killer. It would stretch the force's resources but he would listen to any suggestions to help lighten the load while not ignoring any work on current cases.

He looked at Rocco and handed him a message slip from the front desk. 'There's been a call for you. A Gérard Jeunet? Needs to see you urgently.'

The slip contained a telephone number. Rocco thanked him and went back downstairs, wondering what the old man wanted.

He was beginning to feel a sense of frustration at the knowledge that they were no further forward with either of the main investigations, hampered by lack of information on both fronts. Something had to break soon or they'd be going backwards, with any leads out there beginning to fade and die. And now an officer had been shot dead.

Captain Canet intercepted him, also holding out a message slip. 'Lucas, you're in demand today. I was going to ask you earlier about this address here in town for Koutcheff. The search team made a check first thing after he escaped to see if he'd gone to ground there. They got in but the current occupant, name of Kazelmy, said Koutcheff hadn't been around for a while and he was looking after the place in the meantime.'

'Did they find anything?'

'No. The place was a shambles and didn't look much lived-in. In the wake of what just happened to Pouillot I was wondering if you'd care to take a look when you get a moment? You might uncover something useful.'

Rocco nodded. 'Glad to.' He took the piece of paper and picked up a telephone at a spare desk and dialled the number Massin had given him. First he had to meet with Jeunet. Then Koutcheff's place. Anything was better than hanging around the office and there were plenty of others eminently capable of dealing with any queries that might arise.

Chapter Twenty-Two

Caspar stood at the end of the street where Fouad Hamal had lived, and breathed in a familiar aroma. Darkness had fallen and this part of the city of Marseille known as the Les Crottes was almost quiet, save for a few vehicles moving away from the port area of the Bassin National. He couldn't see the water but he could smell it, carrying more than a trace of fuel, oil, fish and something exotic he couldn't quite place. It was a reminder of his time down here years ago, and the need to keep his head down. The people he'd been up against here then, mostly running drugs and/or illegal arms, had long memories.

The street he was in was a narrow cut-through just off Avenue Roger Salengro. It lay in the shadow of a number of small warehouses on either side, with a block of tired and weather-worn three-storey apartments at one end. It was these apartments he was currently focusing on, and a group of about a dozen people clustered around one of the entrances. They were talking in subdued voices, bidding a sombre farewell to someone inside. News of Fouad Hamal's demise had clearly arrived among the man's immediate friends and neighbours.

He turned away and did a tour of the block. To intrude now would invite attention and be remembered for a basic lack of courtesy. On the way he passed a number of small stores, all locked up tight. Among them was a fruit wholesaler, a moped repair workshop, a clothing shop and a window covered in garish film posters. He recognised actor and singer Jean Gabin, American-French tough-guy import Eddie Constantine, and actress Simone Signoret. Others at the rear of the store were too dark to make out in detail, but were of the same dramatic quality and familiar from walls all over France. Here and in this light they looked sadly faded and neglected, as if from another age.

By the time he was back at the apartment block, the small crowd had gone. He gave it another couple of minutes then approached the entrance.

The building had uneven wooden shutters at the windows, some showing dim yellow lights through the slats. He tried the front door and was surprised to find it creaked open easily, emitting a rancid smell of vegetables, boiled meat and spices.

He checked a list of tenants on a scrappy piece of card tacked to one wall. The Hamals lived on the third floor. He went up on his toes, fast and light on the tiled treads, passing muffled voices and the sounds of jazz music on the first floor and something more Middle Eastern in flavour on floor two, overlaid by the fractious squeals of a small child.

Floor three was silent, with that special air of stillness brought about by the arrival of sickness or death. He tapped on the door and waited.

It edged open and revealed a woman staring out at him with a look of caution... and what he recognised as a combination of resignation and grief. He'd seen it before on the faces of relatives of people caught up on both sides of crimes. On one side shock and loss, the other portraying a reaction from years of waiting for the inevitable knock on the door.

'Mme Hamal?' he said politely. He kept his voice low; he wanted to avoid questions from well-meaning and protective neighbours.

'What do you want?' Her voice was flat and the skin around her eyes had the puffy look of grief. She would have been remarkable at one time, he thought, with long, wavy hair and strong features with a generous mouth that was born to bring forth a ready smile. Now she looked worn down and hollowed out.

'I'm trying to find out who killed your husband,' he said simply, 'and why. I was hoping you could help me.'

Her expression changed but not for the better. 'You're a policeman.' Her expression clearly showed that her trust in the police was in short supply. He wasn't surprised.

'No, madam, I'm not a policeman. But I am working on behalf of the police in Picardie, up north. They want to find out the truth of this tragic matter. Believe me, I'm sorry to intrude.'

She made a harsh sound deep in her throat. 'My husband is dead. What else is there to know? Will it bring him back?' Her voice was on the verge of breaking, and he suspected that any second now she might start yelling, which would bring the building down around his ears.

Caspar held up a hand, palm out to placate her. 'May I come in?' he asked softly. 'I've come a long way. I just need to talk to you and tell you what I know. It's not much but it might help you.'

She shrugged, grief and anger giving way to natural if reluctant courtesy. She moved aside and opened the door wider in invitation. He walked in, listening for signs that anyone else was there but hearing nothing.

The apartment was spotless, a mix of old but traditional French furniture and elaborate cushions and drapes that had clear echoes of Hamal's home country. The air smelled sweet and he saw three vases of cut flowers standing on the floor in one corner, the plants still in their cellophane wrappings.

Mme Hamal excused herself and disappeared into a side room. He heard the sound of crockery and relaxed. It was a good sign. Unless she was about to come out and start throwing plates at him, she was following the Mediterranean custom of showing hospitality to visitors. He sat on a hard-backed chair and waited until she returned bearing a small tray with two cups of black coffee.

'It's much too late for coffee,' she said with an attempt at a smile. 'But I won't sleep tonight anyway, and my digestion is beyond caring.' She handed him a cup and sat down opposite, gathering herself together and waiting for him to speak.

Caspar decided to get straight down to it. She looked and sounded as if she didn't need or want sympathy, but facts. And something in her bearing, sad as it was, told him that if she knew anything about her husband's work, she would either talk about it willingly or not at all. There would be no half measures.

He laid out a few bare facts from what Rocco had told him, minus the details of her husband's death. She listened without comment until he finished by explaining that the police in Amiens believed her husband had been a victim of circumstance; that they had no reason for thinking he had been involved in anything criminal or underhand.

After a moment's silence, she said, 'Thank you. I am happy to know that. But how can I help? I don't know anything.'

'Your husband was a taxi driver, is that correct?'

She nodded. 'Yes. At least, here he was. Back in Casablanca also for a while, but before that he was a government worker.'

'Can you tell me about when he arrived here? For example, was he part of any group or association in the Moroccan community?'

'Never. He was obviously part of it but Fouad did not join groups. He was a solitary man, which was why he became a driver, he said, to spend his time talking only when he had to.'

Caspar smiled. 'Most taxi drivers I know can't stop talking.'

'That's true enough. He was not part of any organised rank, though. He liked to work solo. It was sometimes risky, with occasional threats from drivers who didn't like unregistered cars taking their trade. But Fouad was a man who got on with people, in spite of his solitary nature, so they tended to leave him alone.' Her voice softened at the memory. 'He was a man of peace; everyone liked Fouad.'

'Did you come over together?'

'No. I was born here in Marseille. My grandmother, though, she was from Tunisia. My grandfather was French. I was working in a restaurant not far from here and Fouad walked in one day and smiled at me.' She shrugged. 'He was a charming man and I was smitten.'

Caspar felt he was moving away from getting any kind of solid information, and decided to try another angle. 'Can I ask if you know what kind of government work he did before coming here?'

'Is that likely to help?'

'I really don't know. I'm trying to find connections, that's all.'

She looked away as if trying to recall details. Then she said, 'He told me he once worked on water management for the Moroccan government. I don't know what he did exactly, but it was a technical position. I think he had to travel all over the country checking for water sources like springs and underground lakes – and water off the Atlas Mountains. I asked him once is that right, that there are lakes underground? He said they were called aquifers and that the rock is... what do they call it, full of holes that can hold water. It's vital for providing irrigation for farms, he said.'

Caspar nodded. He didn't think this was likely to lead anywhere, but now he'd got her talking and thinking, he had to keep going while she was in the mood.

'I'm sorry to have to ask this question, but it could be important: in spite of being a solitary man, could Fouad have become unwittingly involved with any criminal elements since he arrived here?'

'Not here.' She shook her head with conviction. 'Not criminal.' But there was a look in her eye that he couldn't read, as if there was something that had occurred to her that she didn't want to mention.

'Madame,' he said softly, 'you can tell me. I promise it will be in absolute confidence. Was there a problem with something... not criminal but perhaps in the ordinary sense... maybe connected to his home country?'

'I think...' She hesitated, then ploughed on as if to get something off her chest. 'I think a call he received the other day and the journey he made to the north may have involved something... political. He did not say, but I could tell there was something that troubled him. He hated anything to do with politics, which he said had caused so much pain and misery in his home country.'

'Was he somehow involved in it?'

'He once admitted that he had had trouble with some of the political factions in Morocco years ago because he had no interest in joining them. Over there, if you did not show your allegiances, especially against France, who they wanted out of the country, you were regarded as a traitor and it could affect your job, and most government work was ruled by the nationalists. Fortunately, he worked most of his time far from the city, so he wasn't under their eye very much.' She took out a handkerchief and twisted it in her hands. 'The factions could be violent, he said, and there was much dishonesty. There had been many deaths and people disappearing, even some of the French farmers who owned land there. It was why he decided to leave, because of the corruption.'

'What sort of corruption?'

She hesitated again, then said, 'I had heard something about it before, of course, with many Moroccans coming to live here. But my world was sufficiently distant for it to be happening somewhere I did not know. It was only on the odd occasion when Fouad talked about it that I realised how horrible it must have been for him and his family.'

'He was threatened?'

'Yes. Because of his work in irrigation planning he had to meet many people – mostly farmers, to talk about where they were sowing crops and where they needed access to water. He got to know several of them very well. That was when he noticed irregularities.'

'Did he tell you about them?'

'Only a little. He told me that some of the farms owned by French people changed hands almost overnight. This surprised him because he had only recently been talking to them about their plans and there had been no mention of them leaving. The farms were big and successful and employed many local people.'

'This was before Morocco gained full independence?'

'Several years before, yes. When he mentioned it to his superiors he was told that it should not concern him and that someone else would deal with it.'

'Did that trouble him?'

'Yes. Even to this day. He was a man of principles; he did not like to think people were being cheated. He had liked some of the farmers very much and wanted to know where they had gone. He could only think they had moved on or returned here to France.'

'Could it have been the political factions that might have had something against your husband? It's been a while since he was there.'

She shrugged, an elegant but sad lift of her shoulders. 'I cannot say. He once said they have long memories, these people. Years, maybe decades will pass, but they remember. I don't know if it's true but... the world is very much like that, I fear.'

'About the telephone call. What happened?'

'The caller said he wanted a lift to the airport. Fouad thought it odd because the buses going there are much cheaper. But business is business so he went out to collect the client. However, he came back after twenty minutes and told me the job was not to the airport but meant collecting a car and three passengers from a garage here in Marseille and taking them up north.'

'I understand.' Caspar took a photo of the Mercedes from inside his jacket, thankfully not displaying any signs of blood on the interior. 'Can you confirm if this is your husband's vehicle?'

She frowned, then shook her head and stood up. 'Excuse me – I need my reading glasses.' She found the glasses and put them on, studying the photo. 'No. He never drove a car like that. He had an old Renault.' She motioned with her chin towards the window. 'It's still parked down the street. The caller insisted that Fouad use a car of their choice, not his own.'

'Is that normal?'

'Not normal, no.' She took a deep breath and removed the glasses. 'He did do some driving work as a chauffeur at odd times, like weddings and such, but not often. Then he would use the client's vehicle. But this… it was different.'

'How?'

'He said they could travel so much cheaper by train if they had to, and he didn't like the sound of the job. But he couldn't refuse.'

'Why not?' Caspar picked up on the words. 'Because of the money?'

Mme Hamal's head dropped along with her voice. 'The money sounded very good. It would have allowed us to visit Fouad's home in Casablanca. When I asked why he was doing it he said I shouldn't ask… that it was something he had to do and when it was over he could go back to driving his own car.' When she looked up at him, her eyes were moist. 'Why couldn't he have said no?'

'Do you know where he went to collect the Mercedes?' Caspar had the address of a garage from the documents in the car but they could have been left there by a previous owner and he wanted to make sure.

Mme Hamal put her glasses back on and walked over to a small bureau, where she took out a notepad. She handed it to Caspar and sat down again. 'He wrote it down. He said he was told not to, but he needed to get the details right. My husband was a meticulous man, you see. And very honest.'

Caspar read the note. It was the same address. And underneath was the name Rocco had mentioned: Benhamid.

'Is this the caller's name?'

'I think it was the name of one of the passengers he was told to pick up.' She took a deep breath, her body trembling, then said, 'To me, Fouad was an open book; I could tell he recognised the name and that it worried him. When I asked why all he said was that it was a common enough name among Moroccans and there was nothing I should be concerned about. I know he was trying to protect me.'

'Did he say where the passengers were going?'

She shook her head. 'No. Only that he had to drive the car north and there would be no stops except for fuel. That was all he told me… also that he would have to make a telephone call when he was further north and he'd be given more instructions about the destination.'

'He didn't mention how far north?'

'No. Just north. He left that afternoon. He said he would have to drive overnight to arrive at the destination by early morning. That was the last time I saw him.' A tear rolled down her cheek. She didn't bother brushing it away.

She probably couldn't even feel it, Caspar thought, her face was so numbed with grief.

He thanked her and wrote down the number of the small hotel where he'd booked a room close to the station. 'If you think of anything else, no matter how small, you can call me at that number any time over the next twenty-four hours. Ask for Caspar.'

She nodded. 'Don't worry, M. Caspar. I won't be going anywhere until I get my husband's body back.'

'Of course. Maybe I can call back tomorrow morning? You never know, something might occur to you… a name, perhaps.'

'If you wish, but I wouldn't want you to waste your time.' She seemed to remember her coffee for the first time and picked it up before promptly putting it down again untouched.

–

As Caspar walked up the street, a car turned the corner and came towards him. The headlights blazed off the walls of the buildings, highlighting a patchwork of broken plaster, ancient shop signs and electricity wires looped overhead like black spaghetti. He kept his head down and adopted an unsteady gait, waving in a carelessly friendly manner, effectively masking his face as the car cruised past. He risked a quick glance at the occupants but the street lights flashing across the windows made it impossible to determine the face of anyone inside. At the top of the street, he ambled erratically towards the opposite corner, glancing back once.

The car had stopped right outside Mme Hamal's apartment block.

Caspar ducked into a doorway and waited but nobody got out. Moments later the car began reversing up the street towards him.

Chapter Twenty-Three

'Inspector Rocco – Lucas?' The voice was familiar but uncertain and faint. It was Gérard Jeunet, the cheese lover and absconder from the Académie Française. 'I'm so glad you've called.'

'Gérard. I got your message. What can I do for you?'

'Can we meet, do you think? Do you have time?'

'Of course.' He sensed some strain in the older man's voice. 'Is it urgent?'

'Urgent enough. In the cheese market, say, thirty minutes?' The phone clicked off before Rocco could reply.

He walked round to the market and stepped through the entrance to be met by the memorable fragrances from his previous visit. There were very few customers and most of the stalls were closed. He made a tour of the building, stepping past piles of empty boxes and rubbish bins ready for collection, and finally caught sight of Jeunet lurking at the far end, close to a fire exit.

He was surprised by the older man's appearance; he looked even frailer than the first time they'd met, with a noticeable stoop to his tall frame and an almost haunted expression on his face.

'Thank goodness you could come.' Jeunet sounded relieved. He put a weak hand on Rocco's arm and pulled him to one side, glancing past him to study the few customers drifting among the stalls. 'I cannot stay long but I just wanted to tell you something I should have mentioned the first time we met. Perhaps we can go to another café I favour from time to time. There are too many people here… I don't feel safe.'

'Of course,' Rocco said, puzzled by the change in the man's demeanour. 'Lead the way.'

The café was closer than the previous one, in a tiny side street with close-knit buildings that left the available sunlight in short supply. The interior was empty of customers and smelled of beer and stale tobacco. Jeunet signalled to the man behind the bar, who brought two coffees and cognacs in quick order.

Jeunet sipped his cognac before downing the rest with a gulp. He pushed his coffee to one side with a grimace.

'Gérard, what is it?' Rocco asked. Waves of tension were coming off the old man like an electrical charge, and he reached out to hold his arm. 'Are you unwell?'

Jeunet shook his head and patted Rocco's hand in gratitude. 'Nothing that nature or medicine can mend, I'm afraid, Lucas.' He took out a handkerchief and blew his nose, then said, 'I must apologise for this ridiculous subterfuge, but I have good reason. It's De Lancourt.' He put the handkerchief away and toyed with his empty glass.

'What about him?'

'You may recall that I told you that I've always opposed his membership of the academy. Well, I heard yesterday evening that he has put forward an application for a vacant seat.'

'Your seat?'

Jeunet waved a hand. 'No, not mine. He knows I would be asked to speak for him if he did, and since I would have nothing good to say about him; he has applied for another with a more favourable outcome. I understand there is a powerful lobby behind him who are making it known that they would welcome his addition to the academy.'

'Do you know who they are?'

'Certainly – some, anyway. I have heard mention of several eminent members of the legal profession in particular. Even a government figure and a judge – and at least three existing members of the academy who support his application. As I indicated to you before, he has powerful friends.'

Rocco wondered where this was leading. He knew from what Jeunet had said before that he had no regard for De Lancourt. But he wasn't sure why it would matter so much to him to be so angry at the prospect of the lawyer gaining the distinction of membership of an organisation to which, in reality, he no longer belonged.

'I'm not sure I follow. You've stepped down, so why does this upset you so much?'

'Because one, the word is that De Lancourt is what the Americans would call a "shoo-in".' He waved a hand. 'I shouldn't use that horrid expression, should I? But you're quite right: since I no longer hold a seat, I doubt anyone will care what I think. But I do.' He paused, then said, 'The other reason is that De Lancourt has a background that I know if it became public would render him ineligible, even subject to serious investigation.'

'Such as?'

Jeunet took a deep breath. 'Murder for one.'

'Seriously?'

'Yes. Before I tell you more, I should mention that I have been recently diagnosed with cancer. The physicians tell me that it's inoperable but I should not give up hope as there are new developments coming along all the time. I'm sure they always tell people that as a matter of course – not that I blame them. There comes a moment when even the most optimistic of people have to acknowledge that their fuel is running down fast and is close to empty.'

'I'm very sorry to hear that. Are you sure?'

'Sadly, yes. I grow weaker by the day, so even I can tell. The fact is I don't want to sail off into the dark night without at least trying to spike De Lancourt's guns.' He gave a weak smile. 'My God, I must be in a bad way – I should have come up with better metaphors. And before you say it, I am not wasting valuable energy on hate, I promise. What I want is justice. Justice that should have come about before now but for various reasons I could not pursue earlier.' He sniffed. 'A case perhaps of mortality giving a man a silent nod to clear the decks and be done with old enmities.'

'I'm listening.' Rocco drank his coffee, happy to wait for Jeunet to continue. Whatever was coming sounded at the very least something the old man needed to get off his chest.

Jeunet reached into his jacket pocket and produced an envelope. 'I have a granddaughter, Micheline, who is studying art and literature at the Sorbonne in Paris. She's a beautiful, bright girl and I love her dearly.' He opened the envelope and pulled out a photograph, and dropped it on the table in front of Rocco. The photo showed a group of young women – clearly students – outside the entrance to a large building. They were laughing and clearly happy, young people with the world and much promise at their feet.

Rocco recognised the domed building in the background. 'What is this, Gérard? Tell me.'

'The photo arrived at my home last night. It was handed to me at the door. There was nothing with it, no note, nor any explanation either in writing or from the man who delivered it.' He pointed to a young woman in the group. 'That is Micheline, with college friends outside the university.'

'You think this is a threat.'

'I know it is.' Jeunet cleared his throat and apologised. 'Forgive me, this makes me emotional. I know it is a threat because of this man.' He pointed to a figure in the background. It was a man in dark clothing, standing away from the group. He was smiling at the camera, it seemed, as if his proximity to the girls was somehow to be admired.

Rocco studied the man. He was in his late thirties, he guessed, of slightly Asian appearance and wearing a leather jacket. He had a broad, tanned face with high cheekbones and spiky black hair, which came to a peak on his forehead. In normal circumstances he might have been looking pleased at being so close to a number of attractive young women. But Rocco already knew this was no ordinary circumstance.

'Do you know him?'

Jeunet nodded. 'I know his face. It was he who gave me the envelope.'

'At your home in Amiens?'

'Correct. You can keep the photo. I was wondering if there is anything you can do? I feel helpless knowing he is out there. It was so blatant. I've never experienced anything like it.'

Rocco sat back. In Jeunet's place he would have had the same feelings of alarm – even anger. Nobody he could think of would deliver such a missive without evil intent.

And the smiling face of the man carried its own horrific message. *She's within our reach.*

'I'll do something about it,' he promised. 'Can you give me her address in Paris?'

'It's written on the back. She shares an apartment with three other students.'

'Good. It's better if she's not living alone – it might put off any idea of an attack. You mentioned wanting justice about De Lancourt. Precisely what has he done?'

Jeunet coughed again, this time with considerable force. Rocco signalled for a glass of water, which the bartender brought over at speed. He waited until Jeunet had regained his composure before offering him the glass, and the old man took a sip and raised a hand in thanks.

'Sorry, Lucas. I must be weaker today than I thought. This has taken a lot out of me.' He sipped more water, then said, 'I cannot tell you everything I know – I'm not sure I have the strength. But if you meet me here tomorrow morning, I can show you documentation to support my accusations. Then you can make up your own mind about what to do.'

'Why have you not come forward with this information before?'

'Cowardice, quite simply. De Lancourt is more dangerous than you or anyone would suspect. If I tried to put what I have out there without help, I doubt I would last more than a few days.' He looked bleak at the thought. 'Also, I have family members who are dear to me and he probably knows that.'

'If that's the case,' Rocco suggested, 'why don't I come home with you now and you can show them to me.'

'I wish I could. Unfortunately they're in a safety deposit box at my bank, and they're closed today, something to do with an annual audit. But they're open again in the morning.' He took a deep breath and exhaled with obvious difficulty. 'Tomorrow, I promise. I'll pick up the papers and have them ready for you by eleven. Right now, I think I need my bed.'

He struggled to get up and Rocco had to help him. He left some money on the table to pay for the drinks and asked the bartender to summon a taxi. Moments later it arrived in the narrow street and stopped outside.

Rocco made sure the old man was able to make the journey and waved him off. Jeunet smiled, and sank into the seat with a sigh.

–

Before doing anything else, Rocco rang Captain Michel Santer, his former boss and close friend in the Clichy-Nanterre district of north-west Paris. If anyone was able to help keep an eye on Jeunet's granddaughter, it would be Santer.

He explained the problem and read out the student's address. The captain immediately understood.

'Don't worry, Lucas,' he said, 'I know this area. I'll get someone to check the building without alarming the young lady and have regular patrols going by. In fact, it fits in with local crime prevention calls we've been making. We'll alert the residents generally to keep an eye out for strangers. If we see anyone matching the description, we'll haul him in. Send me a copy of the photograph and I'll issue it to the patrols.'

Chapter Twenty-Four

After an uneasy night's sleep punctuated by minor flash-backs of his time working undercover here in Marseille, Caspar was up early and walking towards the Bassin National. He'd managed to slip away before the car last night had reached his doorway, and had been forced to leave the area. Instinct told him the vehicle reversing was more than a driver looking for a parking space. His time working here before had taught him that the city's crim-inal element had a very effective grapevine, and pushing his luck would not end well. Right now he needed to speak with Mme Hamal once more to see if she had remembered anything else since they had spoken. It was unlikely but the difference of a few hours often woke memories that in tired or stressed minds had lain dormant.

He pushed the front door open and climbed the stairs, wincing at the traces of grit on the treads. At least this time if a neighbour appeared, Mme Hamal would be able to vouch for him. He reached the third-floor landing and stopped.

The door to Mme Hamal's apartment was wide open.

He moved closer and listened. Nothing. He stepped inside and murmured her name. No response. This wasn't good. In this part of the city, he doubted anyone left their doors open willingly.

He peered round the doorway into the room where he'd sat the previous evening. The cups they had used were lying on the rug, one smashed with a black coffee stain spread across the fabric. Her cup: she hadn't touched the contents. Lying on the floor nearby were two elaborate cushions from an armchair, and the front of the bureau from which she had retrieved the notebook was open, its contents scattered underneath, evidence of a hurried search.

He left the apartment and closed the door softly behind him. He made his way downstairs, stepping lightly. As he went to open the front door, a tiny woman entered with a shopping bag.

'Good morning, madame,' he said politely, holding the door open for her. 'I came to offer Mme Hamal my condolences but she seems to be out. Do you know when she will be back?'

The woman looked at him with sad eyes. 'That's kind of you, young man, but she's gone.'

'Gone? Gone where?'

'A car came for her late last night. Very nice, it was. The driver was polite and told me she'd arranged a lift to stay with her sister near Aix-en-Provence. I said what about the funeral and he said he would bring her back for it.' She pursed her lips. 'Poor woman, her mind must have been deranged with sadness.'

Caspar was about to leave, deciding he'd been here too long already, when something in her comment stopped him. 'Why do you say that?'

'She doesn't have a sister in Aix – or anywhere else. I've known her all my life. She was born an orphan.'

–

Caspar thanked the old woman and left the building with a feeling of dismay at the news. But what could he do about it? It was entirely possible the neighbour had been mistaken. And looking for a 'nice' car in even a small town would be tough; in a city this size, it was a non-starter. He debated telling the local police about the matter, but that would mean filling in forms, and what could he tell them – that a woman he'd met only the day before, who had lost her husband in a shooting up north, had disappeared, apparently collected by a 'polite man in a nice car'? They'd laugh him out of the building. Worse, they'd begin to investigate his background and that might lead to trouble for Lucas; running investigations on another police patch without official clearance was frowned upon.

He decided instead to begin the search for the source of the grey Mercedes-Benz 220. Rue Samatan wasn't far and he decided to walk. Taxi drivers here, like anywhere else, were inveterate talkers and would undoubtedly ask where he was from. He didn't want to get into that and in spite of having lived for so long under different aliases in his police work, he didn't want to fabricate a fake background. Their chat didn't stop once their passenger had disembarked; in the quiet downtimes they might casually mention to colleagues a man from the north who didn't sound quite 'right'.

Samatan was a busy enough thoroughfare to allow him to blend in, yet quiet enough at this time to move easily. The garage entrance was located down an alleyway off the main street. He checked it out and came to a large roller-shutter door pitted with chipped paint and dotted with rusting metal plaques for oil, spark plugs and sundry other auto-related products. He banged on a small door adjacent to the shutter but the sound echoed through the interior.

A small glass panel in the shutter door was filthy with years of dirt, but when he rubbed it away it showed the interior to be empty. Not just empty but scoured clean. Not even a workbench or a box of tools. He checked further along the street but the building appeared to have a front access only with no windows.

As he turned away, a man in a leather jacket and cap appeared from the direction of the main street. He stopped a few paces away and stared hard at Caspar. He was balding and somewhere in his fifties, with the rugged build of a rugby player who'd had more than his share of hard matches.

'You looking for something?' he demanded. A thin cigarette in his mouth bobbed up and down as he spoke.

'That depends,' said Caspar, 'on whether this place can do a service on my car. Are you the owner?'

'Does it look like anyone owns it?' the man replied. 'You'd be better off going elsewhere.' He took the cigarette from his mouth and flicked it into the gutter. 'Anyway, I don't see your car.'

Caspar sensed that, if he pushed it, a confrontation with this man could quickly escalate out of his control. If that happened, he had no way of knowing where it could end, but he figured the man in front of him might have help close by. 'My car's a couple of blocks away. I was looking for somewhere that wouldn't charge me the earth to change the oil and sparkplugs.' He shrugged, and added in explanation, 'I lost my job a couple of weeks ago. Why are you breaking my balls – you think I need this?'

The man looked sceptical for a moment, then shook his head. 'Tough luck. But like I said, find somewhere else.' With that he turned and walked back the way he'd come.

Caspar watched him go and experienced a sense of tension he hadn't felt in quite a while. It was the feeling that he'd suddenly come up against a man who wasn't as random or innocent as he looked. It was an inner alarm that had served him well in many potential tight spots.

He waited for a few seconds, then set off after the man, allowing him to get some way ahead. As he turned out of the alleyway, he saw the man walking along Samatan before ducking into a side street. By the time Caspar got level with the turning, the man had disappeared.

He knew when to cut his losses. Asking questions around here would make him stand out to the wrong people, and he had no wish to have his visit cut short before he'd spoken to anyone else.

As the thought entered his mind, he turned to cross the street and found himself facing three men. He stepped aside to let them pass, but they held their ground, watching him carefully.

'Well, well, boys,' said the man in the centre, a large figure in a smart suit and dazzling white shirt. 'Who have we here, then? If my eyes don't deceive me, it's Casparon the *flic*!'

The 'boys', both in their thirties and even bigger than the man who'd spoken, said nothing, merely staring at Caspar as if he were a bug on the ground.

'Hello, Karim,' Caspar said, and wondered if flinging himself into the street to get away from this man was worth the risk of getting squashed by a truck. The option didn't appeal. 'Long time no see.'

Karim Hadji was a mid-level Moroccan criminal who sailed through life under the guise of being a businessman. He'd been operating along the coast here for years, running his section of the narcotics and contraband trade from across the Med. He had also operated several bars, cafés and small businesses through which his illegal money had been flushed and washed clean. The police had never been able to prove any of it as far as Caspar was aware, choosing instead to go after bigger fish in the hopes that Karim would trip himself up. He'd come close himself to catching Karim, but not close enough. That was largely, he'd suspected, because the Moroccan had inside information on police movements and was able to cover himself in time and make evidence disappear.

Caspar decided to go on the attack rather than take a dive; he knew Karim wouldn't expect anything else. 'I'm surprised to see you out and free. I thought they'd have locked you and your gang up by now and melted the keys.'

The two men with Karim muttered under their breath and edged forward at this affront, but their boss held up a restraining hand heavy with large gold rings. 'Don't bother, boys. This one's a small fish. Hell, he isn't even a policeman any more, last I heard. Isn't that right, Caspar? You handed in your papers?'

'Quite right, Karim. You got too clever for me so I decided to give it up and settle for a quieter life in the country.'

Karim laughed aloud at the idea, causing a small dog in a car parked nearby to start barking. 'A good decision, I think. But tell me, please, what are you doing here? A friend saw you yesterday evening and said to me, "Karim, you'll never guess who I saw lurking along Avenue Roger Salengro last night. It was that undercover cop, Casparon, as sure as I stand here."' He grinned. 'I didn't believe him, of course, because why would you come back here without a badge and a gun? It would be crazy. Yet here you are in person!' He placed a large hand on Caspar's shoulder and said, 'Let me buy you a coffee and we can chat in a civilised manner. What do you say?'

Caspar was about to refuse but one of Karim's men stepped forward and took his other arm. They guided Caspar down the street to a restaurant with an elaborate frontage called Les Goûts du Maroc. It was quiet and cool inside, and by the way the waiters scurried around clearing a corner table, he guessed Karim was more than a regular customer.

'Nice place,' he said, and sat down when the pressure on his shoulder became too clear to ignore.

'Thank you,' Karim said, looking around as if seeing it for the first time. 'It's a bit small but it's all mine. Now, coffee, yes? Then we can have a little talk.'

Five minutes later, Karim had told his two men to disappear and Caspar was enjoying, in spite of himself, some excellent coffee and orange cake.

'So what do you want to know?' Caspar said after a few moments of silence and eating. It was obvious he wasn't going to be allowed out of here unless he talked, so he figured it was best to get it over and done with. In any case, he wasn't down here on business that would affect Karim's affairs, and he suspected the gang boss knew that.

'Well, you could begin,' said Karim, dusting off his fingers with a sparkling white napkin, 'with telling me why you were talking with Fouad Hamal's wife, Simone. I mean, she's a handsome woman but I doubt it was a romantic visit. Am I right?'

Caspar held his breath for a second. So his call on Hamal's wife had been spotted. This was moving faster than he'd expected. 'You heard what happened to her husband?'

Surprisingly, Karim shook his head. 'No. I have been in Rabat for three days, visiting my family. What are you talking about – and why should you be interested in a taxi driver here in Marseille?'

'He's dead.'

'Say again?' Karim looked surprised. So he didn't know everything that went on here.

Caspar gave him a summary of the shooting of three men and their driver by a so-far unknown assassin, and how he'd been retained to find information about Hamal and the Mercedes. Since Karim wouldn't take too long to find out the details for himself if he wished, he decided he wasn't giving anything away. But instinct made him hold off mentioning the Benhamids by name.

Karim frowned. 'I knew Fouad Hamal.' He waggled his hand. 'Just a little, you understand, mostly from the old days in Casablanca. He was a good man. A little… reluctant, like many, to embrace fully the nationalist dream of ousting your country's colonialist boot from the neck of Morocco. In the end he left to come over here.' He licked the tip of one finger and picked up some cake crumbs. 'A wise move, I think. Some of those people over there were – are still – bloody crazy. As for the Mercedes and the garage, if it was from Autos Samat I can tell you it was a front operation only. It's used by whoever needs it, sometimes for storage, sometimes other things, and never for more than a couple of days, cash up front and no questions.'

'Did your contact who saw me mention that Mme Hamal has disappeared? She was taken away in a car last night. If her husband's death was a way of silencing him because of what he knew, could this be a follow-up?' He left the suggestion hanging in the air.

Karim scowled at the idea but didn't deny the possibility. 'No. He did not mention that.' He turned and snapped his fingers, and one of his men appeared like magic from a side door. Karim muttered something to him in a rapid-fire manner and the man nodded before hurrying out through the front entrance. Karim turned back to Caspar and said, 'Don't worry, I think I know who might have done this. I will find her and get her to safety; you have my solemn promise. For some of us this is not a big city. She will be fine.'

'I'm pleased to hear it. So, the Mercedes trail is a dead end.'

Karim nodded. 'Quite so. Even I, with my influence here, would not be able to tell you who would have used it last.' He smiled, signifying that he had the means to find out if he really wanted to, but it would not be worth his while. 'Who were the three men who were killed?'

The question came unexpectedly, catching Caspar off-guard. For a second or two he debated not replying. On the other hand, if Karim had known Fouad Hamal, he may have known others, too, and would soon put the links together. There wouldn't be too many secrets in this town for a man with his contacts. Or so he thought.

'Hafid Benhamid, a Moroccan civil servant,' he said. 'And his two sons, Saad and Mohamed.'

Karim's eyebrows shot up again and he stopped licking at his fingertip. A clatter of dishes echoing from the kitchen highlighted the sudden silence. '*Bismillah*, who would do such a thing?'

'You knew them?'

'Of course. Everyone over there knew the Benhamid family. Especially the two cops, the goat droppings from the old man. They were into everything.' He put both forefingers together and rubbed them back and forth. 'Like parasites, they fed on their own and used others for their own ends – even your countrymen. Something in your eyes tells me you do not know this.'

'Correct. I was hoping to find out more. The Moroccan authorities have been advised of the shooting but they don't seem keen to help with the why or the who.'

'You shouldn't be too surprised,' said Karim. 'There is still much bitterness in some quarters against the French presence. Even though they now have complete control, the Moroccan government does not forgive entirely what many see as the lost years.'

'Is that the only reason?'

Karim waggled his hand back and forth. 'Not entirely. Trust is in very short supply there, too. There are many competing factions and nobody can be too sure who owns who.' Karim placed a hand on the table and dropped his voice, any trace of former aggression completely gone. 'Let me tell you a few things about that family. But first…' He turned and snapped his fingers, and a waiter appeared within seconds with fresh coffee. 'You have time to listen, of course?'

Caspar nodded with a wry grin. 'Do I have a choice?'

Karim laughed, and reached across to pat Caspar's shoulder. 'You worry too much, Caspar. I have no interest in preventing your investigations – but I do have an interest in getting you out of this city as quickly as possible, and in one piece, so I can go back to a quieter life.'

'Competitive pressure?'

Another waggle of the hand. 'Always. And not simply from the street. There are some here and in Casablanca who would like to take my place.' He gave a faint grin. 'I have to play a role, you understand – and to know exactly where I stand in the picture. If they can use an ex-cop like you nosing around to start pointing fingers, they will. Now, more cake?'

–

Half an hour later, after more coffee and cake and a lot of useful, even surprising information, Caspar managed to make his excuses to leave. They shook hands, past or present differences momentarily set aside. 'One thing,' said Karim, before letting go. 'I would not want anyone to think I make war on women. Give me a means of letting you know that we have Simone Hamal safe and well.'

Caspar was surprised. 'Is me knowing that so important to you?'

'You and whoever else, I think so.'

Caspar took a notebook from his pocket and ripped out a page. On it he wrote down a name and number, then handed it over.

Karim studied it and scowled. 'Inspector Lucas Rocco? I know that name. Why him?'

'Because if you want people to know you're not uncivilised, he carries more weight than I do. And he'll want to know she's safe.'

Karim gave an understanding smile and tucked the slip of paper in his pocket. 'What you really mean is you don't want me contacting you directly. I understand.'

As Caspar left the restaurant, he was forced to step to one side as a car pulled onto the kerb and a man climbed out from the back. Caspar noted an official-looking card in the front window and that the driver wore a dark suit and tie. *Someone official having an early lunch on the taxpayer,* he thought.

The passenger, a stocky man with iron-grey hair, looked at him with a faint frown, his mouth open as if about to speak. Caspar ducked his head quickly and continued walking, running through his mental index of past names and faces. The face he'd just spotted was familiar and the look the man had given him was a sure-fire giveaway that the thought had gone both ways.

Grégory something, he thought. *Missurat? Messurait?* Then it came back to him – and with it Rocco's warning that this assignment had to be carried out with as low a profile as he could manage. Well, that was now shot to ribbons.

It was an unsettling moment. Commander Grégory Missurat had been one of the senior members on the task force Caspar had been assigned to down here. Responsible for resources and strategy, Missurat had not been a street cop but one of the background faces – a back-room man. Caspar had met him a few times, although usually along with several other members of the team in group briefings. The last he'd heard on the cop grapevine was that Missurat had since been elevated to the Interior Ministry in a senior planning role. So what was he doing down here?

He summoned a taxi and told the driver to head for the station. With luck he could make the next train out and be gone before the man he'd just seen remembered his name and questioned what he was doing here.

As the taxi pulled away from the kerb, he turned and looked back in time to see Missurat stepping towards Les Goûts du Maroc – and Karim Hadji's outstretched hand.

Chapter Twenty-Five

Detective Desmoulins pulled in to the side of the road on the outskirts of Amiens and switched off the engine. He sat for a while, getting a feel for the area and its layout. It was late afternoon and he could make out through the heat haze the shadow of Pont-de-Metz in the distance. The scene was a stark contrast, with the busy town behind him and the bucolic air of the open countryside ahead. Yet both seemed peaceful and calm, as if the shooting of the young officer had never happened.

It wasn't the first time that Desmoulins had found himself wondering how it was that violent events in life somehow left little or no mark on the immediate atmosphere. Physical damage, yes – that went without saying. Emotional ruin too, more often than not. But nothing tangible in the air. It seemed illogical, as if a tear in the fabric caused by violent death had closed itself off. But he supposed extreme events only left behind that which affected those most closely involved.

Desmoulins glanced at the area close to the corner of the main road and a side street, where a layer of pale sand had been spread across the tarmac and onto the pavement. The patch was roughly the size of a human body.

Climbing out of his car, he walked across the road, stepping past the sand, and approached the house on the corner. It was the address of the only to witness to the shooting, a man named Robert Ledran, who had called the police immediately. According to the officer who'd interviewed him earlier, he appeared to have a strong sense of civic duty.

Desmoulins had read the officer's transcript, and had decided to come back to speak to the witness himself. Being a quiet period in the day and even in daylight, it might allow him to get a feel for what it might have been like when Pouillot had been shot.

As he'd seen before, the houses here were small, narrow and huddled together, a sign of the area's agricultural and industrial past, before the gradual spread of the commune of Amiens and its newer houses had moved across the fields and swallowed it up, the voracious creature called progress. There was probably little the residents here could do about the dull red brick of their houses, but some had painted the standard grey metal shutters in a variety of colours as if making a valiant attempt to show that a frivolous side to their nature really existed.

As he knocked on the door, he saw movement through the frosted glass panel. When it opened, he saw an elderly man in a neatly pressed blue shirt and trousers, with glasses perched on top of his head.

'M. Ledran?'

'That's me,' the man said.

Desmoulins introduced himself and said, 'Could we have a word, please? It won't take long. I hope I'm not disrupting anything.'

Ledran smiled and beckoned Desmoulins inside. 'That's not a problem, Detective. I live alone but I'm never averse to company. You've come about your colleague, I expect. How is he, by the way?'

'He died on the way to hospital,' Desmoulins told him. 'There was nothing they could do for him. But thank you for calling it in.'

Ledran waved the comment away. 'Just doing my duty as a citizen. It was a terrible business. I'm sorry it turned out so bad. Come in and sit.'

'I know you've already spoken to my colleagues about what you saw,' Desmoulins began, taking a seat. 'I was wondering if anything else had come to mind since then? Anything at all, no matter how insignificant.'

The room was small and cramped, with a dining table, a sideboard with elaborate mirrors and a display of old plates, and a comfortable-looking armchair. A scattering of old photographs was testimony to a lengthy history in the house, and family and friends long gone or moved away.

'How do you mean?'

'We find witnesses to something as dramatic as a shooting often have a delayed memory about the sequence of events. Something they didn't think to mention because it didn't seem important, or because they weren't sure of the detail, could be a vital clue we need to follow up.'

Ledran nodded and sat down with a grunt in the armchair. 'I know what you mean. But as I said to the other policemen, I didn't see much. It was dark and my eyes aren't so good these days. I wish I'd seen more.'

'Doesn't matter. Tell me what you can, even if it's repeating what you told the others.'

Ledran nodded. 'Fair enough. Let me see, I'd just put on some milk for my nightly indulgence of chocolate. While waiting I heard a car coming along the main road. We don't get a lot of traffic in the evening here, although I'd heard another car not long before that. Anyway, when I looked out the window, I saw a car had stopped at the side of the road near the corner. A man was standing alongside it.' He nodded towards the window. 'It's not much but take a look – you'll see the place I mean.'

Desmoulins did so. Looking at an angle through the glass showed the corner of the street with the main road, with the area where the sand had been spread out. It wasn't the best of observation points but evidently M. Ledran had seen enough.

'What was he doing?'

'He wasn't doing anything, that's the odd thing. In fact, he looked as if he was waiting for someone. Seconds later he looked towards the street here and laid himself down in the road.'

'He fell?'

'No, I mean he lay down, just like you would if you were going to take a look under your car. I immediately thought that was it: he'd got a car problem. Then I heard another car coming up the street towards the corner.'

'Then what?'

'I didn't see. I remembered the milk I'd put on and was worried it would boil over. Makes a hell of mess when it does that. My late wife, bless her, used to give me earache when I wasn't paying attention. I went and turned it off, and as I did I heard a gunshot.'

'You recognised the sound? Most people wouldn't.'

Ledran gave Desmoulins a sideways look. 'Son, I was in the army in the Great War. You don't go through something like that without knowing a shot when you hear it. Guns – can't stand the bloody things now. When the hunters are out in the fields around Pont-de-Metz I have to stick cotton wool in my ears so I can't hear them.' He stared at the floor for a moment as if slipping into reflection, and Desmoulins stayed silent. Finally, the old man said softly, 'I was close to the end of my military service when that war came along. Too old for all the usual running around and marching up and down, my wife said; time to get a proper job.' He smiled. 'She didn't mean it. She always said how proud she was that I did my service. Unfortunately, it turned out I wasn't too old to be handed a rifle and told to fight. I was proud to do it, of course, but I wish I hadn't had to. I wish none of us had… especially the boys who didn't come back.' He waved a hand. 'Sorry, that's not helping.'

'No matter. Take your time.'

'I hurried through from the kitchen and looked out again and saw a police car at the kerb just in front of the first car. There was no sign of a cop, though – sorry, I mean officer. I don't mean any disrespect.'

Desmoulins smiled. 'It's fine. We're cops. We hear worse.'

'Thanks, son. Where was I? Oh, yes. The man I'd seen first was just getting up off the ground.' He paused and looked unsure of himself, then shook his head and frowned.

'What?' Desmoulins prompted him. Had the old man remembered something?

'I didn't mention this before to your colleague because I wasn't sure. But I thought I saw movement inside the car itself. It could have been the street light playing tricks… and I think I was telling myself why not – if there was a passenger in the car, the driver might still have got out to look if he had a problem. Thinking about it now, though, I realise the other man was in the driving seat, not a passenger. Maybe that meant…' He rubbed his face. 'You'll think I'm an old fool.'

'It meant what?'

'The man on the ground was lying in wait.'

'Say again?' Desmoulins murmured.

'Like on a battlefield… you don't look twice at the bodies lying around. I mean, they're either dead or dying, right? So no threat.'

Desmoulins thought he saw where the old man was going with this. 'Right. So?'

'Well, that's where you'd be wrong. In the Great War there were times when a soldier was hit out in no-man's land, between the trenches. He'd be wounded and unable to roll into a trench or a shell hole, but maybe not too badly to fight. It happened – I saw it a few times on both sides. Along comes a Boche soldier or one of ours, eyes on the next trench and stepping past bodies, then bam – one of them sits up.'

'I see what you mean. You think it was a trap. An ambush.'

'Exactly. I mean, it's only my guess, so don't go putting that down on paper and dragging me into court, young fella. They'll think I'm a daft old goat with a twisted imagination. I don't want people laughing at me.'

'I'll keep it in mind, don't worry. What next?'

'The first man jumped back in his car and drove off. That's when I saw the body lying in the road.'

'What did you do?'

'I went out for a look, didn't I? I couldn't leave the officer out there like that… you don't do that, not if you've got a grain of self-respect. Poor devil… there was a lot of blood; as dark as it was, I could see that. Something else you learn in battle: blood stands out against everything else.' He looked at Desmoulins with a trace of wonder. 'Why is blood so red, do you think? Given a choice, I'd rather have a different colour... something not so shocking. I mean, a nice pastel colour would do me. Would we be a different colour if we had green blood, d'you reckon?'

Desmoulins smiled in spite of himself. He'd have to take that up with Dr Rizzotti, who'd be sure to have an opinion on the matter.

'You told my colleague that you didn't see the first man clearly. Is that still your view?'

'Yes, sorry. Just his outline... his profile, I think you'd call it. He was tall and thin but that's all I can tell you. The street lights here are rubbish; you'd get more glow from a charity candle.'

Desmoulins thanked the old man for his time, and again for calling the shooting in, and drove away towards town. He'd write his report then head home. See what Rocco thought about it in the morning.

Chapter Twenty-Six

Desmoulins was dog-tired. After speaking to Ledran the previous evening and suffering a disturbed night's sleep, his eyes felt gritty and dry. Now he was having to search for faces in the cars going by, assisted by two uniformed officers flagging down vehicles and checking them for signs of Koutcheff.

He'd been hoping to catch up with Rocco first thing, but on arrival at the station he'd been intercepted by Captain Canet and asked to help out as a matter of urgency pending the return of another officer from sick leave. Seeing Rocco, Canet had suggested, could probably wait; it would only be for a couple of hours, and with the force under pressure they needed all the help they could get.

Desmoulins had agreed readily enough but privately thought it was a waste of time. He doubted if Koutcheff would show up in a busy street where he would be spotted too easily. But he also knew the exercise was a public necessity; Koutcheff had already demonstrated how little regard he had for the law, and the local population were all too aware of the two separate shooting incidents, both here in town and out near Caix, and needed to see that the police were taking action to protect them against further incidents. A lack of visible activity by the police would translate into a volley of complaints by the public and the government, especially now an officer had been killed.

A brief break in the flow of traffic allowed the two uniforms to stand in the centre of the road, ready to stop the next vehicle coming while on full alert for any sign of trouble. A careless moment could see another officer gunned down, so there was to be no relaxation while doing their job. It was no surprise that while checking cars and the people in them, they were starting to find drivers without documentation or insurance and, in a couple of cases, that they were driving stolen vehicles.

'Detective Desmoulins?' A man's voice caught his attention, and he turned to see M. Ledran approaching. The old man was smartly dressed and walked with a brisk pace, the former soldier in him not ready to slow down yet.

'M. Ledran. Good to see you.'

'Likewise. There's something I wanted to tell you yesterday. It might be nothing, but it's been on my mind ever since we spoke and I need to get it out. I hope you don't think I'm wasting your time – I can see you're busy.'

'That's not a problem. What is it?'

'I said before that all I could see was the man's outline, right – the one outside the car? But no other detail that would identify him. Sorry. It set me thinking about what he might be rather than who, if you see my meaning.'

'I'm not sure I do. Go on.'

Ledran nodded towards the two uniformed officers standing in the road. 'I don't want to speak ill of your colleagues, but he looked like them.'

'What?' Desmoulins was astonished. He'd known both the officers for a long time and trusted them implicitly.

Ledran said quickly, 'I don't mean exactly those two – I mean *like* them. It's the way they stand: fit, lean and ready to do what they have to.'

Desmoulins studied the two men. They were both slim, standing upright with one hand close to their side-arms and watchful of the people and traffic. He saw what Ledran meant, although it took some thought to process the idea. It didn't mean Koutcheff was out of the picture, but a fellow cop? He'd heard of cops caught playing both sides of the field before, but not here.

Just to be sure he said, 'You think he might have been a policeman?'

'He had the same look. But I could be wrong.'

Desmoulins wasn't reassured. He touched M. Ledran gratefully on the arm and said, 'This is something I will have to take to my superiors. It's just the kind of point we need to narrow the field. Thank you.'

–

Twenty minutes later, he passed the two separate pieces of information from Ledran about the shooting to Rocco, who was studying a message sheet just in. The station was noisy with a hubbub of voices from people protesting their innocence after being scooped up in the vehicle checks.

Rocco pointed upstairs and said, 'Well done, René. Come on – you can tell them yourself.' He led the way up to Massin's office where a strategy meeting was underway with Perronnet and Canet, discussing the extra resources needed to cope with the latest investigations. Dr Rizzotti was sitting in and nodded genially at Rocco. Massin beckoned the two men in and listened to Desmoulins' report. For a long moment nobody spoke, digesting the information and the implications.

'I can't believe it was one of ours,' said Canet, breaking the silence. He looked at the others for agreement. 'Can you? I mean, who – and why? It makes no sense.'

'I agree,' Massin said. 'It might be nothing but clearly Ledran thought it was worth telling Desmoulins what he saw, so we have to follow it up.' He looked at Desmoulins. 'You trust his account, Detective?'

'Yes, sir. He's getting on but he's ex-military and sharp as a needle. There was no drama; he was telling me what he saw.'

Massin nodded. 'Good work.' He looked at Canet. 'I think we need to review any officer who has been disciplined recently. It's a long shot but better to do it now rather than be surprised down the line. Include any who might have had contact with De Lancourt or his men. There could be a connection there.'

Canet nodded. 'Will do. But I have to say, knowing the men, I think it's unlikely.'

'I would expect nothing less of you, Captain.' He looked at the others. 'The question is, whoever the shooter was, why Pouillot and why was he shot in that particular location? Did the shooter live nearby and see his chance to take out a cop for the hell of it? It seems unlikely.'

Canet said, 'It could have been pure circumstance. Pouillot was on a late patrol, and standing orders would have had him covering that area up to the city boundary on the Pont-de-Metz road. From what the witness said, he heard Pouillot drive up the street towards the main road, so he must have driven down one of the adjacent streets, probably checking the place out. But whichever way he did it, it's completely random; the patrols don't follow the same route every time. As long as they cover the ground within a given period they can structure it any way they choose.'

'What are you suggesting?'

'I think he must have been followed to the point where he was shot.'

'By who, though? I still can't believe it could have been one of ours.'

Rocco had been happy to let them talk it out so far. He didn't want to influence them by pointing to the obvious; that was how investigations got derailed. 'It wasn't,' he said finally.

Massin looked at him. 'You know that for sure?'

'No. But Ledran said described the man as being *like* a cop, the way he carried himself. It could also have been a former soldier; like Koutcheff.' He held up the message he'd been given downstairs. 'This just came in from the military records office in Vincennes. They ran through the service records for personnel under the letter K and got this.'

Perronnet said, 'That was quick work.'

'The files were originally set up by the military,' Massin said with dry humour. 'They're better organised than the civil service and they don't take long coffee breaks.' He looked at Rocco. 'What do they say?'

'Koutcheff was in the army for ten years, serving a lot of the time in North Africa.'

Massin stared at the ceiling. 'That makes sense. However, being devil's advocate for a moment, even if it was Koutcheff who shot him, how do we prove it? And merely being in the military doesn't make every man capable of murder.'

'It might if they had the inclination. According to the records, Koutcheff was a member of a unit called the Commandos de Chasse.'

'The what?' said Canet. 'Never heard of them.'

Massin was nodding. 'I have. The Commandos de Chasse were a specialised unit that originated in the conflict in Algeria in the late fifties to track down members of the ALN – the National Liberation Army. They were highly trained in guerrilla tactics and accustomed to merging with the local population and living off the land for lengthy periods. The activities of one or two of the commando groups have been questioned over the years but they have always been described as necessary according to the circumstances.' He pulled a face. 'That might be open to question either way, but if Koutcheff was part of one of those units he would have been capable of what has been described. And by his actions recently, he's certainly not your run-of-the-mill citizen.'

'Just what we needed,' Canet muttered. 'A home-schooled killer come back to haunt us. But why Pouillot? Are you suggesting he was after him in particular?'

'I think he was,' said Desmoulins. 'It seems too planned to have been a random shooting, especially with two of them.'

'Two?' Massin queried. 'Remind me.'

Desmoulins took them again through how Ledran had thought there was another man inside the car when Pouillot was shot. 'He won't swear to it but it's possible the shooter had a lookout working with him. If that was the case, it shows a degree of planning.'

'He's right,' said Rocco. 'It would make sense. I'll follow up on it. If the shooter was Koutcheff, it's a certainty that one of the other men at Les Cyprès was involved. They seem to be a tight unit.'

There was a lengthy silence, then Rizzotti lifted a hand and spoke up. 'Forgive me, but this might involve a question of psychology.' He looked at Massin. 'May I?'

'Go ahead, Doctor. Your input would be valuable.'

'Thank you. If the person responsible was Koutcheff, he might have wanted revenge on Pouillot for taking him in. Simply that. From what you describe I can imagine his training and work in this commando unit would have been extremely intense and dangerous over a long period. I have been reading recently some eminent studies about the effects on the psyche of specialist American troops in areas of conflict. Because of what they have been through, some of them found it difficult returning to civilian life. They tended to stay very close to what they have known – some of them for years. It's not uncommon, apparently.'

'True enough,' agreed Massin, 'but they don't all go round killing people.'

'Certainly. But pride is also part of their make-up. They are specialists, and if Koutcheff has a reputation he's proud of, it's entirely possible that being taken down by what he sees as a simple traffic cop would weigh heavily on his mind – especially if he still works with others who are aware of his past skills. It's possible one of those he works with suggested helping him as a favour. They look out for each other.'

Perronnet said, 'Getting caught so easily was something he'd have found difficult to endure without taking action against the man responsible, is that what you're saying?'

'It's a possibility.'

'That sounds a reasonable explanation,' Massin agreed. 'But would he bother? It would be risky trying to kill a police officer with the whole force already on high alert after the first shooting.'

'Possibly,' said Perronnet. 'However, we already know we're dealing with someone who doesn't have a strong hold on reality. He's happy to ram cars in the street and put a policeman in hospital for no reason that we yet know of; what else would a man with his background and training be prepared to do if his pride had been dented by someone he saw as a nobody?' He glanced at Rocco. 'You're not saying much, Inspector. Something on your mind?'

'An uncomfortable thought,' Rocco replied. 'If it was Koutcheff and he had a policeman helping him, it wouldn't have been too hard to find out the name of the arresting officer from his legal representative, and another cop would have known where Pouillot was on patrol.'

'God help us,' Canet muttered. 'This is getting worse.'

Massin got to his feet, signalling the end of the meeting. 'It's a possibility to keep in mind,' he said. 'Now all we have to do is find who did what. I've had approval for extra officers on loan from Lille, Arras and Saint-Quentin. It might not achieve anything but if it gives the local population more confidence in our abilities to protect them, it will be a good thing. Let us get this done.'

Chapter Twenty-Seven

With all the talk about Georges Koutcheff, Rocco's thoughts turned to the address details Canet had given him here in town. He had no reason for thinking the man would have returned to the flat, and the earlier visit by the other officers would have warned him off. But sometimes even the brightest of criminals did the stupidest things. Or maybe, just maybe, the man was currently hiding right under their noses.

The address lay in a narrow street to the east of the town, not far from the prison. The narrow, three-storey building was squeezed between a refuge and an abandoned vehicle repair workshop, and the fabric wore an air of sad neglect. The scattering of vehicles parked along the kerb on either side were in poor shape, which told him something about the local population. A group of youths was gathered outside the building smoking and laughing, and they turned to watch as Rocco locked his car and crossed the street towards them.

One of them, a skinny individual with giant acne spots and a half-hearted growth of facial hair, recognised Rocco and demonstrated his knowledge to the others by saying, 'Hey – it's the big *flic*! Hi, Rocco – sorry – Inspecteur!' The others muttered between themselves, moving around in a semi-threatening dance to show off their *couilles*, but backing away quickly when he kept on walking right at them.

'Hello, Bakri,' he acknowledged to the skinny youth. 'I thought you'd got yourself a job and were staying out of trouble.'

'I am. I have.' Bakri grinned. Rocco had hauled him in for possession of drugs several months ago, cutting him loose when Bakri gave him information on a supply line coming into Amiens. It had done little to stop the supply, merely causing a brief hiccup. But he felt sure Bakri had the ability to turn a corner if he worked at it.

'Doing what?'

'I'm an apprentice panel-beater.' He mentioned a metal workshop on a nearby industrial estate. 'I spend all day hitting sheets of metal with a giant hammer.'

'Good for you. Enjoying it?'

'Love it. I'm going deafer by the day but it's letting me work out all my aggressions. My counsellor says that's a good thing.'

Rocco eyed him for signs of leg-pulling, but Bakri looked genuinely proud of what he was doing. 'I suggest you ask your boss to get you some ear plugs. If he doesn't, I'll come round there and shut him down.'

'Right.'

Rocco looked at a line of name plates to one side of the front door. The tenants' names were either scrubbed out, vaguely illegible or, in the case of one, bore a lurid photo of a young blonde woman named Coco on the second floor with too much flesh on display and her tongue sticking out like a slice of salami.

'Koutcheff,' Rocco said to the group. 'Which one is he in?' He was actually talking to Bakri but he didn't want the others knowing it. There was every chance the youth would be found dead in a rubbish skip if they thought he was talking to the police.

'Koutcheff or Coco?' one of the other youths muttered nastily. 'Forget it – you don't look as if you could handle Coco. She'd chew you up and spit you out in bubbles.' He laughed at his own wit until Rocco fixed him with a glare.

'Ignore him, Inspector,' Bakri said, throwing the offender a warning look. 'He doesn't mean any harm. Koutcheff's in number three, first floor. He hasn't been here in a while, though. What's he done?'

A short, muscular kid with a badly executed tattoo of a snarling lion's head on his bicep stepped forward and said excitedly, 'Koutcheff's the *mec* who crashed his car the other day and put a cop in hospital! I read about it. It was crazy – I wish I'd seen it!' Then he noticed Rocco staring at him and backed down. 'Sorry – no offence.'

Rocco left them to it and walked into the building. He checked the ground floor at the back out of habit and found that the building had no rear exit. Always worth knowing. The air smelled of urine, stale tobacco and the unmistakable aroma of marijuana, and the walls were scrawled with graffiti and splashes of paint. If the place had once had light bulbs, they were long gone. Nice place to bring up a family.

The door to number three was a thin plywood panelled affair and partially open. He knocked and pushed it back.

A young man with a head of wild hair appeared from what looked like a makeshift kitchen. He was dressed in a grubby vest, crumpled trousers and had the aura of death walking. Rocco put his age at about twenty, although he looked older. Drink or drugs or unlucky genes.

He was carrying a gun.

'What are you doing here?' the man demanded. 'This is private property.' The words tumbled out of his mouth as if he had no real control over what he was saying. The gun, however, was very real and pointing vaguely in Rocco's direction. 'You think you can come in here uninvited and take what you want? Is that it?'

Rocco looked around at the poorly furnished room, which contained a filthy settee, a small table and a couple of battered and mismatched armchairs, covered in cigarette burns and stains he wouldn't have wanted to touch. A small table held a collection of beer and wine bottles, all empty, spaced apart like the columns of a Greek temple.

'I suppose I might if there was anything worth taking and I wanted to pick up some nasty bacteria. Who are you?'

'Bac-what?' The man looked confused by the words.

Rocco took his hand out of his coat pocket and gave the man a close-up look at the business end of his service weapon. 'Hold the gun out to the side or I'll shoot you. Do it now.'

The gun moved out to the side and the man looked sick, his eyes fixed like black buttons on Rocco's weapon. Rocco relieved him of the gun and checked it out. No bullets and the barrel was filthy, showing that it hadn't been fired in a long time. He put it in his coat pocket.

'Name,' he said. 'Before I lose patience.'

'Yannick. Kazelmy. Sorry. People call me Yannick.' The man's eyes went dance-about and he looked ready to drop to the floor in shock. 'I didn't mean... they've been stealing stuff from me. I got sick of it. Bloody kids have no respect for property. I only showed that to frighten them off.'

'Stuff? What stuff?'

'Clothes. Cigarettes... some drink. Even furniture, when nobody was around. They don't care. Can I sit down?' He staggered backwards before Rocco could answer and sat on the settee with a crash. 'Sorry – been working late and had too many drinks, y'know? You're a cop, aren't you? They've already been here, the uniforms, asking questions. Am I in trouble?' He blinked as if to clear his head and gestured at Rocco's pocket. 'Because of that? Stupid, I know... but it couldn't have gone off. No bullets.'

'Maybe not,' Rocco told him. 'Mine might have. How do you know Georges Koutcheff?'

'Georges who?'

'The man who normally lives here. How come you're here instead?'

Yannick nodded blearily. 'Ah, right. Big, skinny *mec*, used to be in the military – is that him?'

'That's the one.'

'I've spoken to him a couple of times, but I don't know him as such. I bumped into him one night in a café near here, you know, and I told him I'd been thrown out of my last place and he told me I could crash here for a couple of days.'

'Just like that?'

'Yeah, just like that.'

'When?'

'When what?' Yannick's head fell back and he gulped before recovering, eyeballs rolling.

'When did he say you could stay here for a couple of days?'

'Not sure... about three weeks ago, I think. He wasn't using it, said the rent was all paid up so it was all right to stay as long as I stopped anyone else moving in. Decent guy. Not many of those around.'

'Yes, he's a real credit to the community. Do you know where he is now?'

'No, sorry. He hasn't been back. When he does I'll have to leave, I suppose. Lend me a cigarette, will you?'

'I don't smoke – and lending cigarettes isn't a thing, is it? You can't hand them back.'

Yannick laughed, his face suddenly animated. 'Are you kidding? Of course it's a thing – especially if you don't have any. Smoke now, pay back later, right? It's the way the economy works, see – on the streets, anyway. Where have you been?'

'Too busy working to attend lectures on the modern economy, evidently.'

'Oh, right. Funny.' Yannick laughed and then looked as if he was about to be sick.

Rocco moved out of range before the floodgates opened. 'Did he leave any stuff here?'

'No, nothing. To be honest I don't think he used it much, which is crazy, isn't it? How many people pay rent for a place they don't use?'

Rocco ignored the question. He'd heard the sound of movements from the floor above. 'Who lives up there?'

'A couple of people… one man and a woman named Coco. Separate rooms, though.' He sniggered. 'You probably saw the card downstairs, right?' He gave a silly smile as if at some private joke.

'What's so funny?'

'I just thought, Rocco and Coco in the same building.' At Rocco's deliberately blank look, he said, 'Rococo, get it? Architecture.' He lost the smile. 'I read it in a book once.'

'Good for you. If I take a look around am I going to find anything I shouldn't?'

'Absolutely not. Help yourself.'

Ten minutes later, Rocco came up empty-handed. If Koutcheff had hidden anything of value here, it was somewhere it wasn't about to be found without ripping the place apart.

Rocco gave Yannick his card and said, 'If Koutcheff comes back here, ring the station and leave a message for me.' He didn't hold out much hope of Yannick doing any such thing; if he had a grain of sense he'd bolt for the hills before Koutcheff showed up. But it was worth a try.

Yannick nodded repeatedly, his Adam's apple bobbing up and down like a yo-yo. 'Of course. Right. Rocco. Whatever you say.'

Rocco left him to it and went back to his car. The group of youths had disappeared, leaving a scattering of hand-rolled cigarette butts and several beer bottles on the ground as if taunting him with their juvenile machismo.

Chapter Twenty-Eight

The café where Rocco and Jeunet had shared coffee the previous day was quiet apart from two men who looked like farmers, and the owner wiping down the bar with a cloth. Rocco murmured a general greeting and ordered a *café crème*. He took a table at the back and hoped Jeunet wasn't going to be long. The need to solve both the shootings on the Caix road and the killing of Officer Pouillot was now more than a little urgent.

As with any case, the first twenty-four hours were the most critical for picking up information and clues; beyond that any trail began to go cold and the memories of possible witnesses began to fade. With the case against Koutcheff and his connection with De Lancourt, however, this meeting could be vital in opening up new leads and he didn't want to waste the opportunity.

Ten minutes later, when there was still no sign of the former academy member, Rocco approached the bar.

'You know M. Jeunet?'

The man nodded. 'Of course. He is a valued customer – an important man in Amiens. You were expecting to meet him here?'

'I was.'

'It's not his usual day. Could there be a mistake? He is a man of fixed habits, as you might know.'

'I know,' said Rocco. 'But he insisted on it. Do you know where he lives?' He produced his card but the man waved it away with a smile.

'I know who you are, Inspector. And yes, I can tell you where he lives.' He reached under the counter and produced a small notepad and pencil and wrote down a street name and number. 'It's not far from here – you can walk it within minutes. He has a nice town house behind the cathedral facing the canal. He has lived there many years.' He looked concerned. 'I hope nothing is wrong – he has not been well recently.'

Rocco thanked him for his help and walked round to the address on the slip of paper. He found the house, an elegant building painted a light shade of beige, and rang a metal bell-pull to one side of the sturdy wooden door. The jangle of the bell sounded but there was no sound of a response. He rang again. Nothing. Maybe Jeunet was on his way to the café via another route.

As he turned away, he noticed that the front door was not completely closed. He pressed his knuckle against the wood. It swung open, emitting a stale smell of trapped air.

His gut told him this wasn't good.

'Gérard? M. Jeunet?' But there was no response.

Stepping inside, he listened for sounds of movement. He closed the door gently behind him and walked through the ground floor, which consisted of a through hallway, a large living room and dining room, a kitchen and a conservatory room overlooking a neat garden. The kitchen was neat and clean, and a table in the centre held an aluminium cafetière and a large mug, both unused. Another bad sign; Jeunet would have prepared coffee at the very least.

Rocco walked up a wide staircase lined with a selection of paintings and photographs, the latter an insight into Jeunet's past life, the mix of coloured and monochrome snaps looking dated. The faces staring down at him made him feel like an intruder.

He called out Jeunet's name again, but the sound was lost in the high ceilings and largely unused rooms. Finally, he reached a bedroom with the sheets twisted and tossed to the floor. This was obviously the master bedroom. Next to it was a bathroom decorated with ancient tiles and a bath and sink that had been here forever.

And Gérard Jeunet.

The former art historian was lying fully clothed but huddled on the floor in a darkening pool of blood. He'd been beaten around the skull with a large hammer lying nearby, the head and part of the handle dark and shiny with blood.

Although he knew the result, Rocco bent close enough to confirm that Jeunet was dead. A light touch showed the man's skin to be still warm. This must have only just happened!

Drawing his service weapon, he stood still for a moment, head cocked for sounds of movement. He felt a hot rush of anger at such an evil crime and hoped the perpetrator was still on the premises. Nobody deserved to die in such a brutal manner, especially an elderly man with precious little time left to him.

A loud click echoed clearly up the stairs in the silence. *The front door.* He ran down as fast as he could and saw the door was now wide open. He burst out into the street and saw a figure running away. The choice of what to do was simple: phoning for help would result in losing the suspect. If he could keep the figure in sight, he might be able to get a member of the public to call for assistance.

Rocco set off in pursuit, anger at Jeunet's murder driving him, his long legs covering the ground easily. But the man in front of him was also quick and looked fit, moving with the ease of a practised runner and shouting at the occasional pedestrian to get out of his way.

Rocco wondered where the man thought he could run to. The city wasn't huge but it had a warren of smaller streets and cut-throughs that would give a good runner ample opportunity to lose his pursuer if he knew his ground and could keep going. Rocco, unfortunately, wasn't intimately acquainted with the city and had to rely on keeping the man in his sights. He was also burdened by his clothes and heavy shoes, and hadn't been able to holster his gun yet.

They traversed one busy street then another, startled drivers having to brake hard to avoid a collision and showing their displeasure in the customary way of drivers everywhere, by leaning on their horns and shouting abuse. Rocco narrowly escaped being flattened under the wheels of a large truck and bounced off a parked car, a jolt of pain going through his arm.

The runner dodged into a quiet residential side street and appeared to be slowing. Rocco eased off the pace himself to conserve energy. If he could get a pedestrian to call for police help...

The runner turned again, entering a narrow street. As Rocco followed, he could see ahead of them a small square alongside a section of the city's canal. Putting on a burst of speed, the runner crossed a bridge and arrived at a wider street on the far side.

Rocco could feel himself flagging. He had a pain in his side and chest, and his legs were becoming wobbly as fatigue took over. He had to catch the man soon or he was going to lose him. Worse, he had a sense that the runner had followed a predetermined route and knew where he was going.

Suddenly the roar of a car engine sounded behind Rocco and someone shouted a warning. Risking a look behind him, Rocco saw a vehicle charging towards him only metres away and clearly intent on running him down.

He threw himself sideways in desperation just as the car reached him, and he felt something snatch at his coat. It was enough to send him sprawling and he bounced and rolled into the side of the street, tucking himself instinctively behind a lamp post and bracing himself for a deadly impact. A blast of hot air and exhaust fumes washed over him as the car rushed by, its tyres squealing as the driver pulled away from hitting the lamp post.

Rocco got to his feet in time to see the car stop alongside the runner. A side door opened and the runner looked back briefly before jumping in. Seconds later they were gone, leaving Rocco wincing with pain from his bruised body and trying to catch his breath.

'Are you all right?' a man's voice asked, and a strong arm helped him to his feet. The man was wearing an apron and Rocco saw a café across the street. 'That bloody idiot nearly killed you!'

'I'm Inspector Rocco,' Rocco gasped, nodding his thanks. 'Please ring the police and ask them to send officers to meet me at Gérard Jeunet's house. They'll know where it is. Tell them what you saw.'

The man nodded. 'Of course. But are you able to walk? You should see a doctor.'

Rocco nodded. 'I'm fine. Please ring the station. It's an emergency.'

Leaving the man hurrying inside the café, Rocco made his way back to Jeunet's, where he made a repeat search of the building, noting signs of random disorder with drawers and doors left open, the obvious signs of a search. A room on the first floor, which appeared to have been Jeunet's study, seemed to have suffered most, with an ornate desk completely ransacked, the contents spread on the floor and one of the drawers broken. This was no simple robbery. Whoever had done this had gone to some lengths to focus on this room where Jeunet had done his work.

A voice called out from the front door and a uniformed foot patrol officer stepped inside, alerted by the station. Rocco explained what had happened and told the officer to secure the front door and wait for back-up, then located a telephone and called Dr Rizzotti at the station, giving him the basic details.

'Understood,' Rizzotti said. 'I think we've had a couple of calls already but not about Jeunet. I'll have the team close the house and get to work. Before you go, I just saw a friend of yours in reception. He's asking to speak to you urgently. Caspar, he said, is that correct?'

Rocco was surprised; he'd been anxious to hear from Caspar but he hadn't expected a personal delivery of information. He asked Rizzotti to see that the despatcher looked after Caspar and that he'd be with him in a few minutes.

Chapter Twenty-Nine

'Is it good news or bad?' said Rocco, joining Caspar in a vacant side office. A coffee pot and cups were on the table and he guessed Caspar had settled in for a long wait. He hoped that meant he'd got some useful information to hand over. He needed something to push the investigation forward before it settled into a mess of supposition and speculation. He helped himself to a coffee and sank half the cup in one, hoping the caffeine would counter the aches that were coming to the surface with a vengeance.

'Depends who it's for,' Caspar said, and stared at Rocco, eyeing his dusty clothes and a tear in his trouser leg. 'What happened to you? You look as if you've been in a scrap.'

Rocco explained briefly, then got Caspar back on track. 'If it's bad I'd rather you tell me now. Get it out of the way.'

Caspar related his chance spotting by Commander Missurat and the fact that he had heard the man was now with the Interior Ministry. 'If he didn't remember me there and then, he will have done by now. I could see it in his face. Sorry, Lucas, but I really didn't expect to see anyone – especially not when I'd just been having a cosy chat with Karim Hadji. You remember him?'

'I do.' Rocco knew Hadji as a long-time criminal who would never change his spots. Not one of the worst he'd come across down there but still one of a bad bunch.

Where Hadji had seemed to differ from his crooked peers was his uncanny ability to stay out of serious trouble. He was surprised any member of the Ministry would be in close contact with the man without a team of lawyers. If it was a solo visit, it raised all sorts of worrying questions. 'Did he see the two of you together?'

'I think so. The last glimpse I had was Karim giving him the big welcome, although to be fair, he might have been as surprised as I was at seeing him and was playing the part. But the car had a local plate with an official badge in the window so Missurat must have been in the city on business.'

Rocco put it to one side. 'Forget it. If he reports seeing you there's no reason why you shouldn't have been down there visiting friends and happened to bumped into Hadji by chance. Is Hadji likely to tell him what you talked about?'

'He would if he saw a benefit in doing so. He's a criminal; he'd sell his own mother if he had one. But he did mention that he's under pressure, which I don't recall him ever worrying about before. He always seemed to rise above that. I assumed he meant from his competitors but he could have been talking about the cops, too.'

'Or perhaps he's been seen in the company of men like Missurat and the others don't like it. If so, he's playing a dangerous game.'

Caspar gave Rocco a rundown of his talk with Mme Hamal and her abrupt disappearance, followed by his coffee and cake meeting with Hadji. Rocco listened without comment, making a few notes and allowing Caspar to talk at his own speed. Debriefings were best done with minimal questions until the end. Stops and starts did nothing to help the flush-out of information, especially where the person giving the details had been forced to memorise everything.

'I wish I could have done something positive about Mme Hamal,' Caspar said ruefully. 'I hope Karim keeps his promise.'

'You did what you could,' Rocco reassured him. 'The police would have asked who you were and why you were there, and there's no saying that she wasn't picked up by friends of her husband. Anyway, it sounds as if Karim will sort it out. What was the good news?'

'It turns out Karim knew the Benhamids from way back. The old man was basically a crook in a boring job and a respectable suit. His sons were ruthless thugs who would do whatever their father told them. He said they'd been involved in property deals selling land formerly owned by French farmers confiscated under national-isation rules. His sons enforced the "law", dealing with landowners who were reluctant to leave. Most of the deals were small-time plots out in the countryside where nobody would notice.'

'So much for being a trusted civil servant.'

'It was the best cover he could have had. Working in the land ministry, he had access to who owned what and which French farmers were having to leave once they knew their time was up. Who would suspect him of such a thing? At the time, anyone in real power or close to it in Morocco would have been too busy fighting for position in the new government to worry about an insignificant pusher of paper like Benhamid. They were careful about their deals, paying off officials who needed paying and using false names to take over the property and land. Some of their deals even extended to Algeria where land joined Moroccan farms. More payouts over there. It was a racket and Benhamid wasn't the only one. Karim knew of several sales Benhamid had arranged to local Moroccan farmers on a silent commission basis, and if nobody was interested in unoccupied land he'd simply set them aside and look for a buyer later. After a while the details would get conveniently lost and the land registry was so full of holes and poor paperwork, nobody would notice.'

'But would he have been in a position to get the French farmers to sign over their property? They'd have wanted the best price they could get to leave the country and get back here.'

'That's where Karim got really interesting. He reckoned a mid-level functionary like Benhamid would only have been able to hide the small-to-middle-grade stuff; the bigger farms that were French-owned would have needed paperwork to make it look legal so nobody at the top would question it. Having his sons along for a bit of silent persuasion probably worked with the smaller and less able landowners; they'd have been happy to get out with whatever they had in the bank and their skins. But the bigger farmers were different; they'd have needed persuading by someone they knew and trusted that their best course of action would be to cut their losses and get out with whatever they could carry. Leave it too late and they might end up on the street with nothing.'

'Someone they trusted – you mean one of their own?'

'Yes. But that's not the worst of it. Karim told me – although this is going to be impossible to prove – about rumours of at least two, possibly three French farmers and their dependants disappearing not long before the French departed. I vaguely remember reading about it in the press some years ago.'

Rocco recalled it, too, although he'd been in transition from the army to the police at the time and not given to a lot of reading. 'How disappeared?'

Caspar shrugged. 'To use his words, they were there one minute, gone the next. The houses were deserted, all the goods still in place. Their vehicles and document-ation were all gone, leading locals to believe that they had cleared out for France or maybe one of the other territories where they could set up again.'

'Do you believe all this?'

'Actually, I do. I admit I got the feeling Karim might have been involved with Benhamid himself on one or two occasions; it would fit with his character. But I don't think he had anything to gain by telling me this – or, at least, nothing I can think of that would be worth misleading us. Maybe he has a hidden agenda over there, I don't know. The thing is, Karim said he knew one of the farmers very well. The man was from Bordeaux and a former legionnaire, tough as old boots, who would not have left his farm without a fight. He reckons the man and his family are probably buried out in the desert somewhere nobody will ever find them.'

Rocco nodded. 'So the three people who know everything about this are all dead... apart from, perhaps, the intermediary used by the Benhamids to acquire the farms. I don't suppose Karim told you who that might be?'

'No.'

Rocco felt a stir of disappointment. Caspar had uncovered some important information but there were still too many questions for which he had no answers. Certainly, there was now anecdotal evidence that might explain why the Benhamids had ended up dead; being involved in illegal land deals and possibly murder would certainly involve acquiring enemies over the years. Jealousy was always an unwelcome companion to criminal conspiracies, especially if one party made more out of their endeavours than another.

'Will Hadji make a statement?'

Caspar shook his head. 'Never. Sorry, but that's the nature of the man. He has too much to lose.'

Rocco wasn't surprised. Hadji probably had too many enemies of his own back in Morocco who would not relish him talking about what he knew. And Morocco was not far away; a quick hop across the Med and he'd be easy meat. It was unfortunate but the information he now had did nothing to explain why the three men had been travelling north in France or where they were going. Had they been trying to escape their past and someone had caught up with them? And who would have been in a position to have them killed? It was clearly not a random event and must have been planned with some degree of care to achieve the means and the location. Was it someone high in the Moroccan government... or someone who had been working with them and felt either threatened or betrayed?

Caspar sat back, a clear sign that he'd said all he had to say. He looked relieved to have got it all off his chest.

Rocco stared at his notes. A few blanks had been filled in but it would take more work to build a more complete picture.

'What's going on here?' Caspar asked, nodding towards the door. 'I get the feeling there's a rush on.'

Rocco told him more about the murders of the Benhamids and now the murder of Pouillot. 'It's stretched us a bit, but with what you've found out we might now get further forward with the Moroccan thing. If we could get a lead on who would have benefited most by the Benhamids' death, it would help. As for the mad commando, that's just a matter of time until we track him down.'

'Commando? Seriously?'

'Apparently. He was in a normal infantry regiment in Algeria before transferring to the Commandos de Chasse in 1958. He'll be used to hiding and evading discovery.'

'He will, that.' Caspar frowned, his mouth open.

'What? Do you know something?'

'You know they were in Morocco, too, don't you?'

Rocco said, 'I didn't. His service record only mentioned Algeria.'

'I'm not surprised. I heard about them from some of the Moroccan community when I was working undercover down south. They were rumoured to have made cross-border incursions in pursuit of ALN insurgents but the government always denied it and insisted they were internal to Algeria only. The Moroccans I knew said different, that they'd been in deep cover for some time, coming and going, some singly, some in groups.'

'Doing what?'

'Well, if you believe the rumours, they were in live training – and killing people.'

Chapter Thirty

Rocco thanked Caspar for his excellent work and saw him down to the front entrance, where a taxi was waiting to take him to the station. With the job done, the former policeman was anxious to get back home to Lucille and make up for his time away.

'Give her my regards,' Rocco said. 'And I'll take you up on that meeting once this business is over.'

Caspar grinned. 'You'd better. She already thinks you've become a useful figment of my imagination.' He grabbed Rocco's hand and shook it with vigour. 'Thanks for the job, Lucas. You know I'm always up for more.' He squinted at Rocco's ruined trousers. 'And it looks like you need a bit of help.'

'I'll keep it in mind. Now go home.'

After the taxi had left, Rocco thought over what they had discussed. There was now a whirl of information in his head about the two cases, all of it needing to be dealt with urgently. But the fact that had come back to bug him most was Jeunet's promise of some papers that would tell him more about De Lancourt's history. He had no idea how it would fit into Koutcheff's actions or even if it did. Maybe it owed more to Jeunet's intense dislike of the man and his ambition to be a member of the Académie Française, but there was a nagging thought in Rocco's head that would not let go. Was it his own instinctive dislike of De Lancourt for being so defensive of his employee's extreme actions that was driving him or had Jeunet ignited something far deeper?

'I can show you ample documentation to support my accusations... they're in a safety deposit box at my bank... I'll have them ready for you by eleven.'

Rocco remembered Jeunet's words and wondered if the old man had been killed before getting to the bank. He hadn't seen any papers during his brief search, but he'd been looking for an intruder, not paperwork. Maybe it was time to go back for a closer look.

As he walked past the reception desk, the duty officer handed him a slip of paper. 'A call came in while you were busy, Inspector. The caller left a message and said only call back if it was a no.'

The caller was Eliane and the message was simple. *This evening at 7? I hope you like chicken!*

Rocco found he was smiling in spite of himself. When he looked up, he saw the duty officer was grinning, too. Damn, this would be all over the office inside ten minutes.

'Don't even think of it,' he growled at the man. He went to his locker and changed into a spare pair of trousers he kept for emergencies. Going round looking ruffled might be excused by people who knew the demands of the job, but turning up to dinner with Eliane was a whole different matter.

Looking slightly more respectable, he returned to Jeunet's house and found a small crowd gathered outside a cordon set up by uniformed officers. A reporter named Serge Houchin, who freelanced for a number of papers and had proven himself particularly pushy in the past, shoved himself to the front and thrust a tape recorder microphone under Rocco's nose.

'Come on, Rocco, we know something's going on here. Our readers have a right to know what it is. This is the house where Gérard Jeunet lives, isn't it? What's happened in there and why are the police not telling us? What are they hiding?'

Several other voices supported his questions until Rocco held up both hands and they went quiet. He noticed Houchin gave a familiar smirk of triumph.

'Actually, M. Houchin, it's Inspector Rocco to you, and a bulletin is already being read out as we speak to press members at the station. But being here instead, you'll have missed it.' With that he eased past Houchin, who had suddenly lost his smirk, and went inside the house, closing the door on further questions.

Rizzotti met him inside and chuckled. 'Nicely done, I must say. He was almost shouting through the letterbox until I asked the officers to set up the cordon further back.'

'You should have offered him a drink of something chemical. That would have slowed him down.' He explained that he was looking for details of Jeunet's bank in the town or any financial documentation that might have been left lying around. 'Can I look in the study?'

'Go ahead. I've been concentrating on the body and the immediate area. I haven't looked anywhere else yet.' He looked concerned at the way Rocco was holding himself and said, 'I hear you took a tumble. Can I do anything?'

Rocco shook his head. 'Just bumps and bruises. I'll survive.'

He excused himself and went up to the study to check the desk. The top was bare save for a newspaper, several unopened letters, a small bundle of dried flowers and some notebooks. The notebooks contained jottings that appeared to relate to artistic matters but nothing that constituted a dramatic revelation about anyone named De Lancourt. The drawers were hanging open and the contents had been dumped on the carpet by the intruder. Among them was a plastic loose-leaf binder bearing the logo *BF* – Banque de France. Inside were details of Jeunet's accounts. It was enough; at least he knew where the account was held.

Rocco walked round to Rue de la République, where the bank had its offices, and asked to speak to a manager. A large man in a smart suit and with slick, black hair stepped out from a doorway and approached him. They shook hands.

'Good day to you, sir,' the man said smoothly. 'How can I help? Is it about an account you wish to open?'

'Not really,' Rocco said. 'I'd like your help with regard to a case I'm working on.' He handed over his card and the man perused it.

'Inspector Rocco, of course,' the man said, and led him into a small office and closed the door. 'I have heard of you. I am Alexandre Gréville, the deputy manager. Our branch manager is away on sick leave, I'm afraid, but I have every authority to assist you, within reason. You know, of course, that there are restrictions on the precise information I can give you?'

'I realise that. I don't need account or personal details. I just need to know if Gérard Jeunet came in this morning to collect some papers from his safety deposit box.'

Gréville frowned. 'I'm sorry – is there a criminal matter involved here? Only I would have to call my superiors at head office to—'

'A crime has been committed, yes,' Rocco told him, sensing a whole avenue of obfuscation and regulations about to open up before him if he didn't get to the point quickly. 'I'm afraid M. Jeunet is dead. His house was broken into earlier today and he was beaten to death. He has been helping me with some enquiries and I simply need to know if he collected some papers he was going to give to me today. That's all.'

Gréville blinked in alarm and touched a hand to his chest. 'My God, that's awful. Poor man... I can't believe it.' He flapped his other hand and said, 'I'll check with the cashiers to see if he has been in. I would normally deal with that sort of issue but I have been involved elsewhere. Can you wait one minute?'

'I'll do that.'

Gréville was as good as his word and was back within sixty seconds. He looked genuinely shaken and Rocco felt bad at having been so blunt. 'I'm sorry,' he told the banker, 'I was too blunt. My apologies.'

'No, Inspector, please. You have your duty to perform and... poor M. Jeunet... always such a gentleman.' He took a deep breath and nodded. 'Indeed, he came in first thing. In fact, he was waiting on the doorstep when my assistant arrived. He seemed poorly so she let him in so that he could sit down. He has some standing in the local community, being who he is. As soon as she was able, she unlocked the door to the deposit boxes and M. Jeunet took what he required.' He blinked hard. 'Was that why he was killed, Inspector? Should we not have allowed him to take the items?'

Rocco shook his head. 'No. It's not your fault or your assistant's. Can you describe what he took away with him?'

'I cannot, but I will ask Mlle Servallon. She might have seen it.'

The man hurried out again and came back with a young woman with long blonde hair and thick spectacles who stared at Rocco as if he were about to arrest her. Rocco smiled and said, 'There's no need to worry, young lady, I just need to know what M. Jeunet collected this morning. Was it papers, perhaps, and in what form?'

'Certainly, papers. But I could not see them – they were inside a brown envelope.' She glanced at Gréville and explained, 'I wasn't watching, you understand; our clients are guaranteed absolute privacy. But he was holding the envelope as he walked past me.'

'Did he place it in his pocket?' His heart sank at the thought. If the envelope was in his jacket, it was likely the intruder had found it.

'No. Inside the paper.'

'Paper?'

'Oh, sorry. He was carrying a copy of *Picardie La Gazette.* He tucked the envelope inside, thanked me for my help and left.'

Rocco held out his hand and she reluctantly shook it. 'Thank you,' he said gently. 'You've been very helpful. You, too, M. Gréville. I appreciate it.'

He left the bank and returned to Jeunet's house. The crowd had diminished to a few onlookers, and he walked into the building and made straight for the study. He could hear Rizzotti's voice coming from upstairs but decided not to bother him.

Rocco spotted the newspaper on the desk and opened it. Inside was a brown envelope just as Mlle Servallon had described. If this was the documentation Jeunet had mentioned, he had wisely taken the precaution of placing the envelope almost in plain sight where nobody would think of looking for it.

Inside the envelope was a selection of closely typed sheets of paper and newspaper cuttings with handwritten notations showing their origin. These were, Rocco noted with interest, from *Le Figaro*, *Le Monde* and *La Croix*, centre-right, centre-left and liberal. Was this Jeunet being careful to take a balanced view or merely a coincidence?

It didn't take long for him to scan the contents. Among a list of names, he saw De Lancourt mentioned several times, along with his photo and that of an older man, a former family member. The other news cuttings were reports from Morocco four years ago of burned farmhouses, bodies and dead farm animals, and a tableau of the victims' faces. Another tableau held faces of people who had disappeared without trace in what the report described as mysterious circumstances. In nearly all cases, the deceased and missing were French farmers with holdings in Morocco. This no doubt explained why the events had found traction in the national newspapers. But what had happened thereafter?

Rocco pocketed the papers without looking further. If true, along with what Karim Hadji had told Caspar, it was explosive stuff. It was time to get all the facts in front of Massin to see if they could be useful, or whether this was merely the result of one man's dislike of another having grown more than it warranted.

Chapter Thirty-One

The commissaire and his deputy were in a discussion about resources when Rocco knocked on the office door.

'Come in, Inspector,' Massin said, and pushed away a collection of papers. 'Take a seat. You look as if you could do with it. I hope you have something to show us?'

'This has all come at once,' Rocco explained, placing the envelope on the table, 'because I have two sources of information. It might take some time.'

'If it helps us solve these cases, fine,' Massin said, and asked Mme Ignace to bring coffee.

Rocco explained about the results of Caspar's visit to Marseille and the details of his talk with Karim Hadji. It allowed him to segue easily into the meeting with Jeunet and the man's claim to have details about De Lancourt that would implicate him in, among other crimes, the murder and disappearance of French citizens in Morocco.

'I hear one source of information is now closed to us,' Perronnet interjected sombrely. 'I liked Gérard Jeunet – he was a gentleman. Was it Koutcheff's work?'

'No,' Rocco said. 'It wasn't his style and I'd have recognised him. It was probably one of his men but I'll have to take another look at them to make a positive identification.' He confirmed the details of Jeunet's death and his chase through the streets after the suspect.

'Fortuitous or good planning?' Massin muttered. 'Why not have a car waiting near the house?'

'Probably to keep a low profile. The killer had most likely reckoned on getting in and out without being seen and simply walking away. A car hanging around outside might have attracted attention.' He switched back to his report about De Lancourt, and the two senior officers exchanged looks of disbelief but kept silent throughout, pausing only to thank Mme Ignace for the coffee. On top of Jeunet's murder, their sense of shock was understandable: having a putative member of a nationally recognised body accused of serious crimes would take some swallowing at first glance. It was a scandal box that few would want to open without irrefutable proof. And, as they all knew, there was a big gap between accusation and conviction, which could be further lengthened if the accused had the distinction of high office behind him and the ability to fight his corner supported by powerful friends.

'I should advise you all at this point,' Massin interjected, 'that De Lancourt has been in touch with a number of highly placed individuals in government circles and the administration about what he sees as harassment against himself and Koutcheff and trespass on his property. So far I have received half a dozen requests to curtail our investigation or face legal challenges. Two of the requests came from members of the Interior Ministry and three from colleagues in the legal profession.'

Rocco looked at him, wondering what he was leading up to, and was relieved to see a faint smile on Massin's lips. 'I haven't answered them yet but I will be doing so today. They probably won't like it, but we'll have to see. If any of what has been alleged is correct, they will have a hard time defending the indefensible. Please continue, Inspector.'

Rocco spread the papers on the table and let the two men absorb the details. There was a heavy silence as they read, save for the rustle as they exchanged sheets and the occasional murmur of incredulity. What was apparent was the moment they saw the same name in the papers as one in their current big investigation.

Benhamid.

'Unbelievable,' Massin declared eventually. 'I remember some of these details in the press at the time... but as I recall, it was largely blamed on the activities of ANL insurgents and anti-French nationalist groups in Morocco trying to accelerate the demise of the protectorate over there. I don't remember hearing De Lancourt's name, though. But this... it might explain a lot we had not heard of.' He waved a hand over the papers. 'And now the Benhamid connection... I can't quite believe it. If true, it's immense. And what's this thing with the name change? Does Guy De Lancourt sound so much more important?'

'It must to him,' Perronnet muttered. He was staring at the sheets of typed paper with a cynical expression. 'If we believe the assertions here, it certainly implicates De Lancourt – however he spells it – as being somehow involved... in fact, of being connected to some of the disappearances among French farmers. Tying this information together with what Casparon was told about Benhamid having someone helping him, it definitely points towards De Lancourt being the respected figure among other French landowners. It's shocking. He's supposed to be a leading lawyer in Paris, not some scheming international criminal!' He slid the sheets to the centre of the table and stabbed a finger on one of them. 'It's all there.'

Massin nodded. 'He certainly kept it very quiet that he, his father and grandfather owned farms in Morocco and over the border in Algeria. It needs verifying, of course, but maybe it was something he didn't wish to publicise – although the historical activities of families should hardly be a cause for criticism.'

'Unless the properties were acquired illegally,' suggested Rocco. 'It also says the properties were signed over to local owners during the course of 1956. It doesn't say they did it for free or where the money went.'

'Profiting out of illegally held property?' Massin commented. 'That's quite an accusation.'

'If the family owned land and farms out there,' Perronnet pointed out. 'The validity of ownership can be checked through land registry in Morocco and his tax records back here. France agreed Moroccan independence in 1956. Is that significant?'

Massin lifted his shoulders. 'Possibly. The timing is certainly odd. But only the Moroccans can help with all that. My question is, why would they? They haven't helped us with regards to the Benhamids, and this paper-work implicates them, too. Perhaps that's why they left Morocco and came here: their actions had finally come to light and they decided to get out before they could be questioned. The question still remains, though, escape to where?'

'And how would they sustain themselves?' Perronnet pointed out. 'As I understand it there was no money found in the car and very little on their persons. That suggests they might have access to funds here in France… or someone who might help them.'

Nobody spoke for two or three long minutes while they digested the idea. Then Massin stood up.

'This is an unholy mess. What I don't understand is why Jeunet didn't present all this detail before. Why wait until it was effectively too late?'

'Because,' Rocco said, 'he had an idea of what it might have meant to himself and his family to expose De Lancourt without more proof.'

Massin nodded slowly. 'A fair point. If we believe all these allegations – which they are so far, let's not forget that – there are serious questions that need answering by Casablanca, not to mention some embarrassment in Paris over alleged cross-border activities of our own military personnel. However, this was several years ago in another country and the Benhamids aren't going to confirm their part in it. As for De Lancourt's alleged part, the claims are all unsubstantiated and come from the words of one man, Gérard Jeunet, who actively opposed De Lancourt's election to a national body based on personal feelings and what he had heard and read in the press.' He took a turn about the room. 'We can't ignore it or pretend we didn't see it. Quite apart from the murders of the Benhamids, there is now the death of Gérard Jeunet himself and, historically, French citizens in Morocco.'

'What are you saying?' Rocco asked.

'Simple. We will have to place these details with the Interior Ministry. Only they have the responsibility and the muscle to take this matter further. We'll reconvene in the morning and make sure we have all the paperwork in place.' He gave a thin smile. 'If anything does, this should light a petard under their collective shirts.'

Or not, Rocco thought darkly. The Ministry's usual response to bad news involving people in high office was to put a clamp down on all announcements on the basis that digging into the nation's darker secrets was to be avoided at all costs – even if it got in the way of a police investigation.

That meant he would have to help things along a little. And the best way of doing that was to put pressure on De Lancourt himself and see if the lawyer would buckle.

Rocco became aware of Massin watching him. The commissaire had become accustomed to Rocco's strength of feeling about the Ministry and their aptitude for inter-ference, and would no doubt be aware that telling him to hold fire in the middle of an investigation was unlikely to last long.

'What are you thinking?' Massin said, giving Rocco a knowing look. 'Is there something else we should know?'

Rocco had been in two minds about revealing that Caspar had spotted Missurat with Karim Hadji, mainly because he couldn't see what it would prove either way. If no questions arose from Missurat or anyone else in the Ministry about Caspar, it might be because of an ongoing investigation they wished to keep under wraps. Equally, if Missurat was up to something less official, the last thing he would want was to bring himself under a spotlight. He decided to tell Massin anyway. Better to have a clear deck than not.

'Interesting,' Massin said. He tapped his fingers on the desk, then said, 'What do they call it – a potential can of worms or a wasps' nest? I suggest we wait and see. It could be entirely innocent, of course, although why a Ministry official would be calling on a known criminal is a little unusual. I'll keep a note of it just in case. We've got more important things to worry about. What else?'

'Our original case,' Rocco said. 'It might be useful to visit De Lancourt to see if he knows anything about Koutcheff's whereabouts. He might have heard something by now.'

'If he has, what makes you think he'll say so?'

'Because his loyalty to a gun-happy employee won't last long if there's the possibility that his reputation will suffer.'

Massin pursed his lips. 'You could be right. Unfortunately, I happen to know that De Lancourt is in Paris for two days overseeing court cases involving a couple of his clients.'

'Not a problem,' said Rocco easily, scooping up the papers and cuttings he'd found in Jeunet's house. 'There's plenty more I can do. I'll go and finish my report to go with this lot.'

—

Rocco found Dr Rizzotti in his office, staring at something in a glass jar.

'Not more bodies, Lucas,' Rizzotti said in mock despair. 'I can't keep up! I'm thinking of retiring to the country to grow roses.'

'Do you know anything about growing roses?'

'No. I don't.' He sighed and waved Rocco to a seat. 'What can I do for you?'

Rocco placed a folder containing the Jeunet papers and his written summary in front of the doctor. 'I need copies of this lot. Can you do it?' He nodded towards a cupboard where he knew Rizzotti kept his camera and developing equipment. Rizzotti had railed against using local commercial companies after some of his crime-scene photos had been lost in transit, and had opted to rely on his own expertise instead.

Rizzotti looked through the papers and newspaper cuttings, then glanced up at Rocco. 'Is this evidence in the Benhamid shootings?'

'It is.' He waited for Rizzotti to say something, but the doctor merely lifted an eyebrow.

'And?'

'Massin wants to send them to the Ministry for evaluation, in view of the Moroccan connection… and the De Lancourt link.'

'Yes, I'd worked that out for myself. It's the logical next step. But this is heavyweight stuff, far more the Ministry's concern than a regional station like this. Is there a problem with that?'

'Only if the papers go missing. It's the only evidence we have showing a strong reason why the Benhamids were killed.'

'You want me to take photos of them for safe-keeping, don't you? I saw you eyeing my camera cupboard.'

Rocco sensed reluctance. He reached out to take the papers back. 'I'm sorry – I should have thought this through – I don't want to get you involved.'

Rizzotti gently batted his hand away. 'Get off, you giant oaf. I didn't say I wouldn't do it. I'm just concerned for you, that's all. Take my advice: don't mention this to anyone outside this office and I won't either.' He slipped the papers and the summary back in the folder. 'I'll have these back on your desk first thing in the morning and I'll keep the prints down here until you need them.' He smiled. 'They'll be perfectly safe among the corpses; you're pretty much the only one with the stomach or the interest to come down here.' He looked up with a smile on his face as Rocco turned to the door. 'Have a pleasant evening.'

Rocco looked back. Damn. The rumour mill had already swung into action. It reminded him that he didn't have a lot of time to waste before meeting with Eliane. It was already late.

First, however, he needed to swing by Les Cyprès on the way. With De Lancourt in Paris, now was the best time to do it.

Chapter Thirty-Two

There was nobody in evidence when Rocco drove through the gates at Les Cyprès and followed the drive to the house. A light showed behind the side window next to the front door, but the place had the look and feel of an empty building.

Rocco knocked and waited. Moments later, he heard a sound behind him and turned to find a man standing a few metres away. He was carrying a rifle at an easy slope, vaguely pointing in Rocco's direction. The man was tall and slim, with a hard, angular face and a scrub of hair cut very short. He looked relaxed enough but Rocco wasn't fooled; he'd seen men like this before. Calm and seemingly unthreatening but capable of swinging into action at a moment's notice.

'I'm a police officer,' Rocco said softly. 'Point that thing somewhere else.'

The man took his time, but did so. 'I know who you are. You're the cop who came here looking for Koutcheff. What do you want now? The boss isn't here.'

The boss. The title didn't escape Rocco's notice. It was common parlance among men with a common focus and part of a tight-knit group – an acknowledgement that they had a leader, like some units in the military.

'What's your name?' he queried, stepping away from the door and closer to the man.

There was the briefest hesitation. 'Samsonov. Stefan.' It came out stiffly, a man accustomed to stating his name automatically when asked without embellishment.

'Do you have a licence for that weapon?'

'It's for killing vermin and rabbits. All farms have them.'

Rocco changed tack; it was pointless arguing and a waste of valuable time. No doubt De Lancourt would have all the appropriate paperwork. 'Where are the other men, M. Samsonov?'

'They're here, around the place somewhere.' A wave of the hand indicated the house and grounds.

'I'd like to see them. Are they in the staff quarters at the back?'

Samsonov blinked as if uncertain of himself, then said, 'Wait here. I will get someone to talk to you.' With that he turned and walked away stiffly, the rifle held close by his side.

Rocco followed at a distance. He wasn't sure whether he was being played or not, but he didn't want to lose the initiative gained by having arrived here unannounced. If the men promptly scattered into the grounds, he'd have no hope of tracking them down.

Samsonov disappeared into the staff building and closed the door. Moments later, Rocco saw two faces appear at the windows. The word was out. He waited outside, hands clasped behind him, relaxed. It was a deliberate stance these men would have seen many times in their lives, the stance that said *senior officer. Do not mess.*

Moments later the door opened and a figure appeared. It was Bruno Dujols, the man he and Claude had met in the woods.

'Inspector,' he said. He sounded nervous, his eyes flicking back and forth. 'Can I help?'

'What exactly is your position here, M. Dujols? Are you in the chain of command?'

Dujols surprised him by chuckling. At least that was what Rocco assumed it to be. It was more like a repetitive gulping sound. 'Me? Hardly. I'm just one of the group here. Why would you think that?'

'Because Samsonov said he'd get someone to talk to me and now you're here. That suggests you're someone with authority. And you came into the woods the last time we were here.'

'I simply pass on instructions to the others and report back when needed. So maybe I do have some kind of position, of a sort. What exactly do you want? Samsonov told you the boss is away in town.'

'Town?'

'Paris. He's working. You know he's a lawyer, right?' The man was gradually becoming more confident, the tortoise emerging from his shell. Rocco could see he had small eyes but they were bright, with an intelligent gleam. It made him wonder how many others had missed that over the years, seeing only the lowered head, the lack of eye contact.

'I know. How many men are here right now, M. Dujols?'

Dujols hesitated, then said, 'With me, it's four. Why do you need to know that?'

'Thank you. I'll ask the questions then I'll get out of your hair. What are their names?' He took out a notebook and pen.

'Well, there's Raphael Debac, Samsonov you've met, and Jean-Baptiste Salairat. And me.'

'What about Georges Koutcheff?'

'Pardon?' Dujols' eyes widened.

'You heard me. Koutcheff. Big, physical and prone to violence. Hard to miss here, I'd have thought.'

'He's not here.' The voice dropped along with the eyes. 'He never came back from town. Last we heard, you lot had got him... then you hadn't.' A shrug. 'I don't know where he is. Sorry.'

'Nobody else? I heard there were more of you.'

'There were.'

'And?'

'Two left a day or two ago... I can't recall exactly.'

It was like dragging water out of dying man's grasp. 'What were their names?'

'Ivan Garbus and Aziz Touati.'

'Why did they leave?'

'They hadn't been here long. They didn't fit in. They were a bit older than the rest of us and there were arguments.' A shrug. 'One minute they were here, the next they'd gone. It happens; people move on.'

'Arguments about what?'

'All manner of things. They talked like old veterans and said we younger men didn't know what real soldiering was about.' He lifted his shoulders. 'They were wrong, of course, but it annoyed the others.'

It was a common enough feeling between old soldiers and younger men. 'Why were they here? I thought De Lancourt only helped younger men.'

'I don't know. He doesn't always explain why he does things.'

'Was that all you can tell me about those two?'

Dujols tilted his head to one side as if in thought, then said, 'Pretty much. They didn't get on with Koutcheff, I know that. He was rough on them... told them they were past it and should move on. It happens, Inspector, right? What do they call it – lack of chemistry?' He gave a sideways grin as if he were telling tales on the big boys. One of them, at least.

He's getting cocky, thought Rocco. *Maybe he's not so happy here, either.* 'Where did they go?'

'I don't know for sure. They left during the night… sometime after midnight.'

'How would you know that?'

'Because I'd pulled the first watch and went round checking doors and windows… the usual stuff. Their bunks were empty, all their stuff gone. The boss was really annoyed.'

'Where do you *think* they went?'

'I honestly don't know. Far away, if they had any sense. There was nothing for them here.'

'What do you mean?' It was a minor point to pursue but he sensed that pushing with this man might get results.

Dujols looked tense, as if he'd said too much. 'Nothing… I mean, they wouldn't get a friendly hand-shake and a welcome from Koutcheff if they did come back. Like I said, they didn't fit in.'

'I suppose not.' Rocco snapped his notebook shut. 'I'd like to see Debac and Salairat.'

'What, now?'

'Why not? I'm here, they're here – at least I figure they are; I saw them looking out of the windows. And bring Samsonov back with you – without the gun.'

Dujols nodded and seemed resigned. 'Fine. Can you wait here, please? I'll go and get them.'

He turned and ambled away. Five minutes later he reappeared with two men in tow, both looking less than happy, and Samsonov bringing up the rear, minus the rifle.

'Debac,' said Dujols, pointing at a man with the battered appearance of an ex-boxer, 'and Salairat.' This man was slim, muscular and with a challenging stare.

Rocco made descriptive notes in his notebook, then said, 'Do either of you know where Georges Koutcheff is right now?'

'No.' Salairat's response was firm, unhesitating. Rocco had come across many men like him before: deny everything, admit to nothing.

'Me neither.' Debac's response was slower. His voice held the muffled nasal tone of a nose long past repair, and sounded as if breathing might be a permanent problem.

'What about the other two... Garbus and Touati?'

Debac spat on the ground dangerously close to Rocco's foot. 'Garbage, the pair of them. Oldies who should have retired a long time ago.'

'Retired from what?'

'Life, mostly. That's all I'm saying.' With that he turned and walked away, followed by Salairat.

Rocco watched them both carefully and was immediately hit by the way Salairat carried himself. Springy and relaxed, like an athlete. It was him – the runner. He knew it without a shadow of doubt, even though he hadn't seen the man's face.

'Do they both drive?' he asked Dujols. He had to restrain himself from calling Salairat back. All in good time. As angry as he felt about the senseless murder of Jeunet, he had no firm proof save for his own eyes, and that wouldn't stand up in court.

'Debac, certainly. He was a fast-patrol driver in the military. Salairat probably does but I've never seen him behind the wheel. Why?'

'Just asking.'

'Is that all?' Dujols said. 'Only I have work to do.'

Rocco looked past the building at the trees in the background. Thick with conifers, the overall appearance was gloomy and forbidding, full of shadows and varying shades of dark. If sunlight penetrated its confines, it wouldn't go deep.

A good place for someone to hide, he thought. Especially a man on the run.

'What's back there?'

Dujols looked. 'Trees. Why?'

'Just trees?'

'Mostly, yes. Koutcheff and a couple of others used to shoot pigeons down there. I've only been there once.' He shivered suddenly, although Rocco couldn't tell if it was real or not. 'It gave me the creeps, the thoughts of the tunnels and dugouts that were never filled in properly. Some of them are really deep. Did you know they even had basements?'

'Yes. I heard that.'

'Well, I think most of it must have fallen in on itself now. But God knows what's still down there, like ammunition and stuff. You'd have to be mad to go in there.'

Create enough fear about a place and it was by instinct off-limits except to the most foolhardy. He wondered if that was what Bruno was doing.

'I'll give it a miss,' he said casually. 'I've had my share of battlefields and trenches.'

Chapter Thirty-Three

It was just on 7 p.m. as Rocco drove through the pillared entrance to the ruined chateau where Sébastien and Eliane Cezard had made their home. He'd called in briefly at home to clean up and make himself halfway presentable in a fresh shirt and trousers, which also gave him time to cast off all thoughts of his current cases and focus on the here and now. He'd found his talk with Dujols oddly unsettling, as if there was something he'd forgotten to do, and decided it had to be related to the woods behind Les Cyprès, which were still an unknown quantity. That was something he'd have to attend to tomorrow.

There was no denying he felt unaccountably nervous as he followed the cobbled drive through a wild garden featuring a mass of bushes, ancient flower borders and lawns, and too many trees to count. This was outside his normal experience; dating and notions of a romantic nature had not been a part of his life for a while. Instead, work had taken over, which wasn't much to boast about.

What the hell was wrong with him? He'd faced guns, explosives, knives, drowning, baseball bats – and most recently nearly being run over by a car. This should have been easy. But it was proving anything but.

As he'd seen on previous visits, the terraced grounds possessed a shambolic charm, with few signs of regular upkeep, yet which somehow seemed to fit perfectly with the reduced state of the chateau itself. Maybe it was the way things were supposed to be once an impressive building had passed its best, with nature taking over however it saw fit and each individual piece of flora fighting for its place without the help or hindrance of man.

It didn't seem as if Sébastien or Eliane had much interest in gardening, but even if they had it would have taken far more than the two of them to keep the place going to anything like its original state.

The building consisted of three floors of solid stone blocks, although one wing had become seriously deteriorated, leaving just the front and one side intact, a mere shadow of its once elegant state. The roof was a newer construction that lent the building, in Rocco's eyes, the appearance of an old lady in a skewed top hat. Heavy wooden shutters covered the large front windows on either side of the ground floor, like closed eyes on an old face; only the steps leading up to the impressive front entrance somehow managed to rescue the overall appearance from complete and crumbling ruin.

As he climbed out of his car, Eliane appeared at the front door. She was smiling and clad in a light, green-and-yellow dress. She skipped down the steps to meet him and gave him a kiss on each cheek. She smelled of soap, a hint of perfume and lemon with – was it a touch of apple? *Damn it, man, stop overthinking!*

'Lucas, such perfect timing. Dinner is almost ready. I'm so pleased you could come.' She stopped, noticing the way he was carrying himself. 'Is something wrong?'

He waved it off. Damn it, he'd tried to hide the stiffness in his leg but she clearly had eyes like a hawk. 'A work thing,' he said. 'I took a tumble. It's nothing a glass of this won't heal.' He handed her a bottle of white wine and a small bunch of flowers. He had to resist touching his cheek where she'd kissed him, and wondered if this constituted a date. If it was, he hoped he didn't make a mess of it.

'Mmm… Pouilly-Fuissé – I love it. And the flowers are delightful, thank you. I bet you didn't get these from Mme Drolet.' She giggled. 'Did you go out shopping just for these or did you send out one of your men with strict orders on what to get?'

'Not guilty,' he protested. 'I prefer to make my own mistakes.'

'No mistakes, I promise you. Come on.' She led him up the steps and inside, along a corridor lined with paintings into a living room overlooking the rear garden. 'I'll just put these in water. Please sit. I won't be a minute.'

Eliane was back minutes later with two glasses of wine. 'This place echoes too much when Pa isn't here. But I love it.' She nodded towards the double doors onto the garden. 'Shall we go outside? It's too good an evening to waste indoors. Am I talking too much?' She sipped her wine a little too enthusiastically and made a small choking sound. 'I'm sorry – that's not very elegant, is it?'

'Actually, it was,' he replied, and handed her a handkerchief from his top pocket so she could mop a tiny dribble of wine from her lip. While she did that, he took a sip from his glass then stepped out of the doors onto a terrace, breathing in the soft evening air and enjoying the silence. This really was a magical spot and he could see why Sébastien had settled on it. Perfect for painting and a great place to bring up his daughter.

'Are you nervous, Lucas?' Eliane was looking at him with watery eyes and holding the handkerchief beneath her mouth. He hadn't seen anything quite so elegant in a long time.

'Yes,' he murmured, and struggled to change the subject. 'You said your father's in Brussels discussing a commission. How's that going?'

'I've no idea – he doesn't always tell me what he's doing until he receives a written confirmation. One thing you learn in his business is that people with money don't always hold onto it long enough to pay the bills – and he's been stung more than once.' She placed a light hand on his elbow and led him off the terrace across a stretch of grass towards some trees. 'So, Inspector, tell me what you're working on at the moment. Anything exciting?'

'Not really.' He struggled for words; what could he say without tripping over his current cases, one involving a policeman shot on duty and the other involving… well, more deaths. Great way to taint the evening's mood in no time flat. Instead he said, 'I have seen some impressive paintings recently. Perhaps I've had a sheltered upbringing – I didn't know art collection was so big in this part of the world.'

'Near here? Where was that? I wonder if Pa knows about it.'

'A place called Les Cyprès out near Petit Montgallet.'

Eliane's hand tightened on his arm momentarily and when he looked round her expression had morphed from one of pleasure to something distinctly different. 'Ugh – you mean De Lancourt? The man's a monster. Pa says he knows nothing about art, only how to make money by stealing it from others.'

'That's a pretty serious allegation.' He looked down and gave her a smile to rob the words of gravity. 'But do tell.'

'No, forget I spoke – I'm sorry, Lucas. This is supposed to be a pleasant evening – which it very much is, I promise. I was speaking out of turn.'

Rocco sipped his wine, then said, 'If it helps, I don't care for him, either.'

'Really? Thank goodness. He's vile!' She paused, her face flushed with sudden passion, and he guessed that this reaction was deeply seated and might have arisen out of something to do with her father.

'You know you shouldn't bottle things up, don't you? It's bad for the complexion.'

She blinked and subconsciously lifted a hand to her cheek. 'Is that so? Who told you such a huge fib?'

'My mother. She was a very wise woman. And she had a great complexion.'

Eliane smiled, relaxing again. 'In that case I had better get it off my chest, hadn't I? I wouldn't want you to be having dinner with an old hag.' She looked down into her glass for a moment, then said, 'It was over a year ago; De Lancourt asked Pa to value two paintings he'd been offered. They were portraits of important figures in the community in the last century – a magistrate and a physician, I think. They were being sold by a local family member who had fallen on hard times and needed some urgent medical treatment available only in Switzerland. Pa had never met De Lancourt before, but he'd heard of him many times because De Lancourt has always wanted an entrée to the art world. I believe he thinks it will make him even more important than he already thinks he is. Anyway, Pa agreed to take a look and said they were fine pieces of art and worth a considerable sum, which De Lancourt seemed pleased about.'

'What happened?'

'De Lancourt went back to the woman and offered her less than half their true value. She refused at first because she'd heard they were exceptional pieces. But she couldn't think of who else to approach and when her health deteriorated, she agreed to sell so that she could afford to go to Switzerland for the treatment. A month later she returned, having discovered more information about the paintings' provenance and demanded that De Lancourt pay her closer to the valuation. He refused and told her that Pa had advised him that they were of no real consequence and that he should pay as little as possible. She happened to bump into Pa one day and asked him why he had done such a terrible thing. He, of course, knew nothing about the sale until then. He was furious, and told her she should seek advice from a lawyer. He even gave her two names of lawyers with connections to the art world. Two weeks later she took her own life.'

'Because of that?'

'Yes. A friend of hers said she felt humiliated at being taken for such a fool and couldn't face the ridicule.' She looked directly at Rocco. 'That's why I dislike him – why we both do. The man's a fraud.' She took a deep breath and leaned closer to him, then planted a kiss on his cheek, leaving a faint hint of perfume in the air. 'There, that changes my mood to one of pleasure rather than anger. Shall we go inside and eat?'

The food was delicious, a creamy *poulet au cidre*, which Eliane admitted was largely of her own device due to a variation in the ingredients. 'There's a traditional list to follow if you want to make it a specific Brittany version,' she explained, 'but I like to do my own thing and change things around a bit. I hope you like it.'

'It's incredible,' Rocco said, slicing into the breast of tender, browned chicken. At least he now knew where the aroma of apples had come from. It made a pleasant change to his normal diet, which was on-the-run food prepared as quickly and as simply as possible. 'Makes a change from anything I can throw together.'

Eliane blushed with pleasure. 'Don't tell me your mother of the perfect complexion didn't teach her son to cook *something*. I'm afraid I can't quite believe that. Even Pa, whose mother was something of a tartar, gave him a few recipes for survival. Go on, what can you cook? Maybe you could cook dinner for me one day.'

'Sure. If it's chicken, I can manage that – or maybe a steak if pushed.' He stopped, blushing, realising that his mouth had run away with him. Cooking for himself was one thing; he had simple tastes and a palate ruined by a lifetime of snatched meals and too much strong coffee. Cooking for someone like Eliane was likely to be a quick lesson in humiliation.

'You're on, Lucas Rocco.' Eliane was grinning at his confusion, her face alight with humour and pleasure. She jumped up. 'Stay here. I'll get coffee – a bad habit this late, I know, but I'm feeling reckless.' She added, 'Then I'll have to kick you out – which I don't want to do but I have another job interview in the morning. It's early and in Abbeville and I don't want to be late.'

'I'm sorry,' he said, feeling guilty. 'I didn't ask how the Doullens interview went.'

'I'm on a shortlist, so I suppose that's good.' She turned back at the door and said with a smile, 'Maybe next time you can stay longer.'

She disappeared before he could respond, and he felt a rush of confusion and something else he could only think was light-headedness.

Chapter Thirty-Four

Before leaving for Paris, Rocco rang Michel Santer. The captain was a mine of information on all things police and criminal around the capital, and had more contacts at his beck and call than anyone Rocco could think of. He also loved to gossip and eat, preferably conjoined activities. If he was lucky he'd be able to get to Paris, have a quick meeting with Santer and do what he needed to do and get out again and back to Amiens without anyone noticing he'd been gone.

'Lucas? I was just thinking about you.'

'Why,' Rocco said. 'What have I done?'

'You haven't been to see me for far too long.' Santer laughed. 'What can I do for you?'

'Do you have access to the Paris court attendances today?'

'I don't, but I know a woman who does. Who are you looking for – one of your criminal friends from the sugar-beet fields of Picardie?'

'Wheat, actually. It's the big thing this year, they tell me. And the name is of a lawyer – Guy De Lancourt.'

'Pff… that *cafard*. Sorry – I'm maligning cockroaches everywhere. Give me two minutes. I have to make a phone call.'

Rocco waited, drinking the last of his coffee and thinking pleasurably over the previous evening with

Eliane. He was fairly certain he hadn't made too much of a fool of himself, but if the kiss she'd given him on the front steps after coffee was any indication, he thought not.

'Lucas? Hello, Lucas – are you there?' It was Santer, disturbing a pleasurable train of thought.

'Yes. Sorry, Michel. Still waking up.'

'You'd better get a move on, my friend. Your lawyer friend is appearing at the *cour d'assises* at two o'clock this afternoon. However, I know an excellent little *resto* near the Pont Neuf that is very quiet and none of the legal profession would dream of going there, so we'll be able to talk in relative privacy.' He named a restaurant along the Place Dauphine.

'Sounds good to me,' said Rocco. The bill would no doubt be eye-watering, but it was a price worth paying if he got the information he needed. 'See you there.'

Rocco drove fast, willing traffic out of his way and only resorted to using his siren twice. If he got picked up by traffic cops he'd have a hard time explaining himself, but he kept his fingers crossed and the kilometres flew by.

He parked away from the Île de la Cité – the island along the river Seine that houses, among other buildings, the magnificence that is the cathedral of Notre-Dame – and walked across the Pont Neuf from the north bank. He spotted Santer immediately, although the captain was dressed in smart casual clothes rather than his customary uniform and looked very different to his normal self.

'I almost didn't recognise you,' Rocco greeted him, shaking his hand.

'It's called blending in.' He eyed Rocco's coat. 'You should try it sometime; you look as if you've come to arrest someone.'

'Maybe I have… eventually.'

Santer grinned. 'That's what I like to see – Rocco ready for a fight. I checked the court journal to be sure and De Lancourt is definitely on at two. I see it's a fraud case with links to a serious crime. That's not yours, is it?'

'No.'

They walked up the street together and Santer led him into a small entrance and up a flight of stairs. As he'd predicted the place was quiet and they were able to get a window table away from the few other diners.

Santer took care of the ordering. 'Let me do this one,' he told Rocco. 'I can see you're on edge. By the way, nothing to report on the young student. She's been warned and is only going out with her friends, never alone. I've asked for regular patrols to go by the building at night, just in case.'

'Thank you. Actually, I should have mentioned it before, but there's probably no reason to keep watching her.' He told Santer about Jeunet's death, which had probably rendered any threat against Micheline no longer necessary or useful.

Santer scowled. 'I'm sorry to hear that. So they went for a direct attack?'

'It looks like it.'

'It's a bad business. So, this De Lancourt thing – what is it about?'

Rocco summarised the Benhamid murders, pausing only while their food was being served. Santer listened without interruption, accustomed to being briefed by officers who had usually come in shortly after dealing with stressful incidents and needed to unload while still able to recall crucial details.

'Apart from De Lancourt being an obnoxious human being and a lawyer to boot,' Santer said at last, clearing his plate, 'why the interest in how he works? Or is it simply getting to know the enemy? Only, you do know he's a firebrand, don't you? You're taking on a pot-load of trouble going up against him.'

'I know – I've met him. But I need to know more.'

'Well, if you've met and haven't been eviscerated, I'm impressed. I mean, all the top lawyers are the same, to one extent or another, but this one is like a great white shark looking for his next target.' His hand mimed a shark cruising through the water. 'Worse still, De Lancourt has the reputation of not needing to be hungry to rip his next victim to pieces. I know some extremely good prosecuting lawyers who are terrified of him because he can fillet them in seconds if they haven't got their details absolutely spot on down to the last dot and comma. Even then they can't be sure he won't skewer them with something totally unexpected that he's dug up at the last minute.'

Rocco had known Santer for many years and worked with him on a number of occasions, and respected his judgement and experience. Santer clearly didn't like the lawyer but he was surprised at the level of grudging respect in the captain's tone.

'You sound as if you almost admire him.'

'He's clever, that's all. No admiration intended. You'd do well to remember that, my friend. Put any cop in front of him in a court of law and he almost drools with expectation. They don't stand a chance. Arguing fine points of detail is his speciality. I know of very good up-and-coming lawyers who've sat in on his cases to see if they can learn how he does it. It's like watching legal theatre… violence without the bloodshed, death by a thousand cuts.'

'I'll bear it in mind.'

Santer finished his coffee and checked his watch. 'You'd better get going. I'd come with you out of interest but I have other duties to perform.'

Rocco said goodbye and thanked Santer for the lunch, promising a re-match at a later date. Then he walked to the court and gained entrance by showing his police card.

The courtroom was old, historic and smelled of rich wood, polish – and an underlying air of melancholy. Rocco sat at the very back and waited while the contestants and other parties filed in and took their seats. He wasn't interested in the details of the case being heard, rather De Lancourt's manner of dealing with it. From what Santer had said there would likely be blood coating the walls if he ran true to form.

Within minutes of the case getting under way it was evident that De Lancourt, immaculately dressed and suave, and backed by his retinue of assistants and researchers, treated the courtroom like an actor did the stage. He was intent on controlling events by sheer force of personality and showed himself happy to use every trick he could summon to badger and diminish the opposing counsel's words. He even challenged the three judges facing him if a point seemed to go against him, although always careful not to push the court etiquette too far.

What was most evident to Rocco was that he had all his facts at his fingertips and most of the opposition's, too. It was clear he had mastered the art of research and, allied with an acerbic attitude barely kept in check, he gradually sliced and diced the opposition's arguments until he emerged victorious. The other man, younger by at least two decades, looked shocked by the icy ferocity of the attack, which it plainly was.

Rocco had soon seen enough. As soon as a recess was called, he slipped out of the court, deciding it was time to get back to the station. Maître De Lancourt was no pushover and had the intellect and sharpness of mind to fight his corner, especially if there were even tiny doubts about the opposing arguments. As he'd told Santer, it was something he had to keep in mind.

As he rounded a corner in the corridor, he found himself facing a uniformed court security officer with his palm raised. Another man stood in the background.

The first man said, 'Can I see your authorisation, please?'

'Why?' said Rocco. 'I'm here on police business, observing a case.'

The man hesitated, then said, 'I would still like to see your identification.'

Rocco produced his card and the man perused it carefully. 'That's fine, thank you, Inspector. My apologies, but could you come with me, please? There is someone who wishes to speak with you.' Without waiting he turned and walked along the corridor, weaving his way through the flow of people, and turned one corner, then another, before opening a small door at the end. Rocco followed to see where this was going, aware of the other officer falling in behind him.

The door opened into a small meeting room with high windows, heavy wooden panels and an undeniable air of gloom. The furniture, also heavy, consisted of a table, several chairs and a picture of an eminent figure Rocco didn't recognise in flowing robes with a small dog at his feet.

And Guy De Lancourt.

The door closed behind Rocco, effectively shutting off all sounds from the corridor outside.

'What are you doing here, Rocco?' De Lancourt's voice was low, but with an undercurrent of real edge to it as if he were fighting to keep it under control. His face was suffused with blood and Rocco began to understand how the opposing counsel just now must have felt. As Santer had described him, the lawyer was every inch the shark, looking for a kill.

'I happened to be in town and decided to observe a case. Why do you ask?'

'Which case – mine? Why would you be interested in that?' He waved an impatient hand. 'Don't bother answering that.' He stepped closer, shooting his cuffs in a display of apparent calmness that was anything but, his eyes betraying his anger and his breath warm against Rocco's face. 'You would do well to go back where you came from, Rocco, and not go up against me. I am an enemy you really do not need.'

'I'll take your word for it. Why are you so concerned about a simple country cop? What was it you said when we first met? *Most of the police around here have yet to shake the farmyard mud off their boots.* That reminds me, did you hear about Gérard Jeunet?'

'What about him?' The lawyer frowned at the change of topic.

'He's dead. Beaten to death in his home – with a hammer. It seems the person responsible was searching for something. Fortunately, they weren't very good at their job because the papers were right in front of them all the time. Now we have them.'

De Lancourt didn't react. 'I'm sorry – but how is a common burglary of interest to me?' He stepped to one side as a distant bell sounded. 'You will have to excuse me – I have a meeting to go to—'

'Connections, *maître*. Connections. It's one of the fundamental tenets of investigating crime. I understand Jeunet opposed your election to the academy.'

'Rubbish. He was an insignificant little man pursuing a vendetta. I will be elected in spite of him.'

'For someone insignificant, he seemed adept at gathering information. You haven't asked what it is.'

De Lancourt shrugged. 'Why should I – it's of no interest.'

'It should be. His area of research was farming families in the past hundred years or so, with land in Morocco. Specifically, what happened to at least three families during the transition to independence.'

The air fairly crackled with electricity as De Lancourt glared at Rocco, the blood draining from his face. Rocco immediately understood why: he was no longer on the familiar ground of the courtroom, where he reigned supreme and the rules and etiquette of that place allowed him to guide and control the outcome. Out here it was different; he could not control what came out of left field.

'Cross me, Rocco,' he hissed with venom, beads of his spittle touching Rocco's face, 'and I will come after you and your pathetic job, which I can have taken away with a simple telephone call!' He snapped his fingers in the air and his voice dropped. 'But don't think I will stop there. I will also come after those you hold dear; every single one of them. You will regret ever hearing of me. I hope we are clear.' With that he stepped past Rocco, opened the door and was gone.

Chapter Thirty-Five

De Lancourt watched from a narrow side window on the first floor as Rocco strode through the ornate gates and disappeared from sight. The brief encounter with the policeman had left him drained in a way he had never experienced before, not even in his junior days in court facing senior counsels who had the skill to send him scurrying back to his room with his tail between his legs. Yet here was this hick of a man who had managed to unsettle him with just a few words. How could that be? Maybe there was more to it than that. He'd long been accustomed to the psychology of the courtroom, where words were the primary weapons in use and getting under an opponent's skin was the norm. But the physical signs displayed by adversaries were almost as important, and it was probably this that had contributed to his feeling of discomfort. Rocco had shown no signs of being disadvantaged here, in spite of it being more De Lancourt's own turf. In fact, he had been surprisingly relaxed, even confident. It made De Lancourt wonder what else Rocco had learned from the meddlesome Jeunet that he hadn't seen fit to mention, such as events in Morocco that he had long ago forced to the back of his mind. He walked the length of the corridor he was in, imagining the fuss that would be made by his opponents should any of those events become public, and kicked at a chair in fury. He'd worked too hard for this, and weathered too many objections from interfering idiots like Jeunet to see his plans and ambitions thwarted at this stage.

De Lancourt shook off the feeling and made his way to an office where he could use a phone in absolute privacy. It was time for action, not emotion. He dialled a number with angry stabs of his finger, taking deep breaths to reduce his heart rate. It would not do to appear rattled to anyone else, especially the men he relied on. It was answered within three rings by Bruno Dujols, the communications operator at Les Cyprès.

De Lancourt had made a habit of using the full names of the 'boys' and their previous military experience where possible, to remind them of their status and skills. In his mind, this form of structure made everyone's position clear from the outset. Dujols, although an unimpressive-looking individual with a decidedly un-military air, unlike the others, had been a skilled radio and communications expert in the army, accustomed to passing complex information and instructions up and down the chain of command. That had made him useful at the house for acting as a link between De Lancourt and the men. But Dujols had another skill that had been used when De Lancourt needed to know a little more about someone with whom he'd had a disagreement: he was a natural at watching people covertly. He looked so ordinary, few people bothered giving him a second glance and he could melt into a crowd with ease.

'Inspector Rocco, M. Dujols,' De Lancourt muttered into the phone. 'I want you to follow him, find out who he knows or holds dear, where he lives – everything about him. He's currently on his way back to Amiens from Paris, so be ready to fall in behind him and go where he goes. But be careful – he's very experienced.'

'I understand, sir. What if he does spot me?'

'I suggest you make sure he does not.' He paused for effect, then said softly, 'I would hate to find that you've caused me any embarrassment. That would be very unwise.'

There was an audible gulp. 'What about my work here?'

'Get M. Debac to stand in for you. Also, tell M. Samsonov and M. Salairat to stand by. They will be needed.' Raphael Debac had also been a radio man, whereas Stefan Samsonov and Jean-Baptiste Salairat had been field men, accustomed to taking physical action of an entirely different nature, which he had found useful on several occasions in the past.

'Yes, sir. Anything else?'

'Where is M. Koutcheff right now?' He knew his so-called secretary should currently be in hiding after shooting the policeman, although following orders had recently proved not to be his strong point. The futility of the shooting had enraged De Lancourt, putting his own reputation in peril by association, especially with the forthcoming elections to the academy. He'd actually considered for a brief moment turning the man in to the police. But the advantage of being seen to be public-spirited, with whatever benefit that might bring in the press and among the public, would be more than outweighed by the knowledge that Koutcheff could spill his guts to the authorities going back years if he felt inclined. The alternative might be to have one of the others deal with him on a permanent basis, which he was sure they would relish. Koutcheff was not the most popular among the boys.

'In the woods, sir, as you instructed.' Dujols' voice was flat and unemotional. It reminded De Lancourt that there had been bad blood between the two men, caused by Koutcheff making it plain that he considered the radio man weak. Giving Dujols this assignment might be a good way of keeping keep them apart. Koutcheff had already shown signs of being a ticking bomb and another death or assault would be a fatal setback he might not be able to weather.

'Tell him to stand by as well. And make sure you report in regularly. Understood?'

'Yes, sir.'

De Lancourt cut the connection and wondered how soon to bring Rocco's world crashing down on his head. That would teach the infernal man to mind his own business. Maybe if Koutcheff got killed in the process it would solve two problems at once.

Chapter Thirty-Six

The atmosphere Rocco found on arrival back at the station was more or less as he'd expected. Forewarned by a radio message from René Desmoulins that two men from the Interior Ministry had arrived unannounced, he'd guessed that their presence would have an unsettling effect. The mood was subdued and most of the staff had their heads down, busy enough not to be noticed, and all wondering at the reason for the visit.

It was easy to see why. As a spot on the national radar, Amiens was not the most compelling of places for Ministry people to choose for a visit on a whim. Although a regional centre, there were other cities with more pressing problems for the suits to fix or amend, and there had to be a reason that brought two such individuals here with apparently little or no notice.

Rocco entered the main room downstairs and was immediately spotted by Mme Ignace, who pointed a finger upstairs with a faint expression of sympathy. No doubt she knew more than she would let on but it was enough for him to take a deep breath and get ready for trouble.

Massin saw him coming and beckoned him into the room, where he and Perronnet were seated at the conference table. Across from them were two men in dark suits, looking to Rocco like members of an undertakers' convention.

'Inspector Rocco,' Massin introduced him, 'M. Thomas Pancaud and M. Gilles Goubier, from the Ministry.' He gave the ministry a capital M, Rocco noted, out of respect for their office, although there was no mention of their ranks. He shook hands with both men, neither of whom offered much of a smile in return, before taking a seat at the end of the table.

Pancaud, he decided, was the senior of the two; smooth of hair, fleshy of face and with a carefully tailored suit around a comfortable frame, he oozed confidence and authority. Sixty-something and a career civil servant, he guessed, good at passing on unpopular news to the lower orders. The man had the Jeunet papers before him on the table, which he'd clearly been reading.

Goubier was a slightly different fish, he guessed. Forty-something and hard-faced, with the look of a former police officer pulled out of the ranks and elevated to a promising career on the decision-making ladder. A listener with the ability to bite.

Pancaud said, tapping the papers, 'Inspector Rocco, I thank you for bringing these details to our attention. Before we go any further, do you have any specific know-ledge of the background to Jeunet's allegations, or any addition to your written report from yesterday, which we should have in our possession?'

'No,' Rocco said. 'It's all there, although confirmation of some points from the Moroccan authorities would help. I'm sure they will be happy to help if asked.' He didn't feel sure about it at all, given their lack of cooperation so far, but he wanted to get that point in before it got lost by the roadside.

Pancaud didn't disappoint him. He shot Massin a brief look of concern and said, 'Let me explain something, Inspector: while we are anxious to investigate these claims, and even compelled to do so for good order, they are for the most part the unsubstantiated allegations of a man who is hardly a friend of the person at their centre. I hope you agree?'

'Was.'

Pancaud blinked. 'I beg your pardon?'

'Gérard Jeunet is dead. It's mentioned in the paperwork in front of you. I believe he was murdered for those very papers.'

'So you say. Can you prove it? Do you even have a suspect?'

'Not yet.' Instinct made him cautious. He knew it had to have been Salairat, but he didn't want to put that name out there when he wasn't entirely sure these two men were behind the investigation.

'Not yet. Maybe never, wouldn't you agree?' Pancaud ghosted a smile without humour and added waspishly, 'After all, you don't still have, if my information is correct, the man accused of brutalising a police officer in the course of his duties, who escaped from this very building and who is suspected thereafter of shooting the very officer who arrested him in the first place.' He glanced at Massin. 'Or do you have him sequestered away somewhere ready to spring on us?'

'That's part of our ongoing investigation,' Rocco said. 'I thought you were here regarding the allegations against Guy De Lancourt contained in those papers, who also happens to be the employer of Georges Koutcheff, the man being hunted for the shooting.'

Pancaud said nothing for a moment, followed by, 'Rocco, I think we have to realise that there is an issue of public confidence at stake here, arising from this commissariat allowing this man's escape from custody, but also from the wider issues involved. However, I don't wish to be unfair since the latter is on a level I'm not sure you need understand.'

Rocco heard an intake of breath from Perronnet and felt a tremor through the table as Massin shifted in his seat at the implied insult to his staff and the commissariat in general.

Rocco adjusted his appraisal of Pancaud's position; if he was able to throw accusations like this around so openly, he must carry more weight than the average member of the Ministry. 'I think I can unravel that, don't worry—'

'The fact is,' Pancaud interrupted him, 'that it has been decided that digging over these historical claims is at best an exercise destined to satisfy a dead man's rivalry. At worst it risks dragging France into a dispute with another country, which does not suit our current situation, politically.'

Massin said evenly, 'Historic claims? All this happened within the past four or five years, M. Pancaud. In any other crime investigation it would fall well within our normal scope of discovery.'

'Especially,' Rocco added, 'when the claims amount to the murders of French citizens in Morocco with the possible collaboration of a fellow Frenchman and members of our military from over the border in Algeria. Or are you suggesting we ignore the concerns of their families?'

Goubier spoke for the first time, looking at Rocco with open cynicism. 'So, we should open up all the files because of these baseless accusations – is that what you're saying?'

Rocco looked at the younger man and said, 'They should be investigated, yes. Or have you abandoned your sworn duty as a police officer?'

By the expression on Goubier's face, he knew he had scored a hit. He didn't get a chance to follow it as Pancaud raised a hand.

'Gentlemen. Allow me to intervene. Inspector Rocco, given your rank and your distance from events in Paris, you have to allow us to make decisions on this matter. We came here today to see if you had anything more... persuasive to add to these papers. It seems you do not. If you continue to press this line of attack on a prominent citizen against our judgement, you could find yourself working at an even greater distance from here in one of our more remote *territoires* overseas.'

'So, you're going to sit on this evidence.' It was an open accusation but Rocco was past caring.

'No.' Pancaud was almost breezy. 'We will assess the gravity of these assertions and announce a decision in due course. Or are you going to object to that, too? If so, I could terminate your position here and now if you wish.'

There was a brief silence as the threat hung in the air, then Massin spoke. 'You do not have that authority.'

Pancaud's eyes swung towards him in surprise. 'You think not, Massin?'

'He's right, actually,' Perronnet said softly. 'Regulations state that in a matter of dispute or disagreement it is for the relevant immediate superiors to decide on action pertaining to an officer. If unresolved, it goes before a disciplinary panel. The Ministry has no say in it. Some might wish they did but that would be a dangerous situation and cause serious repercussions among senior officers all over the country. I doubt you or the Ministry would want that aired in the press… unless it involves a truly serious breach of national security or duty threatening the state. And Rocco's record argues distinctly against that.'

'Doing what?' Goubier demanded.

'Well, he's never murdered anyone as far as I know. However, he is on record as having played an important part in preventing an attempt on the life of the president himself, not far from this very place. That action included uncovering one of the instigators, a man inside the president's own security detail. In some quarters that might count for something, don't you think?'

'It sounds to me,' Goubier responded, looking to his colleague, 'as if a clear-out is needed here.' He got to his feet. 'It might serve as a warning to anyone else who feels like challenging the Ministry.'

'Young man,' said Massin icily, 'you probably have your eyes on higher office, but making threats like that is beyond your call. I would urge you to sit down and keep quiet before you talk yourself and your senior colleague into a corner.'

Goubier seemed set to argue but was prevented by Pancaud motioning him to sit.

'Nobody is threatening anybody,' he said calmly. 'We are simply here to resolve a situation. You may no doubt be aware that Guy De Lancourt is going forward as a potential member of the Académie Française. It's an important and honoured post and it would ill-suit the country to have any kind of scandal involving that august institution.'

'That should not be allowed to impede an investigation,' said Massin, 'if the evidence shows there is a just cause. How are you going to proceed with this?'

'I intend to take this... evidence presented here' – Pancaud tapped the folder – 'and try to find the truth of who committed the alleged killings in Morocco. If that was a member of the military, then an appropriate punishment should follow. That should conclude the matter.'

'So,' Rocco murmured, 'shoot the messenger, not the person who sent it.'

Pancaud's smile could have frozen hot coffee. 'If that is what happens, so be it. We don't live in a perfect world, Inspector. Get used to it.'

Chapter Thirty-Seven

Bruno Dujols had lived his life in the army and outside in the certain comfort of knowing he did not stand out. In military circles that meant he either got overlooked altogether in the shadows of the more confident and brash individuals, or he got picked for insignificant jobs where physical courage and fighting skills were not the primary requirements. Every army in the world, he had told himself, had people like him, and they each had a role to play. In his case it was mostly radio work back at base or in communications units in the field. Action of a different kind.

Then one day he'd been tasked to follow a known agitator in Algeria when his unit had been short of personnel. Surprising even himself once he'd got over the palpable fear of being open to danger, Bruno had found himself in his element. Hiding in plain sight or merging into the background, he'd enjoyed the near-invisibility, no more than a flyspeck on the wall, as one of his colleagues had cruelly described him. But, he reassured himself, a flyspeck with purpose.

The criticism hadn't bothered him; he had a skill that few others possessed, and that knowledge had given him a place in the scheme of things that required little chance of physical action while being able to stay low on everyone's horizon.

Now he was once more out from under the gaze of the other men at Les Cyprès and glad of the freedom. Finding himself even remotely close to the mad pig Koutcheff was always unsettling and mostly unavoidable, but now he could put some distance from De Lancourt and the hot-house atmosphere of the barrack-room surroundings behind the main house. It would give him time to decide on what he did next.

One thing Bruno was sure of, he was going to have to leave Les Cyprès soon and everyone associated with it. One other skill he'd acquired while being a radio operator was listening to those around him while not being acknowledged. The flyspeck on the wall thing again. It meant he'd heard more than he'd ever let on and more than he wanted to. And every hint of conversation he'd heard recently had convinced him that the time was almost there for the walls to come down on De Lancourt and his faux-benevolent organisation of damaged war veterans, and for himself to be long gone before that happened. And if he'd needed any convincing of that, it was the threat he'd just heard from De Lancourt: *make a mistake and you will not survive.*

Bruno took one of the cars De Lancourt kept in a garage at the rear of the property and drove into Amiens. The black Peugeot 403 was a few years old and, like most cars of its age, scarred and inconspicuous enough to pass unnoticed. He parked along the street from where he could watch the commissariat. Sooner or later Rocco would turn up there; all he had to do was be patient and wait.

Too many people who had never done surveillance work thought you simply had to go out and look for your target. In reality it made sense to wait for them to arrive at their home, their work or their favoured eating places. Most people were creatures of habit governed by a daily activity that changed little. It made them easy to watch and follow. All he had to do with Rocco was build a picture of his habits. He had the workplace; all he needed now was a home address and the rest would fall into place.

Chasing after the big detective unnecessarily just so he could tell De Lancourt he'd made visual contact was a waste of effort and far too risky. He knew his own strengths but a policeman of Rocco's experience would likely possess the kind of antennae Bruno knew he had not encountered before. Sooner or later he'd be spotted.

In any case, Rocco knew what he looked like so he'd have to be doubly careful. Having seen the imposing figure up close at Les Cyprès had been enough to give him the shivers, and he had no wish to see him from the inside of a cell.

Bruno made a tour of the area on foot around the station, noting a café where the cops congregated during what must be shift breaks, and the rear car park of the station itself, which was jammed with vehicles and equipment. Safe to say that Rocco probably wouldn't find a space there, confirming that the front would be the best place to keep watch. He even followed a couple of men in plain clothes who had the definite brand of cop about them. It gave him a chance to settle into the routine of seeing without being seen and using a variety of moves to keep his profile low while not losing sight of those he was observing.

Just over ninety minutes after receiving the call from De Lancourt, as he finished another tour to stretch his legs, he spotted Rocco heading along the street to the station. Big and confident, the man's profile in the long, dark coat was a perfect giveaway, especially in this weather. Maybe Rocco had ice in his veins and didn't notice the heat. But at least it was going to make Bruno's job easier than he'd thought.

Bruno watched Rocco enter the building, then turned and walked to the Peugeot to wait for him to reappear. This was the boring part of the job, the part with little risk and lots of time to think; the part he loved most.

–

Bruno didn't have to be watching too closely for Rocco when he emerged from the station's front entrance some time later; the tall figure was tough to miss, even from a hundred metres away down the street. He got ready to turn on the ignition, certain Rocco wouldn't see him at this distance, and waited to see which way the inspector would turn. He glanced at his watch; it was late in the afternoon and quite possibly home time. He'd already covered that eventuality by bringing sandwiches and water with him from Les Cyprès. Wherever Rocco went, whether to his home or elsewhere, it would likely turn into an all-night vigil and he wasn't going to give De Lancourt or anyone else the opportunity to criticise his performance for losing sight of his target.

Bruno felt a chill in his gut as Rocco turned out of the entrance to the station and walked towards him. This was something he hadn't counted on; he'd figured Rocco would have left his car in one of the side streets behind the station, as the yard was full. If Rocco decided to walk past him right here, there was no way the big cop wouldn't smell his presence. He slid down in his seat, peering through the spokes of the steering wheel over the dashboard. A hundred metres, then eighty, then sixty; another twenty and there was no way Rocco could miss him.

Then Rocco turned down the next street by a bureau de change.

Bruno felt a surge of relief and started the car. By car or on foot? Always a difficult decision in the first stages of a surveillance. If he followed on foot and Rocco got into his car and took off, there was every chance he would lose him. End of mission. End of his life, too, probably.

On the other hand, he was in a vehicle that was no different to so many others in this town, and there was no reason why Rocco should spot him. By car it was.

Slipping the car into gear, he drifted along the street, turning right where Rocco had gone. The big detective was just arriving at another turning on his right. Bruno stopped just short and hopped out, edging close to the corner building until he could peer round. Rocco was climbing into a dark blue saloon facing this way. He scurried back to his car and jumped in, waiting until Rocco's car appeared and drove on by. Then he settled in behind it, careful to keep his distance and place at least two vehicles between them.

While he drove, he found his thoughts turning to the last question Rocco had asked him about what lay in the trees at Les Cyprès. It had been unsettling at the time if only because he didn't even like thinking about it in case the big cop was able to see his thoughts written clearly on his face. It was true what he'd told Rocco; that he'd only been in the wood once. He'd been sent to help clear out some old logs for the fire several months ago.

The sombre surroundings had been instantly scary, reminding him of another wood a long way from here when he'd been a kid. Placed in an orphanage after his mother died and his father disappeared, he'd been small and skinny as a whippet, a natural target for the older kids who needed someone on whom they could vent their various frustrations. Escaping one day, he'd found a thick belt of trees not far from the orphanage. It had proved to be a mixed blessing; while offering him solitude and safety away from the bullies, it had also been a place of nightmares to an over-active imagination. Dark and chill, even in hot weather, he'd hated and loved it at the same time, until it was time to leave the orphanage and he'd been jettisoned out into the world, eventually winding up in the army.

The difference between that wooded area and the one at Les Cyprès was the latter's underlying sense of brooding history and menace. There were the ancient trenches underfoot from the Great War, and the solid, squat shape of a bunker, covered in creepers and dark green, almost black with a coating of mould. He hadn't mentioned the bunker to Rocco in case he demanded to be taken there. He didn't need to be told how a cop would think; Rocco would want to know if Koutcheff was likely to be hiding inside.

He forced himself to focus on following Rocco and not to dwell on the fears haunting him. Koutcheff was indeed in the woods, being supplied with food and water from the main house. That made the mad bastard too close for comfort in Bruno's opinion. Worse still, if Rocco did go searching among the trees, Koutcheff and the others would automatically pin the blame on him as the likely culprit. He resolved not to say anything. If Rocco did get to the bunker, so be it; he'd have to do it without his help.

Maybe he'd keep that piece of information in his pocket for now.

Thirty minutes later he was winding through a succession of quiet, twisting lanes in open countryside, with little or no other traffic. He was forced to slow and drop back as much as he dared before speeding up, playing chicken and hoping not to find Rocco waiting for him around the next bend. The stop-start tactics raised a fresh wave of doubts about the wisdom of what he was doing, until he found himself entering the village of Poissons-les-Marais. He passed several small houses, a ruined water mill and a café, before entering the village square. This housed a single shop, the entrance to a small school and a church with a brooding sense of menace. He stopped and cast around and saw Rocco's car down a side lane a couple of hundred metres ahead, its brake lights flaring before it turned left and disappeared.

Bruno pulled into the side of the square, his thoughts racing. What would he do if Rocco spotted him? More to the point, what would Rocco do? He swallowed hard and turned off the engine. Going anywhere near where Rocco had turned would be foolhardy. He left the car and walked across the square past the church, climbing a slope towards some trees at the top of a hill. A narrow view between two houses gave him a bird's-eye view of the street where Rocco had stopped, and he could just see the rear of the car in the garden of a house at the far end.

It was good enough. He turned and walked back into the square and back along the road until he reached the café. He went in and ordered a *canon* of red wine to stiffen his nerves, then used the phone in the back. As he'd expected, Raphael Debac answered the phone.

'Well, if it isn't the little sneak, doing what he does best,' said Debac, openly contemptuous. 'Who are you snitching on now, Dujols?'

'I've followed Rocco to a village called Poisson-les-Marais,' said Bruno, ignoring the taunts. 'I'm going to stay on him to see where he goes next. Tell the boss – if you can remember that much.' It was a silly bit of bravado but he was past caring. If he never had to go back to Les Cyprès he'd be a happy man. He disconnected before Debac could make another cutting remark. He'd deal with the fall-out later.

Bruno returned to the car and drove down the lane. It was all or nothing. Acting perfectly normal while in pursuit of a target was the safest tactic. It was trying to pretend you weren't there that was most likely to give you away.

He passed two houses, neat and red-bricked. Then an enclosed farmyard behind large wooden gates and a succession of cow pats on the road outside. He glimpsed a manure heap inside, gently steaming and being picked over by chickens. Then two barns filled with straw bales and another house, this one small and neat with a busy vegetable garden being tended by an elderly woman with grey hair, and finally an elegant chalet-type structure behind a sheet-metal gate and a line of tall iron railings.

And Rocco, just stepping out of the front door with a large plastic water jug.

Bruno ducked his head and drove on by, trying to picture the cop doing housework. De Lancourt hadn't mentioned whether Rocco was married so he took it that he was single.

Driving out of the village, he passed a succession of fields on either side, empty of crops but one or two containing grazing cows, distant and tiny, like toys. He saw a track to one side and stopped before reversing in.

Bruno sat there for several minutes with the engine running, unsure of the next move. He was dismayed to find a taste of acidity rising in his gut and flooding his mouth. He'd experienced this before on some surveillance missions whenever he'd got too close to a target. Among those who'd known what he did there was, he'd realised, a kind of acceptance. For them, weapons and action were what they knew and understood, going in hot with the blood pounding in their veins and enjoying the thrill and the smell of gunfire. But the idea of following a man or a group on foot, as he had done many times, was an alien concept to them.

Bruno found it easy; you could blend in using doorways, crowds, crossing the street or even overtaking your quarry on the opposite side and getting ahead of them. Nobody expected to be followed from the front.

But this was something else: driving a car in open country and with your target an experienced police detective was something he hadn't reckoned on. As if his body recognised that, he felt a surge in his stomach and pushed the door open, vomiting on the track.

Bruno grabbed the bottle of water he'd brought with him and rinsed the vile taste from his mouth. Then he turned and looked back, half expecting Rocco to be standing behind the car. But there was nothing to see save for a few trees, the rolling fields and a scattering of disinterested cows.

Chapter Thirty-Eight

Rocco was getting itchy feet. His head was full of the discussion with the Ministry men and, with nothing to be accomplished before morning, he had to find a way to overcome the annoyance at their attitude and find some calm. He thought about ringing Eliane; that would calm him down, unless he was reading too much into their recent contact and was about to make a prize *couillon* of himself. Maybe it was better to drive over there instead. If he ran out of courage on the way and turned back, at least it would help pass some time.

He took a walk around the garden first, working on the kind of things he might say to explain why he was there. Just happened to be in the neighbourhood? Not clever and totally lame. Enjoyed our meal and wanted to deliver a return invitation? Also lame – that's what telephones were for. Loved your garden and wanted to see it again? A blatant fabrication, which might make her wonder whether he was really interested. Or not. She'd probably laugh at him? He doubted it. Hoped not.

Rocco stopped alongside the fence bordering his garden and the orchard next door, breathing in the warm air. The fruit trees were buzzing with insects, the branches laden with a variety of apples, pears and cherries, and he reflected that this really was some kind of paradise. He had no idea who owned the orchard and had never seen signs of anyone gaining access through the sagging and rusty wrought-iron gate from the road. Maybe Mme Denis would know.

Stepping over the fence, he walked between the trees, his feet raising a pleasant swishing sound in the long grass. A few early fallers were lying on the floor, and he had to wave away some wasps rising up to greet him, fat and lazy from gorging themselves on the bruised and sugary summer fruit.

A flash of light caught his eye. He stopped. The sun, flaring off something further down the lane. He moved closer to the far side of the orchard and saw the outline of a car parked in the entrance to a field. There was nothing there and he doubted any tourists in the area would have discovered it unless by accident.

The sight of the car in such an unlikely spot jerked him back to the situation in hand.

He'd become vaguely aware of a black Peugeot on his way out of Amiens, just another car on the road, ordinary and mundane like a hundred others. He'd noticed it again as he headed towards Poissons. The road to the village was long and twisty and didn't lead anywhere particularly strategic, which meant it was quiet enough for him to spot and dismiss any vehicle that looked vaguely familiar, or one not obeying the rules of the road. That left only a stranger, which was always of interest.

After a few kilometres, when he'd diverted deliberately off the route home and joined up with another road towards Poissons, it was clear the car wasn't there by accident. He'd also caught a view of the driver's profile in his rear-view mirror: a single occupant following him.

But why? And who?

Moments later he'd lost sight of the car after passing a junction, and had put it out of his mind. These two cases were getting to him, he was sure, and he was starting to see ghosts where there were none. Then, as he arrived in Poissons and turned in to his gate, he'd seen the nose of the Peugeot appear at the top of the lane off the village square. He'd parked the car and gone inside, grabbed a large plastic water jug and gone back outside to the water pump just as the car drove by. It was a bad angle for a clear view of the driver, but he had a feeling he'd seen the man before. If he ran it through his brain long enough, he'd have a face and possibly a name.

But right now he was feeling impatient. He hopped over the fence at the far side of the orchard and made his way across the adjacent field. It was cooler out here away from the trees, and he welcomed the fresh breeze on his skin. He'd never been a fan of walking when he didn't need to, but he was finding this exercise rather pleasant. Hopefully he wouldn't live to regret it when he got closer to the mystery car.

Rather than taking a direct path towards the vehicle, he swung wide and approached it from the side. He could see the driver's profile more clearly now and realised he did know him.

It was Bruno Dujols, De Lancourt's... whatever he was, who passed on his boss's instructions to the other men.

Rocco stepped over the wire fence and was right alongside the car before Dujols noticed his presence. When he did, he sat up as if he'd been scalded and reached for the ignition.

Rocco drew his gun and pointed it at him, shaking his head. He motioned for Dujols to get out of the car.

Dujols climbed out, looking terrified. It was quite a change from when they'd talked at Les Cyprès and Rocco wondered what had brought this on. It wasn't unknown for informers in the criminal world to be full of bluster when surrounded by their colleagues, but to change dramatically when they switched sides, as if suddenly conscious of the reality of what they'd done. Being a tough guy with your fellow criminals one second, then turning *mouchard* – informer – was a whole different exercise when you knew you'd become a target for those same fellows.

Dujols confirmed it without being asked. 'I need protection,' he said, his voice shaking. 'Koutcheff will kill me if I finds out I've talked to you. And the others will want to get in De Lancourt's good books by helping him. You have to get me away from this area before they come looking.'

'That depends on what you are prepared to tell me,' Rocco said. 'A quid pro quo is what they call it.'

'Quid what?'

'You do me a favour and I'll see what can be arranged.'

'Yes… all right. What do you want to know? You realise, don't you, that I'm just a cog in the machinery – a nothing. I do what I'm told, nothing more.'

'Yes, I've heard that argument before. So busy following orders you had no free will to think for yourself.' He paused, then said, 'Why are you following me?'

A shrug. 'I was told to.'

'By De Lancourt?'

'Yes.'

'Why?'

'He wants to know more about you.'

Rocco nodded. Know your enemy. If there was one thing a good lawyer – or a bad one, if it came to that

– would always do, it would be to research the opposition. Going into an adversarial situation was just as vital with a legal argument as it was a physical one.

The only way in which it differed was that following De Lancourt's threats in Paris, this was no war of words.

'Fair enough. Here's one thing you can tell me: where is Georges Koutcheff?'

Dujols' eyes went wide. 'I don't know – seriously. He's still in the area but nobody knows where exactly.'

'What about the woods behind the house?'

'Maybe. I mean, I don't know for sure… but probably, yes. If De Lancourt knows anything, he's not saying.'

Rocco had a thought. 'What about the wine cellar?'

'What about it?'

'Is that all it is?'

Bruno blinked. 'Yes. I mean, it wasn't at one time, years ago. It was a cell. It's even got hooks in the walls where the beds used to be. De Lancourt says they used to put troublesome patients down there and forget them if they kicked off too much.' He shivered. 'Creepy place it is – I've been down a few times to get bottles when he's told me, but it makes me feel claustrophobic.'

'Could someone stay down there for long?'

'Like Koutcheff, you mean? Maybe, if he had to. But I wouldn't bet on it.'

'Why not?'

'Because Koutcheff's an animal; he likes to be out in the open and he'd never agree to being locked down there. He'd need a way out and that place doesn't have one.'

It didn't chime exactly with Koutcheff's manner in the police cell when Rocco had talked to him, but that was probably because the former soldier had known that sooner or later his boss would get him out. Maybe he didn't see being confined inside the house quite the same way.

'De Lancourt relies a lot on Koutcheff, doesn't he?'

'I suppose so. It goes both ways.'

'What do you mean?'

'They go back a long way. Koutcheff knows things about him... things De Lancourt wouldn't want known to the public... or the law. If Koutcheff started blabbing, De Lancourt would be for the chop, I reckon.'

'What sort of things?'

'Pardon?'

'What sort of things does Koutcheff know? Give me an example.'

Dujols took a deep breath like a diver about to go off the high board. 'I know they were involved in Morocco together. One of the others mentioned that they'd known each other back then, like it was a big secret. I didn't take much notice because I didn't care what they'd done; it was of no consequence. Then one day I took a call for De Lancourt. It was a man calling from Casablanca.'

'Did he say that?'

'Yes. He gave me the number in case De Lancourt had to call him back. The caller didn't give a name but told me he knew Koutcheff from way back and needed to talk to him urgently. I told him to wait because I knew the boss wasn't far away. He took the call, and when Koutcheff came in I heard him yelling at him that it was bad news and everything would be coming out in the open. De Lancourt was furious. He said they both had an interest in doing something about it and to stop them coming.'

'Stop who?'

'They didn't say. I think they remembered I was nearby and left the room.' He gave a fleeting smile tinged with bitterness. 'Most of the time they don't even notice I'm around. They think I'm a waste of space as a soldier compared to the others, so not worth worrying about. Like I'm invisible.'

Think yourself lucky, Rocco wanted to tell him. 'Go on.'

'Later on I was in the office next door when they started arguing about the call. That's when I heard a name mentioned. It wasn't very clear but I got most of it.'

'Which was?' Rocco wanted to press him but he knew getting this kind of inside information, if it was to come to anything, was vital. Pushing Bruno too hard might make him clam up altogether.

'It was something like Benhamel... Benhamet. Like that. I'm sorry – they weren't talking very loud. That was all I got. After that, every time I saw Koutcheff he gave me the evil eye like I'd done something wrong. I think he was wondering how much I'd heard.'

Benhamid. It had to be. Rocco let out a long breath. It brought together two events that had seemed uncon- nected. Now they were not.

'There's another thing.' Bruno's eyes were alight, as if he'd recalled something else he needed to get off his chest. 'The two older men, Garbus and Touati, who left a few days ago – the ones they said didn't fit in?'

'What about them?'

'I got on with them fine, unlike the other men and Koutcheff. Aziz Touati was Algerian. He was a nice guy; he'd served with the French military for years. He told me one day not long before they left that he'd been based in the same region of Algeria as Koutcheff, close to the border with Morocco. He said word was that Koutcheff headed up a unit involved in running cross-border raids but it was something they weren't supposed to talk about. Big secret stuff, apparently.'

Rocco had a sudden thought. He took out the photo of the man seen watching Micheline Jeunet and showed it to Bruno. 'Is this Touati?' The photo wasn't perfect but at a glance the man could have been Algerian. He was dark enough.

'No.' Bruno shook his head. 'That's Mavrouk. They called him Tony. Where did you get that?'

'It doesn't matter. Is he at the house now?'

'He was, but that was a while back. I think Koutcheff keeps in touch with him and a couple of others. They share information about jobs needing ex-military personnel, especially in the mercenary sector.'

That was a worry. If Koutcheff or De Lancourt had reserves they could call on, it would increase the risk of tying up this business safely. Men who moved into the mercenary field as paid guns weren't always selective about the jobs they took on, and were likely to meet force with force, even if it came from the police.

'If Koutcheff wanted a back-up driver, who would he choose?' Rocco was thinking about the evening Pouillot was shot. M. Ledran thought he'd seen another man in the car.

'Debac, most probably. They've always been thick and he likes to think he's tough. Why?'

'No matter,' he said, putting the thought aside. 'Getting back to the raids, do you know what they were for?'

'They were chasing insurgents who'd crossed the border into Morocco. Us going over there was against international law but I know the high command had got fed up with insurgents using the border rules for their own ends and being out of range of retribution.' He shrugged.

'To be honest I couldn't see anything wrong with it. The insurgents had killed some men I'd known and a fair number of civilians in the process, especially in Algeria, so I reckoned they had it coming. Getting away with it by skipping across the border wasn't right.'

'How big were these units?'

'Four-man groups, usually. They were fast-moving and hard to track. They knew how to blend in. When they came back they didn't talk to anyone about what they'd been doing so it was obvious they were under strict orders. But Aziz told me he'd seen Koutcheff going off by himself more than once. He said he was the only one he ever saw do that, and he was always fully armed but dressed as a local. He'd be gone for a day or two, then return just as quick.'

'What do you think he was doing over there?'

'I don't know. But Aziz said he always came back looking like one of those big game hunters in Africa, all puffed up and excited as if he'd been in action. He'd get roaring drunk and smoke kif and stay in his quarters, throwing a knife at a dartboard, over and over, Aziz reckoned. The other men used to avoid him like he'd got leprosy until he calmed down. I heard he'd gone crazy once after coming back across the border and done something pretty bad, but it was covered up by the senior officers.'

'Are you prepared to write all this down? Make a statement for the record?'

Bruno's eyes got larger. 'Why?'

'He's a killer. We think he shot a police officer in Amiens and we know he put another one in hospital… and from what you're saying he's done it before. We need to stop him before he kills someone else.'

Bruno swallowed, eyes darting about as if Koutcheff might suddenly appear out of the long grass. 'I don't know… I'd have to think about that. Like I said, I need protection.'

'We can do that. But you have to make a statement first.'

'What, now? That will take too long – going to Amiens and back. Someone might see me.'

'Fine. There's a colleague of mine in the village who can act as a witness. You put down what you know in writing and we'll look at finding somewhere for you to stay. As soon as this is sorted out, we'll make you disappear.'

Bruno's eyes went wide, and Rocco gave him a grim smile. 'Don't worry – that doesn't mean the same in police circles.'

'Why can't it happen now?' Bruno's voice had developed a tremor, as if the full import of what he was doing had finally caught up with him.

'Because if they find out today that you've gone missing, they'll start hiding things. It's better to keep them guessing for a day or two.'

Bruno nodded slowly as if considering the implications. Then he said, 'All right. But only for two days. You have to promise me.'

'Done.' Rocco walked to the passenger door and got in. 'Drive. I'll give you directions, then you can go about your business.'

Bruno climbed behind the wheel, looking as if he'd like to change his mind. 'What do I tell De Lancourt? He'll want to know exactly where I've been… where you've been.'

'Tell him you sat on my tail all day until I left the station, then lost me out in the countryside. I drive fast and know the road. Keep it simple.' He gave Bruno a searching look. 'Unless you've already told him.'

'I have. Sorry.'

Rocco gestured for Bruno to get going before the man crumpled and lost his nerve. 'Forget it. Let's do this. Back into the village and turn left.'

Chapter Thirty-Nine

Three minutes later they arrived outside Claude's house at the opposite end of the village. Claude stepped out to greet them, alerted by the sound of the car engine. 'Surprise visit?' he said, and eyed Bruno with one eyebrow raised. If he recognised him from Les Cyprès, he didn't say so.

Rocco explained what he wanted, and Claude found a large memo pad and pen, and made coffee while Rocco sat Bruno down and told him to get writing.

It didn't take long. Bruno proved to be a fluid writer and covered everything he'd related to Rocco. Rocco read it twice, then Claude witnessed and signed it as having been provided without duress.

'Where do I go now?' Bruno asked, once it was done. 'I don't know anywhere round here where I'd be safe.'

Rocco had been thinking about that. Bruno's nerve was already crumbling at the idea of returning to join his colleagues, and he doubted the man would be able to cover the fact for long that he was seriously on edge. Sooner or later he'd crack, and with De Lancourt being the one person at the house most versed in spotting guilty men, that might come far too soon.

Rocco made a call to Massin and explained what he'd done. Massin was reluctant at first, wary that Rocco had not followed strict protocol in gaining the statement at the station. But Rocco pointed out the danger of that; if Koutcheff had managed to arrange his escape from police custody, it wouldn't be impossible for him to get someone inside to silence Bruno Dujols for good.

'I'm sending Godard and one of his men,' Massin said finally. 'In the meantime, I'll arrange with Lille station to hold him in a secure place pending our next move.'

Rocco breathed a sigh of relief. It was a potential hurdle cleared. If Bruno valued his life as much as he appeared to, he wouldn't give a jot about a departure from police protocol as long as he survived to tell his story.

'Godard's on his way,' Rocco told Claude, then he turned to Bruno. 'While we're waiting, I've a couple of questions.'

'What sort of questions? Isn't this statement enough?'

'Not quite. You mentioned that some of the men who left would come back if asked. Why would they do that?' He'd been thinking about it on the way here and it puzzled him. If De Lancourt really was helping ex-military men with problems, he'd have thought most of them, once out in the wider world, would want to stay out and get on with their lives.

'Because some of them think they owe him,' Bruno replied shortly. 'Most of them go there not knowing what to expect, so they don't stay on long. It's like a temporary posting in the military: come in, keep your nose clean and get on with whatever you're told to do, then move on. It's not exactly a health clinic. But some think they owe him and would come if called.'

'Is that how you feel?'

Bruno pulled a face. 'Not a chance. He knew how Koutcheff and the others treated me and didn't give a damn. As far as I'm concerned, I don't owe him a thing.

He took me on to do a specific job, which was communications. He'd tell me what he wanted the men to do and I'd pass on the orders, take messages and keep records. That's it.'

'What kind of records?'

Bruno gave a knowing smile. 'Nothing you could use. Mostly details about the men who came through there, their tasks around the place and how well they did. He said it was so they had something to show future employers, but we all suspected it was so he had something on us he could use if he needed it.'

'Like military records?'

'Especially those. He knew someone in the records office. Most of the men lied a bit about their past, especially if they'd done time in the stockade. But De Lancourt seemed to know all that.'

The lawyer in him again, Rocco thought. *Get as much detail as you can because you never knew when you might put it to good use.*

'Why would he need it?'

'Security. He'd had some trouble with clients in the past... like serious criminals who'd got heavier sentences than he'd promised and didn't like it. He'd had threats against his life.'

'That's not unusual,' said Rocco with feeling. It was part of the job. He'd received threats himself more than once for putting gang members away. It usually came to nothing; a product of resentment and embarrassment tinged with a heavy dose of gutter bravado. But every now and then someone would get serious and try to follow through with action.

'I get it. But I heard the others talking about it. They said the really heavy threats came from serious gang members. If it got too much, he'd send out Koutcheff and a couple of others to warn them off. It usually worked.'

Rocco could believe it. Most gang members were the macho types who considered themselves the tough guys on the block… until they met up with ex-military men who weren't afraid to use their skills and weaponry to put them in their place.

Claude made more coffee and Rocco allowed Bruno a break. He'd probably got as much from the man as he could for now.

'Is that it?' Bruno asked. 'When does this security escort arrive?'

'Soon,' Claude told him. 'What are you going to do when this is all over?'

Bruno shrugged. 'Get as far away from here as I can, I reckon. It's time for me to get a new posting and move on.' He paused. 'What about the car? If it doesn't go back, they'll know I've skipped out.'

'I'll keep it here for a day or two,' Claude said. 'By then I doubt they'll be worrying about it.'

–

'You've been busy,' Mme Denis called over her front fence as Rocco approached his front gate. He'd walked back through the village after turning Bruno over to the care of Sergeant Godard and a uniformed guard. They were heading immediately to Lille and a place of safety arranged by Massin.

'I've no idea what you mean,' he said easily.

'Criminals follow you home now to get arrested, do they? That's a neat trick.' She chuckled at her own wit and waved a hand to show she was teasing.

Rocco turned and walked over to the fence, where he stooped and gave her a kiss on the cheek. She smelled of baking and apples. Something nice heading his way, he had no doubt.

The old lady actually blushed and patted him on the shoulder. 'What was that for? It's not my birthday.'

'I know,' he replied with a smile. 'Call it one neighbour pleased to see another one.' He meant it; it was almost a relief to speak to her again, a brief shared moment with a refreshingly normal person in what was turning out to be a hectic period. 'You've been keeping me under observation.'

'I haven't got much else to do here – and you do bring a certain level of excitement to this place. Do you need anything to eat?'

Rocco shook his head. 'No, thank you. Just sleep.' He waved a hand in the direction of the village. 'I'd appreciate what you saw not hitting the grapevine yet. That man's life could be in danger.'

'Of course. My word on it. Is it to do with the shooting near Caix?'

'There's a connection – but not him directly. A side issue.'

Mme Denis smiled and disappeared indoors, and he shook his head at her ability to not miss a trick about his movements. It would be all over the village as soon as he gave her the nod that it no longer mattered. For now, though, he trusted her implicitly not to talk about it.

Chapter Forty

The duty despatch officer intercepted Rocco as he entered the station the next morning. 'I've just taken a report of a burned-out car about three kilometres from Caix,' he said briskly. 'It's on an abandoned farm some way off the road. The locals thought it was rubbish burning so didn't bother reporting it until now. But someone eventually went and checked and found the remains of the vehicle. After the shooting over that way, they figured it might be connected.'

'They could be right,' Rocco told him, and took the message slip with the details. Abandoning wrecked cars wasn't so unusual, especially if there was no easy way of disposing of them properly. But the location of this one so close to the shooting was too much of a coincidence to ignore. He spotted Desmoulins and called him over, and three minutes later they were on their way towards Caix.

'What are you expecting to find?' Desmoulins asked.

'Anything. Something connected to the shooting would be good. I can't think how this would be linked but you never know.'

When they arrived at the farm, they found a tumble-down single-storey building with a caved-in roof and an attached barn and small cowshed. A smell of burnt metal and rubber was hanging in the air, but any smoke had long dissipated.

A man in large boots and a set of *bleu de travail* was waiting for them in the yard at the rear of the buildings, staring morosely at the remains of what had once been a car. The blackened shell and twisted metal made the model difficult to identify. With the tyres gone and the wheels buckled, the body had slumped to the ground with some of the side panels hanging loose like the broken wings of a large, exhausted bird.

'You found this, Monsieur…?' said Rocco, and shook the man's hand. It was like rubbing sandpaper, the strong fingers fashioned by years of hard labouring in the fields.

'Baujat,' the man said. 'Arthur Baujat.' He gestured to a rise in the land on the other side of the road. 'I farm just over there. I can't see this place from there but I did see the smoke about three days ago, maybe four, and didn't think much of it. People use this place to get rid of things they don't want. If they don't burn it, they dump it, like that stuff.' He nodded at various bits of rubbish lying around, from broken household implements to worn-out carts, car tyres and ancient mattresses, some of it clearly years old and crusted with moss. 'It was only when I was on my way past earlier that I thought to take a look and found this mess.' He hawked and spat behind him. 'Sorry, Officer – got a chest infection. Bloody thing won't go away.'

'It was good of you to report it, M. Baujat,' said Rocco. 'I suppose you wouldn't have seen anyone hanging around here three or four days ago?'

'No, sorry. I don't get over this way too often. I'm too busy on the farm. Who would do such a thing, eh? There's wrecker's yard not far away – why couldn't they take it there?' He looked about to spit again but stopped himself. 'I can't even see what kind of car it used to be.'

'Looks like a Renault,' said Desmoulins. He bent and pulled at one of the wings, which came away in his hands. The metal was mostly blackened but one end had escaped the ravages of the flames and revealed traces of maroon paint. 'A Renault, definitely.' He bent and dragged his fingers through a layer of soft earth adjacent to the car, then sniffed them. 'Petrol. The soil's saturated. This was deliberate.'

Rocco asked Baujat, 'Do you know if anyone local owned a maroon Renault?'

The farmer shook his head. 'No. There aren't many cars around here. Mopeds, tractors or the bus is how most folk get around. If the car got this far it must have still been working, wouldn't you think?'

Rocco nodded. 'Good point.'

'Bloody criminal setting fire to it. Someone could have used it given the chance.'

Rocco thanked the farmer again for letting them know and the man clomped off, his big boots kicking up dirt.

Rocco did a tour of the car. The number plates were gone and the open boot revealed that nothing had escaped the flames. The spare wheel was now a blackened metal ring with a few traces of rubber that hadn't melted still clinging to the rim. He went to the driver's door. The steering wheel and column had suffered serious damage, and all traces of the plastic inside panels and seat padding were little more than gnarled remnants on the floor and adhering to their metal supports.

Desmoulins tipped up the remains of the passenger seat and shook his head. 'If there was anything here, it's gone. Maybe it had nothing to do with the shooting after all...' He stopped and peered down at the floor of the car, which was mostly burned out, leaving a large hole. 'Hang on.' He reached down into the space beneath the car and brought up a small cylinder clasped between his thumb and forefinger.

It was a spent cartridge.

'A twenty-two calibre,' said Rocco. 'Well spotted. Maybe our luck has changed. We'll get it back to Rizzotti after we finish here.' He took a tour around the yard, peering behind the piles of rubbish and into the cow shed in case anything had been thrown there. But it was bare of anything recent, a mess of mud and creeping vegetation with no signs of footprints to show anyone had come this way.

Chapter Forty-One

Rocco was going through his notes making sure he hadn't forgotten anything when he saw a familiar portly figure enter the building and make his way across the office. The duty officer was hot on his heels and it was clear the lawyer had slipped past the front desk without making himself known.

Rocco signalled to the officer that it was all right to let him go, and walked over to an interview room with Toussaint following. He closed the door behind him and pointed to a chair.

'Something wrong?' he asked. He hadn't forgotten the lawyer's unhelpful attitude at their first and so far only meeting, and wasn't about to put up with a repetition. However, he was surprised to see the man looking shifty, even concerned, with beads of perspiration on his face that might not have been from the warm day outside.

Toussaint sat heavily and dragged out a handkerchief to wipe his brow. 'Thank you, Inspector,' he said, his eyes going everywhere but Rocco's face. 'I appreciate you seeing me – I should have called for an appointment.'

Rocco studied him, trying to discern any trace of guile. It was an abrupt change of attitude and he wondered what the lawyer was up to. 'No problem,' he said heavily. 'I am, as you pointed out, a public servant.' Toussaint blinked and went red at the reminder, but said nothing. 'So how can I help?'

'It's my client – Koutcheff. I fear I may have been the victim of over-enthusiasm in dealing with his case. I would like to clear the air a little... and apologise for any ill-feeling.'

'Go on.'

'I've been in receipt of certain information during the last few days, information that leads me to think that I may have been misled on certain issues surrounding M. Koutcheff and his... activities.'

Rocco said nothing, merely lifted his eyebrows. If Toussaint was here to say something, he had to allow him to lead the way. The last thing he needed was a tricky lawyer suggesting that the police had in some way persuaded him to say something that might implicate his client.

'I was asked to take on this case,' Toussaint continued, wiping his face, 'and yes, I admit I was keen to do so, bearing in mind my recent arrival here in the region. It seemed a useful start to establishing my practice and getting a foot in the door, so to speak.' He paused for a moment, and when Rocco remained silent, said, 'Since then I've heard certain things that have left me uncomfortable about the exact nature of Koutcheff's character and his... connections.'

'Connections?'

'His employer. You know who I'm referring to.'

'I'd like to hear you say it.'

'Guy De Lancourt. It was he who asked me to take on the case via an associate chamber in Paris. They supplied a legal representative, Louis Khoury, to act as a liaison.'

'You mean as a go-between?'

Toussaint pulled a face. 'That's not a term I like but I suppose it's a more accurate description of the arrangement. It seemed perfectly normal – an arrangement that is commonplace.'

'What didn't you like about it?'

'Inspector, I've worked very hard to establish myself. I have what some have described as a certain combative nature, I know that. But the rough and tumble of legal work sometimes calls for it, otherwise it's very simple to find oneself under a steamroller from powerful or influential opponents and clients. However, it became very clear to me that I was merely a link in a chain and that I have been pressured, even lied to about the precise nature of Koutcheff's activities here and elsewhere.'

'Elsewhere?'

'There is a grapevine in the legal profession, Inspector, just as there is in the police. Colleagues hear things and pass them on.' He lifted a hand, adding quickly, 'There's nothing that would interfere with the rule of law, I assure you. Merely information that might protect a colleague from becoming… compromised against their better nature, shall we say.'

'I understand.' He wasn't sure yet whether Toussaint had a better nature but he was ready to be proved wrong. Whatever had driven the lawyer into coming here now was either fear, guilt or some kind of tactic destined to cause a problem further down the line. Hopefully, he wouldn't take too long to spit out whatever was driving him.

'May I ask, Inspector, is there any chance Koutcheff may be apprehended soon?'

Rocco hesitated. It was an odd question. 'There's every chance, yes. But there are no guarantees. As far as we know he's still in the area. Why do you ask?'

'Because instinct tells me the same thing – that he is still here, and I value my safety. That's why I'm here, Inspector. I have no proof that he was involved in the shooting of your uniformed colleague, but having talked to him before he disappeared, I have serious concerns about his mental health.'

'Did he threaten you? If so, you should have said.'

Toussaint shrugged. 'It was not a direct threat but the way he spoke left me feeling very uncomfortable. He is not a man with whom I would care to spend any more time. I'm sure you understand, having spoken to him yourself.' Toussaint gave the ghost of a smile as if eliciting a man-to-man sharing of information.

Rocco wasn't yet convinced that the lawyer didn't have a secondary agenda. 'He's a pussy cat,' he said dryly. 'There's something else bothering you. What is it?'

'I have decided to withdraw my representation of him.' The statement came in a rush, as if he'd been holding it in for a long time and had finally made the jump.

'Well, that's your choice. Why – and why now?'

'Because some comments I have heard over the past couple of days suggest to me that the key players in this matter have… certain history that does not bode well for them or anyone connected with them.'

'Such as?'

'There are strong suggestions, some that I understand appeared in the press some years ago but were possibly set aside by a higher authority, that Guy De Lancourt and Koutcheff were previously connected in relation to property issues in Morocco during the transition of that country to full independence.' He delved into a pocket and brought out a magazine, opening it out on the table.

The article featured was a virtual repeat of the details Rocco had discovered in Gérard Jeunet's file, with a few additional comments. Issued just twenty-four hours ago by a widely read satirical magazine, it pulled no punches in demanding answers from the government, the Interior Ministry and the military to what exactly had happened in Morocco, especially in relation to rumours about the threats against and disappearance of at least three French farmers in apparent land-grabs. It also questioned the establishment of the Commandos de Chasse unit in Algeria and its use in cross-border raids to hunt down insurgents, and rumoured connections between De Lancourt and a middle-management civil servant named Hafid Benhamid.

Jeunet, he thought. This had to have come from him. Had the dying man finally done the only thing left to him to torpedo De Lancourt's chances of gaining the distinction he so wished for? Surely there was no coming back from this for De Lancourt. On the other hand, there had been scandals before that had withered and died, and this might yet prove to be another one.

'Where did you get this?' he queried, without telling Toussaint that he'd already seen the details.

'A friend sent it to me. I'd mentioned the Koutcheff case and he rang me last night to tell me about this publication and suggested I should reconsider my involvement.' He gestured at the magazine with a sweep of his hand. 'There are those in my profession who would be prepared to take it on even knowing this background information, but I am not one of them. I do not have the resources to deal with the complexity of this kind of revelation adequately nor to fight off the results if they turn out to be true.' He shook his head. 'Cowardly of me, perhaps, and I know there are those who will condemn me for pulling out. But some fights can ruin an entire career.'

'Has anyone else spoken to you about this?'

'Not directly. But I gather from other sources in Paris that the story is gathering speed, even at high levels. There are also rumours that the Moroccan authorities have taken an interest in pursuing the case on their side and have serious questions to ask about the three dead men and why they were here.'

Too late, Rocco thought wryly. The Benhamids had been warned by someone in authority in Morocco that the hammer was about to come down. Given the most recent response from Pancaud and Goubier from the Interior Ministry, they were all diving for cover and wanted nothing to do with it for political reasons.

'You sure of all this?'

'I trust the source, yes. If there is a lid on this, I believe it's about to be lifted. Furthermore, I suspect De Lancourt must be feeling some heat because of his connection to Koutcheff at the time and their continued relationship. I will notify him today of my decision to stand down.' He placed his hands on the table and said, 'There's something else. The snuff.'

'I know. You gave it to him.'

'Yes... I— how did you know?' Toussaint looked stunned.

'You were one of only three people who could have passed it to him. Now you've just confirmed it. I also noticed a snuff tin in your wastebasket.'

'But that could have been dropped by a client.'

'True enough. But the shop two doors down the street from your office confirmed that you're a snuff user. It's called detective work. Now, who asked you to bring it in?' He leaned forward for added emphasis, and Toussaint folded.

'De Lancourt. He told me Koutcheff had an addiction to it. To me it was no worse than an addiction to tobacco, but without the danger of setting fire to anything, so I agreed.'

'Why didn't you say so at the beginning?'

'Because you mentioned heroin. I thought maybe it was and panicked. As I said before, I'm sorry for my forceful attitude to you at our first meeting. If there's any way I can make up for that...'

'Wait.' Rocco tore a page from his notebook and wrote down Bakri's name. 'This kid is working in conditions that will ruin his health. You might like to use your position to investigate whether it contravenes any regulations. I doubt it will pay much but you might make a few friends in the unions along the way. Don't tell anyone I told you – especially not Bakri himself. He's trying to stay out of trouble and I don't want him spooked into doing the wrong thing. I don't have an address but he hangs around near Koutcheff's flat.'

Toussaint took the slip of paper. 'Not a problem – I'll find him.' He gave a wry smile. 'So, Inspector tough-nut Rocco has a softer side. Don't worry, I won't tell anyone. They wouldn't believe me anyway.'

Rocco watched him go with mixed feelings. Toussaint was still a lawyer, and no doubt he would come across the man again in the course of the job here in Amiens. His decision not to continue representing Koutcheff was largely down to self-interest, but at least it showed he had some limits beyond which he would not go. Maybe this event might soften his hard-line approach to the police in the future.

Chapter Forty-Two

'Inspector Rocco?' An officer was waving a phone in the air. 'There's someone called Yannick on the phone, says he's found something you ought to see.'

Rocco took the phone. 'Yannick,' he said. 'What have you got?' He wasn't in the mood for wasting time on pointless exercises from someone whose brain was addled by too much strong liquor and who knew what else, but wasn't quite prepared for what followed next.

'You have to get round here, Inspector... quick as you can... only, I'm not hanging around for long and—'

'Whoa, slow down. What's the problem? Is Koutcheff back?'

'No, but he might be, who knows? It's just... I've found a gun. In the toilet.' Yannick was either scared out of his wits or drunk on excitement. His voice was pitched high with whatever was driving him. 'At least, I think it's a gun.'

'What do you mean, you think?' said Rocco. 'Don't answer that – stay right where you are and don't touch anything. I'm on my way.'

Rocco saw Desmoulins across the room and signalled for him to follow. He had no idea if this call was Yannick playing silly games or if he was so high on something he didn't know what he was doing. Either way, going into a situation without some forethought was a sure way of finding trouble.

'Where are we going?' said Desmoulins, grabbing his weapon. He'd learnt before that when Rocco said 'run', it wasn't a social call. He usually meant business.

'A kid at Koutcheff's flat says he's found a gun. I need you as back-up just in case.'

'Suits me.' Desmoulins grinned, and followed Rocco to his car. 'Anything to bring this business to a close.'

Rocco drove fast across town. Luckily, there wasn't a great deal of traffic to get in their way and they were soon pulling up in front of Koutcheff's place. The kids he'd seen before were hanging around, and he took that to be a possible good sign. If they'd seen Koutcheff they'd have followed their instincts for bad news and faded into the background.

Rocco led Desmoulins into the building, ignoring catcalls from the louder element among the youths, only drawing his service weapon once they were inside with the door closed. One glimpse of a gun and the news would be all over the neighbourhood in minutes. Next thing they'd know, the street would be crawling with onlookers and reporters looking for something exciting to talk about.

The building was deathly quiet, as if the very fabric of the structure was expecting them. Or maybe it knew what was about to happen. Rocco nodded Desmoulins towards a hall leading to the rear of the building, then signalled that he would go up and for Desmoulins to follow if it was clear. The stairs seemed to creak much louder than on his first visit, unless it was his imagination, and he varied his steps from closer to one wall or the other. It made no difference; as an alarm it was brilliant or hideous, depending on your perspective.

Reaching flat number three, he stepped to one side, then leaned across and knocked on the door. It flew open and Yannick was standing there in the same grubby vest but minus any kind of weapon. Instead, he had an old army backpack over his shoulder.

The man eyed Rocco's gun with a start and said, 'Inspector. Good job you're here. I was about to leave. I'm packed and ready to go but let me show you what I found first. Then I'm off, right?' He squeezed past Rocco, leaving behind an aroma of sweat, tobacco and something deeply unpleasant, and headed at a fast clip up the stairs. Rocco followed, waiting for the sound of a door opening or footsteps on the floorboards above. He didn't entirely trust this man to be able to tell which way was up, frankly, but it was worth a try.

Yannick turned again at the top and pointed to a door at the end of the landing. It was standing open and Rocco could see it was a toilet with the walls done out in a bilious covering of yellow tiles. Two other doors off the landing were open, and he motioned for Yannick to stay back. 'Wait,' he said softly, the hairs on the back of his neck prickling with tension.

Rocco stepped into one room, then the other. That's all they were: single rooms with the most basic facilities of a sink and a small cooker. One of the rooms was decked out in hideous shades of pink paper and curtains with a scarlet lampshade overhead, and smelled of a shocking perfume that could have stopped an elephant at fifty paces.

Both rooms were empty and looked as if their occupants had cleared out in a hurry. What little furniture there was resembled the few items in Koutcheff's flat, albeit cleaner, and the floors were carpeted. He said to

Yannick, 'You said they were occupied – a man and a woman. What happened?'

Yannick shrugged. 'You did, coming here. I think they heard from the kids downstairs that the cops were interested and took off.'

'Together?'

'Yes. The man looked after her – Coco – but I don't think they were married.'

'Did you say anything to them?'

'Me? No! Seriously... I didn't say a word.'

Rocco shook his head. He didn't believe him for a second. Yannick was the kind who drifted through life in a haze and probably didn't recall what he'd said five minutes ago because remembering didn't suit him. On the other hand, he'd remembered enough to ring the number at the station and ask for him by name.

'All right. Show me this find of yours.'

The toilet looked suitably repulsive and the smell was bad even from all the way back here. How the hell Coco had managed to conduct her kind of business with that in the air was a mystery.

'It's in there, Inspector,' Yannick said. 'I had to use it earlier because the one downstairs is blocked. I was looking for somewhere to hide some stuff and found a loose tile in the wall.' He motioned for Rocco to go ahead. 'Down at floor level on the right.'

'What "stuff"? And if you were leaving, why would you hide anything here?'

'Well, I wasn't going to leave just yet until I found somewhere else. But I needed to hide some... valuables while I was out looking, so I could stop those maggots outside ripping me off. Then I found... what I found, and decided it was time to get out. But I called you first. That was good, right? I did the right thing?' He was hopping from foot to foot as if desperate to use the toilet in front of him. 'Can I go now? Only I need to find a place to crash before tonight—'

'Stop talking,' Rocco said calmly, cutting off the babble in its tracks, 'and show me. Then you can disappear.'

Yannick dropped his backpack and stepped into the toilet. He grubbed around for a second at floor level and stood up, holding one of the tiles in his hand. Where it had once sat was now a square hole in the wall.

'Move,' Rocco said, and nudged him out of the way. If there was anything more lethal down there than dust and woodworm, he didn't want this idiot turning into Billy the Kid and coming up shooting.

The void revealed an assortment of cobwebs around the edges, but he could see there was something inside wrapped in a filthy towel. He put his hand in and felt the outline of the object. Damn. Yannick was right. A gun.

'How did you know it was a gun?' he asked him. 'Did you take it out or touch it?'

Yannick's eyes were bulging at the sight of the weapon. 'No, honest. I was going to, but the moment I felt it I knew what it was. I thought it best to leave it and call you. Is there a reward for reporting this?'

It sounded too genuine to be a trick. 'Maybe. But not right now.'

Yannick looked disappointed. 'Seriously? I could have sold that for a lot of cash. But I didn't.'

'That's very public-spirited of you. If there's a reward, you'll get it. Now get out of here. If you tell anybody about this, you'll be putting your life in danger. I suggest you find somewhere on the other side of town or further away, just in case you forget what I just said and develop

285

a loose lip. Koutcheff is not the sort of man you want looking for you, believe me.'

Yannick gave a sickly grin and picked up his bag. 'I promise. Won't say a word. Don't forget the reward, though, will you?'

'I won't.' Rocco leaned out through the door and called out to Desmoulins, 'One man coming down. Let him go.'

Desmoulins acknowledged the call and moments later Rocco heard the clatter of Yannick's footsteps going down the stairs followed by the slamming of the front door. He wasn't sure he'd been right to let the young man go, but he figured he was the kind of person who would stay where he knew the layout. If he had to find him again, he wouldn't have to look too hard.

As he bent to retrieve the object inside the hole, he heard Desmoulins sing out a warning as he came up to join him.

'Christ – who died up here?' the detective said, and clutched his nose.

'Humanity, mostly.'

Desmoulins eyed the bundle. 'Is that the gun?'

'Feels like it. Keep an eye out, will you? I don't want any surprises.'

Desmoulins nodded and stepped into the pink room, exclaiming in surprise at the décor. Rocco unwrapped the towel. Yannick had been telling the truth; the object inside was heavy and the shape told him instantly what it was. Peeling back the towel, he saw a gun stamped with the model, Unique, and the manufacturer's name, Manufacture D'Armes des Pyrénées.

It was a target pistol with an extra-long barrel and a raised foresight, and looked a fine precision-made piece of machinery kept in pristine condition. No surprise if it actually belonged to an army man like Koutcheff. It held a magazine but he decided to leave that for Rizzotti and the station's armourer to examine in detail. He sniffed the barrel to see if it had been fired recently but there was too much competition from the combined aroma of the toilet and the perfumed bedroom.

Rocco was about to say something to Desmoulins, who was standing in the nearest room by the front window overlooking the street, when the young detective swore softly.

'We've got company.'

Chapter Forty-Three

A car had pulled up outside, blocking the street. Three men jumped out. They were all dressed in leather jackets. It was Georges Koutcheff and two others.

Rocco recognised the tall man immediately but the other two were strangers. Then he took another look. One of them was the man Bruno had named as Tony Mavrouk, the man who'd been keeping close tabs on Micheline Jeunet. The third man was out of the same mould as Koutcheff: tall, fit-looking and hard-faced. All three were staring up at the windows and looked as if they had come prepared for trouble.

Rocco couldn't see any guns but the way they were standing, each with a hand inside their jackets, was enough.

'Koutcheff,' Rocco murmured. 'He's brought reinforcements.'

Damn Yannick, he thought. He'd sold them out, no doubt for the promise of a financial reward or his legs left intact.

Rocco checked up and down the street. If there was going to be trouble, he didn't want innocent people being caught up in any crossfire. It was quiet, but there were a few pedestrians about. The youths who'd been out there earlier had vanished, no doubt their instinct for trouble having warned them off. Or maybe Yannick had spread the word as he left; a parting gift.

Out of habit, Rocco checked the load of his service weapon and saw Desmoulins doing the same. 'We can't afford to be caught up here,' he said, and stepped away from the window towards the stairs. In fact, it would be better not to allow the men inside. The building structure was old and the inner walls paper-thin. Any gunfire would go all the way through, and once the men were in, he and Desmoulins would have no way out. 'With no rear exit, we might have to get creative.'

'How? There are no rear windows either,' Desmoulins told him. 'It's like the building was chopped in half.'

Rocco nodded. That made things a little difficult. It left the front as the only way out.

He was about to take the first step down the stairs when the sound of a soft whistle floated up from the ground floor followed by a voice calling his name.

'Inspector Rocco? It's me – Bakri.'

'What are you doing here, you idiot?' Rocco asked. He was wary but didn't think the young man would be part of what was about to happen.

'I saw Koutcheff coming up the street and wanted to warn you. I might have left it a bit late, though. Sorry.'

Footsteps sounded on the stairs and Bakri's head appeared. He had his hands in the air and was grinning with suppressed excitement as if it was all a big game.

'How did you get in?' Rocco asked him.

Bakri nodded down the stairs behind him. 'There's a side door nobody knows about. It leads into the old garage next door. Come on, I'll show you.' With that, he turned and darted away.

Rocco and Desmoulins exchanged a cautious look then followed. Anything was better than staying up here and instinct told Rocco that he could trust the young panel-beater. As they descended, he listened for sounds of the front door opening. If the men came in it would be in a rush with the standard split of forces going left and right and one in the centre; something they would have trained for many times in their military careers.

It would be wise to not let them get that far.

As they reached the ground floor, Desmoulins moved away to check the other doorways, which were all open. Rocco stepped into a front room and glanced through the window. The three men were advancing towards the front of the building, Koutcheff in the lead. He appeared to be carrying something tucked under one arm. Was that a cushion?

They stopped just short of the steps.

'Rocco?' The voice was Koutcheff's. 'You don't want your colleague to die in there too, do you?' He sounded almost cheerful and Rocco understood why: he and Desmoulins were the enemy and Koutcheff was coming in to dispose of them, the way he'd been trained. It mattered not that they were in the middle of a French city surrounded by innocent people; he had a job to do and nothing was going to stop him.

Damn, he might be right, thought Rocco sourly. Who was going to stop them? There was little chance of any police officers coming here unless by chance, as they were still out hunting the man standing out front. That left Koutcheff free rein to do as he pleased and take his time. As he'd displayed already in so blatantly attacking Pouillot and Cabaud in the street, he appeared to have no restraint when confronting the authorities. Maybe the term 'berserker' was right for him after all.

'Come on!' Bakri's voice was pitched low. He was standing in the rear hallway, gesturing towards a gap in the wall. 'Through here.'

As he spoke, a loud hammering of a fist sounded on the front door, echoing through the house, accompanied by Koutcheff's voice again.

'Come on, Rocco! This is only going to end one way. Come out and we'll let the other cop go.'

Seconds later another bang sounded, this one oddly muffled, followed by a fist-sized chunk of the front door flying off. A hole appeared in the opposite wall and bits of plaster flew through the air.

'That's your last warning!'

Bakri swore in surprise. 'Is he using a silencer? How cool is that?'

Rocco wanted to tell him that it wasn't a silencer but a cushion, and it performed a similar function of reducing noise. He didn't think Bakri would be as impressed. What it told him was that Koutcheff and his men had come here fully expecting to use guns and he, Desmoulins – and now Bakri – would not be leaving here alive.

Rocco signalled for Desmoulins to join Bakri, who was holding a door open. It had been papered over to match the walls on either side, and through the gap they could see the filthy interior of what had clearly been a vehicle workshop, the floor littered with bird droppings and puddles of brown water where the roof had leaked.

'Fooled me,' Rocco said softly, as Bakri closed the disguised door behind them. 'How do you know about it?'

Bakri looked abashed. 'I went to school with Coco.' At Desmoulins' look of puzzlement, he explained, 'She used to work the room upstairs, doing... well, you know. We were friends and she showed me the side door one day. It was her way out if she needed to escape.' He shrugged. 'Her job's not as glamorous as some people think, you know?'

'It never is,' said Rocco. He'd got to know a few night-club performers and sex workers while working in the anti-gang unit in Paris, and there had been more that were sad about their circumstances than not. They lived in as much fear of unstable clients as they did the vicious pimps who controlled them, but many of them found getting out of the profession was not as simple as running away.

A loud crash behind them signalled the forceful arrival of the three men, followed by a rush of footsteps going up the stairs.

'Rocco!' Koutcheff roared. 'You might as well come out or we'll come and get you! We'll make it easy on your little colleague if you come out quietly.'

Rocco motioned Bakri away from the connecting door. They still had to get away from here but there was something he had to clear up first. He looked at the young man and whispered, 'How did you know they were coming?'

Bakri looked hesitant for a moment, then spilled. 'It was Leo. He went to his uncle's café down the street and called them on the phone as soon as you two arrived.'

'Who's Leo?'

'The guy with the tattoo of a lion's head.' He pointed to his bicep. 'On his arm. His real name's Oscar but he doesn't like it so we call him Leo. He likes to think he's a real bad gangster but he'll end up in the gutter one day.'

Rocco remembered. The kid who'd wanted to see Koutcheff's car crash a few days ago. Another tough guy who was bound for disappointment in life.

'Aren't you going to stay and fight it out?' Bakri asked. His eyes gleamed brightly with a mixture of excitement and fear.

'No,' Rocco said. 'We're not. If we did, it might get you caught in the crossfire, along with whoever else is in the vicinity.'

'That makes sense.' Bakri ginned, looking relieved. 'Come on, I'll show you the way out.'

As they made their way across the empty workshop and reached the front door, they heard a knocking sound coming from the other side of the wall they'd just passed through.

Bakri looked back. 'What are they doing?'

Rocco pushed him through the door, one eye on the connecting wall. The three men had moved incredibly fast to clear the building and return downstairs. And they were nobody's fools. They knew there had to be another way out and were checking the wall to see how Rocco and Desmoulins had disappeared.

'Do we take them?' Desmoulins queried. He looked both eager and wary and his fist around his side-arm was white with tension.

Rocco debated trying to capture them, but reason overcame the temptation. As capable with guns as he and Desmoulins were, the three men on the other side were former soldiers and undoubtedly well-versed in house-to-house combat. Any gunfire here would risk hitting innocent people, and while he and Desmoulins would be cautious, he doubted Koutcheff and his men would give it a second thought.

It was time to go.

Chapter Forty-Four

Forty minutes later they were in Rizzotti's office, watching while he inspected the gun found in the toilet wall. By the time Rocco and Desmoulins had got Bakri to safety, found a telephone and called for reinforcements, Koutcheff and his companions had fled. A subsequent search of the building had revealed the toilet door had been kicked in and footprints where tiles adjacent to the one Yannick had removed had suffered the same treatment. Koutcheff, no doubt, less than pleased at finding his favoured weapon was gone.

'It's a Unique model twenty-two calibre,' Rizzotti said, turning the pistol over in his hand and peering along the barrel to the foresight. 'Nice.'

Desmoulins looked surprised. He hadn't taken a close look at it himself yet. 'I didn't know guns were your speciality, Doc.'

'Don't be too impressed,' Rocco murmured dryly. 'It's stamped on the side of the barrel.'

Rizzotti smiled. 'Take away a man's moment of glory, why don't you? Where did you get this?'

Rocco told him. When he mentioned Koutcheff's name, Rizzotti's eyebrows went up. 'So this could be the same gun used in the other shooting – the one that fired this?' He rooted around on his desk and held up the shell

Desmoulins had discovered in the burned-out vehicle near Caix.

'Could be. But can you prove it?'

'Pretty sure, yes. If the strike marks are the same, it puts it very close indeed. From what I've read it depends on a couple of factors relating to the firing pin and rifling. I might have to get out my old college magnifying glass.'

'What's he talking about?' Desmoulins asked with a sly grin.

'Don't ask,' Rocco said. 'We'll be here all day. Can you make a comparison?'

'Sure. Come back in thirty minutes. I'll get Sergeant Maurel down here to take a look and test-fire it.'

Maurel was the station's armourer and experienced with all forms of firearms.

Rocco left him to it and he and Desmoulins walked back upstairs. He was feeling the first flush of something approaching excitement at the thought that they might finally have something to work on. If Rizzotti could prove the gun had fired the bullets that killed the Benhamids, it was enough to get a solid case against Koutcheff – if they could find him. With Koutcheff down, they might be able to bring De Lancourt down with him.

But they weren't there yet. He'd seen too many cases with stronger lines of evidence fall apart at the last minute due to a mistake or a very clever lawyer to be too confident of success at this stage.

Rocco sat at his desk and stared into space, trying to override his impatience regarding the target pistol. If it turned out to have been the weapon used to kill the Benhamids and Hamal, they were on track with a solid lead. If not, they were back several paces.

Something was bothering him, something involving Koutcheff. The former army man was right at the centre of this case, he now knew that. It wasn't just the shootings that involved him but went far deeper, especially with his connection with De Lancourt going back years, if Bruno Dujols' claim was to be believed. Tie that in with the stories of their presence in Morocco and it provided a timeline that even they might have difficulty denying.

Except while Koutcheff was a suspect with a serious bent for violence, his boss, De Lancourt, was very different. As a defence lawyer he spent his life finding chinks in the most solid pieces of evidence, even provided by equally solid members of the public. Then he would destroy them. What Rocco knew he had to do was make any evidence bomb-proof.

A large map hung on the wall of the main office. It was scarred and marked by numerous pinholes relating to past cases and reports, and a few pins relating to current or recent ones. It served as a useful close-up picture of Amiens and the surrounding area. Claude Lamotte knew the land better, road by road, field by field, but that had been years in the making. For a relative newcomer like himself, Rocco needed a bird's-eye view to bring it all together.

He tapped the pin relating to the Benhamid shootings as if it might speak to him with something useful. Reading a map was like a picture book; you had the obvious detail, which was unchanging and static. You knew what was where. What you didn't have was the human element, the trace of people and events and timelines that left no obvious signs on the map itself. They were ephemeral until you nailed down more facts.

If Koutcheff had indeed shot the Benhamids and chased down the unfortunate driver, Fouad Hamal, as he suspected, where had he gone next? And how, if he'd torched the Renault at the deserted farm? He would have hardly hopped on the infrequent bus that served the area, and he doubted Koutcheff would have been stupid enough to thumb a lift. Having set fire to the Renault, he'd have carried obvious traces of smoke and petrol fumes on his clothing, which would have prompted too many questions. And when had he managed to conceal the target pistol in the toilet at the building where he rented a flat?

Rocco did a tour of the office, hoping it might jog his thoughts into a logical construction of possible movements. Koutcheff could only have got back to Amiens if someone had helped him. The same with acquiring the DS, which he'd crashed so spectacularly before laying into the two officers. There was no other way. But he would have had to have communicated with them somehow, and in such a sparsely populated area that would have called for a telephone.

Back to the map. A public telephone, most likely in a café. Anonymous and safe and matter-of-fact. Who even looks at people using a telephone?

He looked around and saw the duty officer, named Weber, crossing the room. He called him over and nodded at the map on the wall.

'You're local, right?'

'That's right. Man and boy.'

Rocco stabbed a finger on the pin where Hamal's body had been found. 'You've shot someone here and dumped the body in a ditch. Then you've driven your car to a deserted farm and torched it,' – he touched the map where the Renault had been found – 'to dispose of any evidence. You have to do this without drawing too much attention.'

Weber eyed the map with an experienced eye. 'It's never busy out there, so that's easy enough. I had a friend out that way when I was a kid. I used to cycle over and we'd get lost in the fields all day.'

'If you were in the killer's position, without a car and needing to get back to civilisation, where would you go to use a telephone to call for a pick-up?'

Weber ran his fingers across the map around the deserted farm, covering two small hamlets with symbols for housing. 'There's nothing here except for farms and farm-workers' homes, so they wouldn't be any good.'

'What about cafés?'

'None. There's not enough trade.' He tapped the map over Caix. 'This is the nearest place of any size. In fact, there's a café on the outskirts called Bar Nicolas. It's a bit of a dump but the owner likes it that way and your killer would have hit on it as soon as he entered the area. There would have been no need to risk going into the centre.'

Rocco thanked him and continued studying the map, checking the scale. Three kilometres, more or less, from the deserted farm to the outskirts of Caix. Koutcheff was fit and a walk like that would have been a mere stroll to a former soldier. Keeping to the fields, he'd have been able to avoid any contact with passers-by. See the café, go in, order a drink, use the phone. Easy.

Then what? He traced the most obvious route from Caix to Amiens. Since that was where he'd crashed and also where the gun was discovered in the toilet wall, it made sense that he must have gone to the flat to hide the gun first before going on his rampage. But why there and not at Les Cyprès, where there would have been a hundred-and-one places to conceal it? Unless, of course, he had been going against De Lancourt's instructions. It was odd behaviour, but Koutcheff was not a balanced individual.

It was a theory, but workable. Hide the gun first, then go where he would be safe and nobody would talk... except that he hadn't done that. Why not?

Theories here were all he had to go on, but the gun was a vital piece of evidence that couldn't be ignored. How did his journey fit the timeline of events from the Benhamid shootings to the fight with the two cops?

Desmoulins approached him. 'Rizzotti and Maurel have finished the test-firing, and you might like to see this.' He held out a sheet of paper. It was a rental agreement for a three-month period on a white Citroën DS. The agreement was made out to G. De Lancourt. 'It's the one he crashed here in town. We tracked this through a company sticker in the glove compartment. He can't deny Koutcheff was involved now, can he?'

'It's another nail,' Rocco said with a smile. It was probably the same car that had picked up Koutcheff from the café in Caix before he'd gone on his rampage. At some point he must have taken over the wheel and left the driver to find his own way back to Les Cyprès.

More steps in the trail.

'Well done. Let's go and see this gun.'

They walked down to Rizzotti's office, where they found the two men sipping coffee and looking pleased with themselves. Rocco felt a sigh of relief. Had it been a fail, it would have been written on their faces.

Sergeant Simeon Maurel was stocky, bluff and past the normal retirement age for officers, but had secured a place as armourer for Amiens and the surrounding regional police units. What he didn't know about guns, he often told junior officers at some length, hadn't yet been invented. He levered himself up with difficulty and stood ramrod straight.

Rocco didn't bother telling him to remain seated; he'd probably be offended.

'So what have you two reprobates found for me?' he asked. 'Or are you still trying to work out how to find the trigger?'

'Don't let him get to you, Simeon,' Rizzotti said genially. 'He's having a hard time at the moment solving a couple of easy cases and we have to feel sorry for him. He'll get over it, you'll see.'

Maurel grinned and picked up the pistol lying on Rizzotti's desk. The way he handled it showed a dexterity that he lacked elsewhere, and he twirled it in his hand with professional appreciation. 'I used one of these – one very much like it, anyway – years ago when I did competition shooting. Amazing piece of work and deadly in the wrong hands.' He looked at Rizzotti and said, 'You'd better tell him what we found or I might get carried away with technical details. I rarely get anything this interesting to look at.'

Rizzotti nodded. 'I'll keep it simple.' He reached into a small tray on his desk and picked up three empty shells. One Rocco recognised as the fire-brushed item from the farm near Caix; the other two were shiny and unblemished. He held up the burned one first so Rocco could see the base of the shell. 'The base is what we're looking at.'

Rocco nodded. 'I understand.'

Rizzotti pushed a series of large black-and-white photographs across the desk, showing the gun and the three shells. 'As you know, each time a gun is fired there's an impression left by the firing pin. It's small, but under a microscope you can see the specific make-up of the mark, which differs from gun to gun. There were only two bullets left in the magazine of the gun you found at the property rented by Koutcheff, and Simeon test-fired them both for comparison purposes. He came up with this.' He held up the two newer shells alongside the old one, then pointed to the photos.

'They look the same,' said Rocco, and felt relieved. At least they weren't dealing with two different weapons. No doubt a lawyer would try to argue otherwise, but that was another battle altogether.

'That's because they are the same,' Sergeant Maurel put in. 'Fire another two dozen or so rounds in that gun and the marks would change slightly with minute wear, it's true. But you're talking, what, a few days apart? Nobody fires that many bullets from a gun like this unless they're in a competition or they have a problem with rats.' He finished his coffee and put the cup down with care, a visual punctuation mark to his final statement. 'That gun fired those three bullets. My word and all my experience on it.'

Rocco said, 'Only two left in the magazine, you say? Out of how many?'

Maurel pursed his lips. 'Out of ten… or six, depending on who you talk to. Overload it and the spring becomes weak and jams. Is there a problem?'

'He's wondering where the rest are,' Rizzotti explained. 'He's very particular that way. But he's not wrong. Find the others and check the strike marks and, depending where they're found, it makes a strong case.' He glanced at Rocco and Desmoulins. 'The fact that you found the first casing proves Hamal was shot inside the car.' He shook his head in wonder. 'Why did he get in? He must have known it wasn't going to end well.'

'He was terrified, probably,' Rocco said. 'And maybe he couldn't run any further.'

'But up close like that… it's cold.'

'Bit careless, though,' Maurel said carefully. 'Leaving the spent shell in the car. Always a risk someone would find it.'

'Comes down to psychology,' Rizzotti replied. 'Career criminals watch out for that stuff, such as chains of evidence. They know a slip-up like that can land them in jail. From what we know about Koutcheff, he doesn't have the same mindset; to him it was done, finished with. Burn the car and who would even bother looking?'

'We would,' Rocco put in. 'Desmoulins did, anyway.'

–

Rocco thanked Maurel and Rizzotti for their work and left them to it. Rizzotti's report would be the next brick in the wall. All he needed now was to find Koutcheff or his men and get one of them to talk. And Rizzotti was absolutely correct: if he could find the other shells, it would add to the evidence trail.

When he got back to his desk, he found a note of a telephone call from Caspar. It contained some good news: Mme Hamal had been found and returned to her home. Karim Hadji, apparently, had been as good as his word.

He dialled Caspar's number. The phone was answered by a woman he guessed was Lucille.

'My God,' she said, when he told her his name. Her voice held a hint of laughter. 'So you *do* exist! I thought Marc had got a secret girlfriend on the side. Hang on, I'll just get him.'

Caspar came on the line. 'Sorry about that, Lucas,' he said quickly. 'She was joking, of course. You got my message.'

'I did.'

'Hadji put out feelers and discovered who was holding her. It was a Moroccan gang thing, apparently. They'd heard about the deaths of the Benhamids and figured Hamal was more involved than he was. Hadji said they were hoping to make a trade using Mme Hamal as collateral in Casablanca.'

'What sort of trade?'

'No idea. Their plans don't always make sense. Anyway, she's safe and well. Hadji's put a shield over her, so nobody will go near her.'

'Good work. Thanks for letting me know. And say something nice to Lucille for me.'

Rocco rang off and picked up a copy of Koutcheff's photograph, then called Desmoulins and led him out to his car. He wanted to check out another potential piece of evidence before he went any further.

Chapter Forty-Five

Rocco drove across country to the scene of the first shoot-ings. He then tracked along the road, first to where Fouad Hamal's body had been dumped, followed by the farm where the burned-out Renault had been left. Beyond that and just over a rise in the landscape lay the small community of Caix. He was trying to figure out where Koutcheff would have been drawn to after leaving the scene of the shootings. There weren't many options.

'He must have had some idea of where he was heading,' Desmoulins observed. 'You don't just march off across the fields and hope to find a phone, do you?'

Rocco agreed. 'He's ex-military – and part of a special unit. He'd have planned what he was going to do and where, at least enough to know the general layout of the area in case he needed a plan B. This whole thing was neat: get the three men to a location where they could be killed, then disappear. With no obvious links to the area, who would ever guess the people responsible?'

'But why?' Desmoulins queried. 'I mean, why get them all the way up here if all you were going to do was kill them? It would have been less risky to send a gun after them down south, well out of the way.'

'There might not have been time. I doubt the Benh-amids made their travel plans known in advance, which meant De Lancourt was probably reacting on the hoof to

305

the news that they were coming. That would have rattled him. Them turning up after all this time would have been the last thing he needed, with selection to the academy on the horizon.'

'So they were looking for a safe haven.'

'Had to be. If they knew their time was up and had decided to get out before they got picked up by the Moroccan authorities, it would have been a logical move: trade on their working relationship in the past for somewhere to hide. Unfortunately, they hadn't reckoned on De Lancourt having gone all respectable and needing to whitewash his past connections.'

'You think that's where they were heading?'

'It makes sense. De Lancourt was the mystery man persuading French farmers to sell up, and with his connections here in France they must have figured he was a safe bet to help them disappear, even if they had to lean on him to do it.'

As they arrived on the outskirts of Caix along what was little more than a narrow, winding lane, they saw Bar Nicolas standing at the rear of a large, open space used as a parking area. There were few other buildings nearby, save for a couple of small, single-storey houses, a farm and what appeared to be a grain store. They could see the roofs of other houses over some hedges, and the solid square tower of the local church looming over them in the background.

Rocco stopped in front of the café, which had the dark shape of a telephone wire looped across to a small pylon on the opposite side of the lane. He could see what would have drawn Koutcheff to this place instead of venturing elsewhere. If he was right about the former soldier having a back-up plan, all he'd have had to do was get to the telephone and wait to be picked up. And right here was ideal; it was quiet, with virtually no traffic and few inquisitive locals to ask questions.

The parking area was empty and fronted by three chopped-down wine barrels sprouting with impoverished-looking plants wilting under the sun. A line of faded plastic pennants in red, white and blue hung limply across the front of the building, which looked tired and run-down with pitted brickwork, tired fascia and weathered shutters either side of the windows.

'Would you go in here if you'd just killed four people and torched a car?' Desmoulins mused.

'We'll soon find out,' Rocco replied, and switched off the engine.

The interior of the café was sombre, dowdy and smelled of stale beer, cigarette smoke and the sour remnant of bodies. The yellowing walls were decorated with posters of tag-wrestling matches past and forthcoming, a large circus poster from two years before with the obligatory representations of a roaring lion, a ringmaster in a top hat, an elephant and a shapely woman in a sequined bathing suit hanging from a trapeze. Elsewhere were several framed photographs of men in hunting gear standing behind lines of pheasants, pigeons and other birds they'd blown out of the sky in the annual hunting season.

The man behind the bar was tall and lugubrious, with lank hair and a three-day beard. He was picking with forced concentration at the side of a stubby wine glass with a grubby thumbnail. He looked up as if surprised at their arrival, but merely nodded and went back to his task.

Rocco ordered two coffees. The man put down the glass and produced two heavy cups in very quick order. The coffee was fresh and surprisingly good.

'Passing through?' It came out as a statement rather than a query. He didn't appear too interested in the answer, but Rocco sensed a shift in his mood. He knew what they were, even if not why they were here. A skill of the trade.

'Not really,' Rocco said, and placed his card on the bar, waiting a few beats while the man absorbed its contents, his lips moving with the words and numbers. 'We have some questions for you. First, your name.'

'Why? What have I done?' The response was automatic, defensive. When Rocco didn't answer, he shrugged and said, 'Collard. Louis Collard.'

Rocco placed the photo of Koutcheff alongside his card. 'You've seen this man before.' There was no room for denial.

Collard nodded immediately. 'Sure, I remember. Hard not to.'

'Why?'

'He turned up early a few days ago, just after I'd opened. A couple of regulars were in on their way to work, but it's not often I see a stranger at that time of day... actually, not often I see strangers at all. What's he done?'

'Was he on foot?'

'I think so. At least, I didn't see or hear a car or moped, not then.'

'Was there anything specific you noticed about him?'

'He was tall, that's all I can say. Not what I'd call a working man – at least not like any men around here. He wasn't exactly friendly, but that's no different to most of my customers, now I think about it. They come in to drink and forget their troubles, not to make friends.'

'Did he use the telephone?'

Collard thought about it, pursing his lips. 'He did. Giving someone orders, it sounded like. I was getting some flak from the other two customers about not having any fresh bread so I didn't really pay much attention.'

'Fine. I want you to tell me what he did from the time he came in.'

'Easy. He ordered coffee, which I'd just brewed, and sank two big cups one after the other. Then he switched to whisky.' He grinned. 'Now that was unusual. Hair of the dog, I reckon, that early in the day. He sat in the corner over there.' He nodded to the end of the room by one of the front windows, overlooking the car park and next to a billiard table, which was the most impressive item of furniture in the place. 'I could do with a few more whisky drinkers like him. Made a nice change.'

'Did he drink much?' Desmoulins asked.

'I can't say.' Collard looked between them, defensive at facing questions from both men. 'All right, maybe three shots, but that was all. I know all about the sobriety rules if that's what you're going to say. But if a man wants to drink himself under the table there's nothing much I can do to stop him unless he decides to bust up the place in the process.' He reached under the counter and produced a sawn-off axe handle. 'That's why I keep this handy.'

'But he didn't do that?'

'No. Nothing like it.' The café owner scratched his head. 'I don't mean to tell tales on a customer, you under-stand – and he was only here the one time – but there was something a bit off about him, now I think about it.'

'Off?'

'In this business we get to recognise signs of trouble. This man didn't do anything, but I got the feeling if there had been a bigger crowd and later in the day, he might have tipped over the edge. All it takes is something said the wrong way and it sparks off.' He shrugged. 'He drank quickly, all edgy like, as if he was on a time limit. I could see his feet drumming on the floor under the table; that's always a bad sign. To be honest I was relieved when he left. There was an atmosphere, you know? Hung over him like a cloud.'

'Did he pay up?'

'Sure. Settled up and walked out as soon as the horn sounded.' At Rocco's blank look, he explained, 'A fancy car turned up and tooted a couple of times. White, it was, a big one.'

'What model?' Desmoulins asked.

'No idea. I didn't get a clear look at it. The customer checked through the window, then finished his drink, paid and left. That was the last I saw of him.'

–

Rocco and Desmoulins returned to the station and Rocco made his way down to Rizzotti's office, where he was greeted with a nod. He sat down and said, 'What do you know about the psychology of killers?'

Rizzotti sat back with a look of surprise. 'Now there's a question I never expected to hear. Where did that spring from?'

'I'm trying to understand what might point towards someone who's killed before. Why he does what he does.'

'All right.' The doctor scratched his head. 'It's a very complex subject and not one I'm that much acquainted with, to be honest. There's a lot been written on it, I know that. Let's try to narrow it down. Is there a specific aspect you're talking about?'

'Post-kill.'

Rizzotti smiled. 'You mean how they react after they've done it? Now that is interesting.' He shuffled some papers around on his desk. 'With some there will be a rush of adrenaline after a killing – as if they've taken a heavy dose of drugs or drink. It's what's called a high. Some men in battle sometimes experience it, others don't. For most it'll be the rush of relief that they've survived.'

'But some will be excited by it?'

'Exactly.'

'How long does that feeling last?'

'It varies, I think. But not long. The system will find other stimulants that take over, or the person involved is forced to focus on something else, such as continued survival or a return to normal. Who are we talking about?'

Rocco went over Georges Koutcheff's actions on the day he'd attacked Pouillot and Cabaud in Amiens, and his appearance in the cell afterwards. He then related what the owner of Bar Nicolas had told him and Desmoulins about his early morning customer and his very obvious heightened manner.

Rizzotti blinked. 'The same day as the shooting of the Benhamids and, what was his name, Hamal?'

'The same.'

Rizzotti stood up and did a tour of his office. 'It would fit, I'll give you that. If he was at all normal – at least if you can call a man who just shot four people normal – he'd have been experiencing a huge sense of excitement, maybe even triumph after the shootings, mostly arising from a job well done... even the survival aspect.'

'Enjoyment?'

'Perhaps not. He might have seen it as a necessary job to do rather than for thrills. You don't go into the kind of scenario of facing two armed policemen – the Benhamids – without thinking it might go wrong, no matter how good you are. If he was like that, the subsequent intake of whisky would have added to, then taken over from the adrenaline rush, so by the time he got back to Amiens he would have been… well, unstable would be one way of describing it. Having a cop car pull up alongside him was probably the last thing he was expecting and he flipped.'

'Could he have been stable enough to have hidden the weapon before being stopped?'

'Probably. Like I said, being made to focus on the survival aspect, in his case hiding the gun and maybe heading back to a place of safety, would have been at the front of his thinking. But it wouldn't have taken much to disrupt that, and… well, you saw the results.' He returned to his seat. 'But this is supposition, not facts. It would help if you had more instances of his behaviour to back it up.'

'I have.' Rocco related what Bruno had told him about Koutcheff's manner and attitude on returning to camp after his cross-border excursions in Algeria and Morocco, and how the other men had avoided him.

'In that case,' Rizzotti said, 'and bear in mind I'm not an expert, I would say there's definitely an example of a psychological imbalance. If, as your informant says, Koutcheff also took kif afterwards, it's a similar process described by the bar owner: a high caused by surviving the killing followed by the need to take a stimulant.' He paused, then said, 'The two officers were lucky. The drink might have been slowing him down by then, aided by fatigue – the body's reaction to stress. If they'd come across him earlier, it might have been a different ending.'

'Would he have been in a mental state to remember the officer who arrested him?'

Rizzotti chewed his lip. 'You mean going after Pouillot and shooting him? You definitely think that was him?'

'He's the only candidate we have.'

'In that case, possibly. That's the best I can say. In his frame of mind, I wouldn't discount it. He'd have been angry enough – and pride would have been driving him to get even. Don't forget this is all supposition; dealing with the psychology of a man accustomed to killing is never a given.'

Chapter Forty-Six

Rocco's phone rang. He was surprised to hear Claude's voice. The normally laid-back *garde champêtre* sounded stressed.

'Lucas – I've been an idiot! I'm so sorry!'

'Why?' Rocco said. 'Slow down – what's up?'

'The bunker at De Lancourt's house, in the woods. We saw rats climbing among the rubble across the doorway.'

'Yes. So?'

'Why rats? I kept thinking about it but it's only just occurred to me: they normally congregate close to a source of food, like in farms and houses, store rooms and the like. I'm annoyed I didn't think of it sooner.'

Rocco felt a tick of something approaching excitement. 'But the main house isn't far away; wouldn't they get food there?'

'Some, yes. Rats are lazy creatures at heart; if they find a food source, they tend not to stray far from it. Rubbish bins, compost heaps, anywhere humans dump unwanted trash, they mark it and go back whenever they need to. Don't forget Les Cyprès has been a food source for them for decades. When it was a mental institute, it would have dumped plenty of rubbish, especially wasted food. What if another source suddenly turned up, closer to hand and away from the main building?'

Rocco stood up, energised. Claude was right. They would have needed something drawing them to the bunker. What better than a dark, remote box where somebody was hiding – probably with food for the taking? If Koutcheff was hiding there, he wouldn't have anything fancy, but rats didn't demand *grande cuisine*. Food was food.

But how did Koutcheff get inside?

Rocco thought quickly. This was going to need more than just him and Claude. To breach the bunker and cover the area effectively would take manpower – especially if they came across resistance from De Lancourt's men. And the lawyer was sure to be ready to intercept any attempt to search his property, even if he was in Paris on business.

'There's something else I remembered,' Claude said. 'Some of those old bunkers had back doors, in case they were overrun and those inside had to get out to fight a rear-guard action.'

'But we didn't see another door. Just the one that was bricked up.'

'That's the thing: a back door doesn't have to be an actual door. They were sometimes tunnels leading away from the bunker and coming up elsewhere through a hidden trapdoor.'

'Where are you, Claude?'

'At home.'

'Fine. I'll need to get permission to move on this and then get a team together. In the meantime, there's something I want you to do.' He explained his idea to Claude, who readily agreed and rang off.

Rocco hurried upstairs, where Massin was busy going through some timesheets. He explained what he wanted to do. Massin looked doubtful, but didn't exactly throw it back at him with a refusal. What he did next explained why. He picked up a folder and waved it to Rocco. 'There's something you should know before you do that. I just received this by courier from the Interior Ministry in Paris. It seems the evidence against De Lancourt has become something of a minor avalanche. The newspapers are on it and even his supporters appear to be folding their tents and slipping away, as the saying goes.'

'And the Ministry is all right with that?'

'They don't have much choice. The evidence is out in the open and they'd be backed into a corner if they tried to deny it all, especially in view of his application to the academy. It would be a stain on the institution and would devalue its position of eminence.' Massin pushed the folder to one side. 'What makes you think Koutcheff will be there?'

'It's the only place we haven't been able to look. He'll go to ground where he thinks he's safe… where De Lancourt has been protecting him.' He explained what Claude had told him about the back door tunnel. 'We didn't see any trace of one because we weren't looking for it. The only way we'll find it, other than by breaking into the bunker, is by searching the grounds around it. If there are signs of anyone coming and going, I'd lay money on Claude Lamotte finding them. If we find the trapdoor, we'll be in.'

Massin chewed his lip. 'We'll still need a magistrate to sign it off, and I know our usual man is somewhere down south on holiday.'

Paperwork, Rocco thought. Another hurdle to clear. Then he had an idea. 'I know a lawyer who owes us a favour. He'll know someone. I'll get back to you.'

'Fine. I'll get Canet and Godard primed and ready to go.'

Ten minutes later, Rocco was knocking on Freddy Toussaint's attic door. The lawyer looked up, blinking behind his large glasses when he saw who it was, but Rocco raised a quick hand to signal he was here in peace. He explained what he needed.

Toussaint looked dubious. 'I can't sign off anything like that. You need a magistrate.' He raised a hand. 'Don't get me wrong, Inspector, I'm not trying to be difficult; it's simply not something I can do and you'd get yourself and your superiors into a host of trouble if you went in there without the proper papers. It would also ruin any case you had against them.'

Rocco nodded, noting the 'them' with interest. 'I figured that. But I thought you might know a magistrate who could help.'

'You mean one who will sign it off without looking at every dot and comma?' He rubbed his chin in thought. It didn't take long. 'When do you need it?'

'Any time now would be good. Like today.'

Toussaint raised an eyebrow. 'You don't ask much, do you?' He stared down at his desk, and Rocco waited. The lawyer was almost there. With a good prompt from his conscience already doing part of the work, and no doubt his venal nature looking for the potential for extra work, all he needed to do was to make the decision for himself.

'All right,' he said finally. 'I know one who's about to retire and doesn't care for people with high-flown reputa-tions and friends. If we describe it as an abandoned bunker on private land and probably hiding a multiple murderer, I think he'll go for it. He's not here in Amiens but I'm sure he'll courier the paperwork across to the station today.' He reached out for his telephone. 'I'll get on it now.'

'Don't you need the details?'

Toussaint grinned. 'Already got them.'

Rocco thanked him and left. He had a lot to do and time was of the essence. He got back to the station and phoned the Lille police station where Bruno Dujols was being held for his safety. He got put through to a room with a telephone, and after a wait of several minutes heard a familiar voice on the other end.

'Well, this is nice, Inspector,' Bruno said with a touch of sarcasm. 'Calling to let me out, are you?'

'Not if you fancy your chances of survival,' Rocco told him. 'But it won't be for much longer. Are there any new faces I should look out for at Les Cyprès?'

There was a pause and Rocco could almost hear Bruno's mind working out why he would wish to know that. He wasn't wrong.

'You're going in, aren't you?' Bruno chuckled. 'Boy, I'd buy a front-row ticket to see that.'

'It's not a spectator sport. You said De Lancourt could call on help if he needed it. What sort of help?'

'Men like Koutcheff and the others. What about it?'

'I want to know if there are likely to be any new faces, men we haven't seen before. Come clean with me and it will help towards you getting out sooner rather than later, and maybe getting help with employment down the line.'

'There's one that I know of in the area,' Bruno said finally. 'Mavrouk, the guy whose photo you showed me. I wouldn't know who else he'd call in, though.'

Rocco described the second man he'd seen outside Koutcheff's place, but Bruno sounded unsure.

'I don't know for sure. That description fits a few, like Samsonov. Sorry. There are a couple out there who've done muscle jobs with Koutcheff before. Mavrouk's done mercenary jobs in Africa, like Senegal and the Central

African Republic, and there's bound to be one or two who've done the same.'

'Government work?'

'Not really. Contract work, like helping put down trouble spots.'

Rocco wasn't surprised; it was what mercenaries were employed for.

'There's something else,' Bruno said. 'The bunker in the woods.'

'The one you forgot to mention, you mean? We know.'

'Yes. Sorry. If Koutcheff's anywhere in the woods, he's inside – although I have no idea how he'd get in and out. It's supposed to be sealed, but I'm not sure if it is.'

'What makes you think that?'

'One of the men said he'd taken some water and food down there and left it in the trees. A couple of minutes later it had gone.'

Chapter Forty-Seven

It was late in the afternoon by the time Rocco arrived in a convoy at Les Cyprès, armed with a freshly signed warrant. He led the charge down the drive to the main house, the wheels of the vehicles kicking up gravel and dust drifting across the grounds like smoke. It was a deliberate show of force to unsettle anyone watching. The van behind him contained a troop of Godard's Gendarmerie Mobile in full kit, followed by another car full of uniformed officers. While the van continued on past the house as planned and pulled up in front of the staff quarters, the other car turned to block the drive to prevent anyone leaving.

Rocco jumped out with Captain Canet and Detective Desmoulins close behind. While Canet deployed his men to fan out with their weapons drawn and to be ready for resistance, Rocco pounded on the front door of the house. In the sudden silence after their noisy entrance, he heard voices raised at the rear of the house: Godard's men doing what they did best.

Rocco knocked hard again. No answer.

Leaving one of Canet's men on guard at the front door, Rocco hurried round to the back of the house, where Godard and two of his men were standing over a man on his knees. It was Raphael Debac. He had his hands in the air and was trying to appear calm but failing, eyeing the armed men around him with unease, his troubled breathing coming in loud gasps.

'Is De Lancourt in?' Rocco asked him.

'He's on his way back from Paris.' A trail of snot ran from his nose and he tried to wipe it away on his shoulder but failed. 'You can't do this, Rocco. It's not right.'

Rocco waved the warrant in front of him. 'This paper says I can. Who else is here?'

Debac regained some bravado and spat on the ground, then clamped his lips shut until Godard stepped up and cuffed him unceremoniously behind the ear. 'Listen, you maggot,' the big sergeant muttered. 'Your friend Koutcheff has already tried to kill one of my men. We're about to turn this place upside down so I'd hate for any of them to find surprises waiting for them. Now, answer the inspector or I might forget my manners and find a reason to shoot you.'

Debac swallowed hard and ducked away at the threat of another blow. 'All right… Take it easy. There's Salairat, Samsonov and Mavrouk. That's it. Nobody else, I swear.'

'What about Koutcheff?' said Rocco. 'We know he's here somewhere.'

'Did that little rat Dujols tell you that?' Debac looked as if he were about to say more when he noticed Godard lifting his gun. 'Wait! I'll tell you.' His eyes were rolling and he was clearly terrified. 'I don't know – honest! I haven't seen him since yesterday.'

'Where yesterday?'

'Here. He spoke to De Lancourt then disappeared. The man's gone crazy… I was glad to see him go – we all were. That's all I can tell you – I don't know where he went and I don't care.'

That left three men for sure, thought Rocco. Four if Koutcheff was out there – and he would be, he was certain of that, whatever Debac claimed. Koutcheff was as dependent on De Lancourt as the lawyer was on his right-hand man and tame killer – although that might have changed by now.

Then he remembered the heavy steel door inside the house, next to the kitchen. He leaned over Debac and said, 'Where's the key to the wine cellar?'

Debac looked dulled by shock. 'What?'

'The cellar – the door next to the kitchen.'

The light of realisation flared. 'The house keys are in a box inside the kitchen door. There's a label on each one – but he's not down there.'

'Like I'd believe you,' Rocco said, and told Godard about the cellar. 'Take men who know what they're doing. If he's down there, he'll be tough to get out.'

Godard grinned. 'Don't worry – I could do with the excitement.' He issued instructions to two of his more seasoned men, and they turned and ran towards the house, drawing their weapons.

While two of Canet's men hustled Debac into the police van where he couldn't do any harm, Rocco stared out across the scattering of trees in the fields bordering the woodland. Then he saw a movement and said to Godard, 'Tell your men to hold their fire. Officer Lamotte is coming in.'

Godard called to warn his men, then said, 'Where?'

Rocco gave a whistle, and seconds later Claude appeared from between two small trees and walked towards them. He was dressed in his working clothes of a drab jacket, brown corduroy trousers and a bush hat, blending in nicely against the background of long, sun-dried grass and trees. He had his shotgun by his side.

'What was he doing out there?' Godard asked.

'Counting active bodies.'

Moments later, Claude hopped over the wire fence and stood in front of them. 'Three active,' he said to Rocco. 'All in the trees. Plus the one you've just taken in.'

'Thanks, Claude.' Rocco turned to Godard and Canet, whom he'd briefed with a sketch of the place before leaving Amiens. 'We have to go into the trees,' he told them, 'and search every square metre, most especially the bunker and the ground around it. Watch out for soft ground and the trenches, and remember, the men out there are experienced and dangerous.'

Godard nodded. 'So are mine,' he said grimly. He turned and said something to two of his men, who ran off and reappeared moments later with a brace of picks, shovels and sledgehammers to force their way into the bunker. 'If they're there, we'll flush them out.'

Rocco had already agreed that Godard would be in charge of the search and the deployment of his men, with Claude Lamotte to help look for signs of anyone on the ground, especially looking for a trapdoor exit from the bunker.

As they moved into position, Massin and Perronnet appeared from the front of the house. Massin nodded and said, 'We're not here to interfere. We just want to see the job done. Carry on.'

It was slow going. The line of men threaded their way cautiously through the trees, stopping every few paces and checking the undergrowth around them. Where the trunks were close enough or the undergrowth sufficiently impenetrable to send men off-line, Godard guided them back with soft commands. It was hot work, with the late afternoon sun still carrying heat in exposed places and the presence of flies and midges adding to the claustrophobic atmosphere.

For Rocco, it brought back memories of the war in Indochina in the even more close-packed jungle, where threat waited behind every clump of harmless-looking foliage.

A soft whistle from Claude in the centre halted the line. He raised his hand and signalled two sets of footprints, then waved to Godard and the line moved on.

The first action had to come from Koutcheff's men – and it did. A shot rang out from a dense patch of young conifers. It caught one of Godard's men in the arm, spinning him around. Instantly, the man nearest to him returned fire, before dropping to drag his colleague into cover behind a tree.

'He's all right,' the man called, adding with grim humour, 'It's a bee-sting.'

Claude, meanwhile, had ducked into the trees followed by another man, to locate the position of the shooter. He returned seconds later and said, 'Good shooting. There's fresh blood on the ground. If he isn't out of action now, he soon will be.'

The search continued, crossing the main trench and several smaller ones, bypassing dugouts after checking there was nobody hiding in them. As they neared the site of the concrete bunker, they saw a shape lying on the ground nearby.

Sensing a trap, Godard signalled for the line to halt, while Rocco edged closer to the bunker and looked at the man lying there. It was Jean-Baptiste Salairat, one of the men he'd seen before. Salairat taken a shot to the chest and was staring up at the trees and struggling to breathe. A rifle lay nearby. Rocco kicked it away and made sure Salairat had no other weapons on him, before asking a man to run back and call an ambulance.

One down, possibly three to go. Samsonov, Mavrouk and Koutcheff. All dangerous.

Godard called the line forward and set up a perimeter around the bunker while the two men with the tools set about demolishing the accumulation of rubble around the bunker entrance. It was slow going at first, and it soon became apparent that some of the 'rubble' was, in fact, cemented together to form a deliberate barrier.

'They'll carry on here,' Godard suggested, 'while we clear the rest of the area.'

Rocco nodded. He called Claude over and got him to circle the area accompanied by another officer to watch his back, while checking the ground for signs of regular use and any indications of a trapdoor.

As Claude turned away there was a frantic flurry of wings and a pheasant burst into the air. At the same moment, a figure stood up just metres away and aimed at Rocco with a rifle. It was Stefan Samsonov.

'Lucas!' Claude shouted, flicking up his gun barrel in one motion and pulling the trigger.

Rocco twisted instinctively out of the line of fire, feeling the brush of disturbed air as the heavy charge of shot went past him and knocked Samsonov backwards into a heavy patch of bramble, where he lay still, eyes wide open.

Rocco thanked Claude for his quick reactions and checked Samsonov for signs of life. The man was dead.

Hopefully that left Mavrouk and Koutcheff.

Even as he thought it, voices sounded off to one side and a man called out a plea not to fire.

It was Mavrouk, arms in the air and looking dishevelled. Behind him, an officer was holding a rifle while another officer put cuffs on him and searched his clothing.

'He's clean,' the officer called.

Rocco returned to the bunker, where the two men had cleared away the rubble and were preparing to make an entry.

Godard stepped forward. 'I'll do this,' he said, and checked his pistol. He nodded to his men to open the door.

Chapter Forty-Eight

The first indication of the horror inside was the smell. It was all too familiar to men in their line of work, and hung heavy in the air. The sight of two shapeless bundles against one wall was a grim confirmation of the cause.

Two men, both dead.

Godard took on the grisly task of checking through the clothing and came up with two thin wallets, moulded and faded by long use. He pulled out documents and looked at Rocco. 'Ivan Garbus,' he read out loud, 'and Aziz Touati. Who are they?'

'They left here not long ago,' Rocco told him, and related what Bruno Dujols had told him about the men not fitting in with Koutcheff and his closer colleagues. 'They clearly didn't get far.'

Rocco bent close to each body and was able to see in the poor light that they had each died of a single gunshot to the head. The wounds were small and identical to the wounds on the Benhamids and Fouad Hamal.

'Inspector?' A uniformed man was standing by a large round metal plate built into the wall of the bunker. A mess of footprints showed in the dirt underneath, and it was clear that this was the back-door entrance to a tunnel. Nearby was a collection of boxes holding bottles of water, fruit and food, most of it beginning to rot.

Koutcheff, Rocco thought. Desperate enough or mad enough to share space with two men he'd killed.

He warned the others not to touch the plate yet, as there was no saying what lay behind it. Koutcheff was the kind of man who might have set a booby trap to catch the first unwary person to step into the exit tunnel. He went outside and called to Claude, explaining the rough direction of the tunnel. Claude nodded and hurried away.

Claude found it after a few minutes. A heavy circular plate a metre in diameter was carefully concealed beneath a layer of dead foliage and branches, all held in place and secured to an underlay of netting. A locking handle was sunk into the plate with enough room for a hand to turn it clockwise. Rocco was impressed. Any one of them could have walked past this spot without giving it a second look.

Godard looked down at it. 'If it doesn't open, we'll have to blow it,' he said. 'Or follow the tunnel through from the other end.'

Neither option was ideal. The first might lead to Koutcheff being killed by the blast, and Rocco was keen to take the man alive. The second option could lead to the first man down the tunnel being killed by Koutcheff if he was still in there, something he wanted even less.

'Block the tunnel door at the bunker end,' he told Godard. 'We need to move the two bodies out of there and let Rizzotti do his work. In the meantime, post a couple of men to watch this end. He has to come out sometime.'

Godard smiled. 'Tear gas would help with that. I've got some in the van if we need it.'

—

An hour later there was still no sign of Koutcheff coming out, although the men in the bunker reported hearing faint movement in the tunnel. The two men who had searched the wine cellar had reported back that it was empty, which meant Koutcheff, if he was still around, had to be here. The waiting led to a level of frustration among them as they wanted to finish the job. But Rocco and Godard were keen to avoid any further injuries. The officer shot earlier had already left for hospital, while Salairat had eventually died of his wounds, his body taken away with that of Samsonov.

Rizzotti arrived and made an inspection of the two bodies in the bunker. He emerged and held out an envelope for Rocco to see. It held two empty shell casings.

'There are lots more of these in a box inside,' he said. 'Most are old. It looks like they're from the same gun, but I'll confirm that in my report.'

'He liked to shoot pigeons,' Rocco explained. 'Why did you pick these two?'

'Because they look fresher and carry faint traces of grease. I'd say they were used within the past week or so. The other shells are dulled by the damp atmosphere inside the bunker.'

Massin and Perronnet appeared but took no active part other than observing, for which Rocco was grateful. Both officers would know that questions were sure to be raised about this operation and were doing their duty.

Moments later, they heard shouting echoing through the trees, followed by a single gunshot. Rocco ran back towards the tunnel exit. Koutcheff must have finally run out of patience, or air, and tried to make a break for it.

Rocco found a circle of men surrounding the former soldier, who was holding a young, uniformed officer in a tight embrace with an automatic pistol pushed under the man's chin. Koutcheff had the air of a madman, twisting and turning and all the while glaring around him in defiance. His hostage looked terrified, staring at his colleagues in a desperate appeal for help.

'Nobody shoot!' Sergeant Godard called out. It was obvious why: the way Koutcheff kept moving around made it impossible for anyone to try to shoot him for fear of hitting the officer.

Canet stepped up alongside Rocco. 'He came out with his hands up,' he reported grimly, 'but as soon as Officer Chenin, there, went to detain him he produced the gun before anyone else could step in.'

Rocco looked at the circle of men. The situation was fraught with danger. If any one of them tried a sneak shot, there was every chance someone else would get hit.

'Tell everyone to back away ten paces,' he said to Canet. 'Give him space to breathe.'

Canet issued the order and the men obeyed, widening the circle. As they did so, a figure appeared from the front of the house, waving his arms. It was a furious De Lancourt, trailed by a uniformed officer who was trying tactfully to restrain him and losing the battle against the senior lawyer's high position.

'Get off me, you idiot,' the lawyer spat, slapping the man's hand away, 'or I'll have your badge for assault of an officer of the court.'

'Let him through,' said Rocco. He looked at De Lancourt. 'What do you want?'

'This is madness,' the lawyer said, looking round at the number of men standing there. 'Why are you all here? It's nothing more than police harassment and trespass—' He stopped speaking, for the first time seeing Koutcheff and his hold on the young officer.

'It's a bit late for a grand speech, *maître.*' The words came from Commissaire Massin, his voice flat with contempt. 'There are dead men here, thanks to that madman of yours. I think you should leave.'

'No!' Koutcheff shouted, spotting his boss. He dragged his hostage back against a tree for added protection and added, 'I want to talk to him now or this man dies!'

'Not a chance,' said Massin. 'You can talk to him at the station.'

'Really? You're willing to play with this man's life?' Koutcheff challenged him angrily, his gun digging into the officer's face. 'One or the other, I don't care which!'

'Let me speak to him,' said De Lancourt loftily. He took a deep breath and adjusted his tie knot as if he were standing in court. 'There's been enough shooting. I can resolve this situation.' With that he walked towards Koutcheff before anyone could stop him, with his hands held out to either side.

'Jesus,' muttered Canet in disgust. 'He's trying to be the national bloody hero.'

'Let him go,' said Rocco softly. 'This could be our only chance.' He looked round at the other men and called, 'No shooting.'

What happened next was lightning fast and completely unexpected. The moment De Lancourt got within two paces of Koutcheff and opened his mouth to speak, the former soldier reached out and grabbed the lawyer by the neck, in the process dropping his hostage to the ground, where he scrabbled away as quickly as he could.

'What the hell—' Massin breathed. 'I don't understand. He'd got our attention already.'

'On the scale of importance,' Rocco said calmly, 'what would you rate the highest, a small-town cop or a top city lawyer with friends in high places?' As calm as he sounded, his mind was racing. Surely Koutcheff didn't think anyone would rate his chances of pulling this off.

Koutcheff's next words were prophetic.

'Nothing's changed,' he shouted at the circle of men, this time grinding his gun into De Lancourt's throat. 'If anyone tries anything, this gun goes off. You all fancy having to explain that to your bosses?'

Rocco held his hands out to each side to draw Koutcheff's attention. 'Nobody's going to shoot,' he said calmly. 'Why don't you put the gun down? You know we can't let you go, don't you?'

Koutcheff gave an ugly facsimile of a smile. 'As easy as that, is it? After everything I've been through, I'm the one who gets the bullet? That's not fair, Rocco. What about this one, eh?' He shook De Lancourt to emphasise his point, the lawyer's head wobbling like a marionette's and his eyes rolling in shock. 'This... this piece of shit has done so much worse than me, I can promise you!'

'Like what?' Rocco asked calmly. The more Koutcheff talked, he reasoned, the less likely he was to pull the trigger and the better their chances of resolving the issue without further bloodshed.

'He ordered me to shoot the Benhamids,' Koutcheff replied. 'Yes, because they were threatening to tell everything they knew about what he'd done in Morocco if he didn't help them. He'd had me knock off some farmers over there... people he needed to get rid of for land deals. And he's going to go free because all his high-flown buddies will see to it? You can't tell me that's not true.'

De Lancourt appeared to come to and stared around at the uniforms as if seeing them for the first time. His gaze finally settled on Rocco. At that he struggled to break free but Koutcheff was too strong for him.

'Don't listen to him,' the lawyer raged, his voice strangled. 'He's a mad dog, can't you see that? An animal I rescued from a trip to the gutter. This is how he repays me, by killing all those people... the Benhamids and the men in the bunker! Shoot him, for God's sake, somebody!'

Rocco ignored him. He sensed Koutcheff was dangerously near breaking point. He could also feel increased tension in the men around him, each one sizing up their chances of taking a shot to end the stand-off, in spite of their orders.

'He'll get what's coming to him, Koutcheff, don't worry,' he said firmly. 'We know what he's done, what he's had you and the other men do on his behalf. But you could help put him away for a long, long time. Let him go, and make a statement; that will do it. There doesn't need to be any more killing.'

'Yeah? Is that your answer? We all pack up and have a nice chat, and everything will be fine? That's not right and you know it!' He adjusted his hold on his gun and screwed it further into De Lancourt's throat. 'Well, that might be your justice, but it's not mine!' His knuckles turned white as he went to pull the trigger.

But that was as far as he got.

Sergeant Godard had managed to edge away to one side without attracting attention. The move – and Koutcheff's total focus on holding De Lancourt – gave him a clear shot. He brought up his pistol and fired once. The bullet caught Koutcheff in the shoulder and knocked him off his feet, his gun falling away and landing at the base of the tree.

'That's for Pouillot,' Godard murmured softly, and reholstered his gun.

De Lancourt fainted clean away but nobody moved to help him. Only Koutcheff, wounded but not fatally, made any noise, railing against everything and everyone, most of all his employer.

Chapter Forty-Nine

'We should take our shoes off,' said Eliane. 'The grass under the trees can be very damp.'

Rocco had joined her on the patio behind the chateau, where an ice bucket and two glasses stood on a small table. She poured wine for them both and they clinked glasses. 'As you can see,' she said, 'I was hoping I'd see you this evening.'

'Well, here I am,' he said. He told himself to stop staring but it wasn't easy. Eliane was dressed in in a light summer frock that set off her figure, and she looked the epitome of light and warmth. 'Is your father back?'

'No. He was until this morning, but he's had to go back to Brussels to make some preliminary sketches. He'll be a few days yet.' She removed her light sandals with careless but elegant flicks, before looking pointedly down at Rocco's brogues and waiting until he took them off.

It had taken two days to get clear of the Interior Ministry enquiries into the events at Les Cyprès, but he'd finally managed to leave it all behind for a short while. He wondered with bemusement what was coming next.

'And socks.'

He took them off, too, then carefully rolled up the hems of his trousers to mid-calf level.

Eliane giggled when he wiggled his toes.

'What?'

'Nothing,' she said quickly, adding, 'Sorry – I suddenly had this vision of M. Hulot.'

He looked at her with suspicion, aware that she was suppressing a laugh.

'Is he someone I should know?'

Her eyes widened. 'You're not serious! I thought *everyone* knew Hulot. Jacques Tati, the actor? *Monsieur Hulot's Holiday?* It's a great film.'

'Ah. Sorry, I haven't had a lot of time for films recently.'

'Don't apologise.' She leaned in close and gave him a soft kiss on the cheek, leaving behind a hint of delicate perfume. 'In any case you're a lot better-looking than Hulot, so it's not a real comparison.' She blushed and turned away to pick up their glasses. 'I'm not saying another word on the subject.' She handed Rocco his glass, then stepped off the patio.

Rocco joined her, pleasantly jolted by the sensation of soft, cool grass against his bare feet. After all the action of the last few days it was a refreshing change of time, place and atmosphere, and he could already feel the tension beginning to slide off him like a second skin, taking with it the sub-surface memories of death and corruption. Those would take longer, but he was sure they, too, would go.

'Is everything done with De Lancourt?' Eliane asked, linking her arm in his. 'I was getting worried I'd never see you again.'

'For now, yes. I'm sorry I wasn't able to come by sooner.' At least it looked certain that De Lancourt would see the inside of a courtroom from the dock this time, alongside Koutcheff, his wounded but increasingly talkative employee.

They walked side by side towards the trees, onto a path of sorts where the grass had been mown short.

'Did you do this?' Rocco asked.

'Me? No. I paid a man in the village. Pa doesn't like paths spoiling the wildness, but I thought it might be worth doing. Just in case.'

'In case?'

She didn't reply, giving only an enigmatic smile that made his heart soar. Even the birds seemed to be singing at full volume.

'How are your feet?' Eliane queried at one point.

'Fine. Wet, but fine.' He was actually finding the sensory perception liberating. Or maybe it was entirely due to Eliane alongside him.

They arrived at a point where the mown path went arrow-straight through the trees, and Eliane stopped. She said, 'I think we should turn back. I wouldn't want to risk either of us getting pneumonia.'

'Quite right,' he said. He was wondering if he dared kiss her when she turned and kissed him instead. It went on for some time and while he couldn't be sure, he could have sworn the birds were singing even louder than before.

Eventually they walked back to the patio and Eliane topped up their glasses.

'Are you hungry?' she asked.

'I am.'

'Me, too. I can put together a salad, if that's all right?'

'Perfect. Why not?'

'Mme Drolet said you were a red meat man.'

'Not true. Let's not talk about Mme Drolet.'

'Agreed.' She gave a gentle laugh, then looked out across the garden. 'I've always wanted to walk in the grounds here at dawn, but never have. Can you believe that?'

'What stopped you? It's right there.'

She glanced at him and flushed, clearly hesitant.

'What?' he prompted her.

'I've never found anyone I wanted to walk with. Until now.'

Rocco wasn't sure what to say to that. But the thrill in his gut made him realise he was pleased. He worked at processing a suitable response, and in the end settled for banal, it being safer. 'It's a big garden. I'm sure it would be delightful.'

'It's two hectares. Pa had it measured.' She waved a hand to the right of the chateau. 'Our nearest neighbours are over that way. Out of sight… and well beyond earshot.'

'So, nobody to hear you scream when you get bored.'

'I never get bored here. It's my peaceful place.' She smiled. 'Can I tell you a huge secret – and I hope I don't shock you?'

'Of course. Although if it threatens the security of the state, I'd have to report it.'

'It doesn't, I promise.' She stopped and said in a rush, 'When I said I always wanted to walk, I actually meant early in the morning. *Very* early, before the world wakes up… and defying all convention.' Her voice had dropped and she looked at him as if checking whether he understood. 'Does that shock you?'

Rocco was becoming accustomed to the sudden switches and swerves in the conversation, but this was a whole new level. He wanted to laugh and shook his head. 'I'm a cop; we're not allowed to be shocked. It's in the rule book. And defying convention is something I'd like to get used to.'

'Thank goodness for that,' she breathed, and they kissed again until both were breathless. Eventually they parted and she said, 'Let's go inside and you can help me make dinner.'

Rocco reached out and gently pulled her back. He wasn't ready for a break in the proceedings, not yet. She giggled and folded into his arms. 'Or,' she murmured softly, 'we can leave eating until later.'

'How much later?'

She fluttered her eyelashes at him. 'We'll have to see, won't we? Are you in a hurry to be back at work?'

'I can't,' he said, and lifted one leg to show his bare foot. 'I'm not properly dressed.'

Acknowledgements

For the brilliant team at Canelo, who turned this gathering of paragraphs into a proper book; especially Kit Nevile, for his eagle eye and wise words.

David Headley, of DHH Literary Agency, for his continued help and support in getting my books to publication.

Rocky, the cat, who adopted us during lock-down and helped make it so much more bearable (although he's of no practical help whatsoever with the writing).